*Abbey*

Life is a constant journey from birth to death.
The landscape changes, people change, and
needs change.

Sometimes life just happens and you have to
deal with it.

———————

**With Thanks To**

**My Wife Sheila**

**and**

**The fresh eyes and minds of Marlene Lavell and Bev Fisher.**

**Other Writings by Ron A Sewell**

**A Basketful of Sleepers**

**The Angel Makers**

**You Can't Hide Forever**

**The Collectors Book One**

**The Collectors Book Two**

**(Full Circle)**

**The Collectors Book Three**

**(Tower 34)**

**The Collectors Book Four**

**(Diamonds and Sand)**

**The Collectors Book Five**

**(Finders Keepers)**

**The Collectors Book Six**

**(Black Gold)**

**And the Point Is**

**Finding Linda**

# Part One

## One

### Chelsea. London

With no lectures to attend, Abbey dressed in blue jeans, a white sweatshirt, and black Doc Martens. On passing the entrance door, she collected the morning post. One envelope grabbed her attention, the rest she dropped into the waste bin.

She was halfway through her first coffee of the day when she slit open the remaining letter from Peters, her legal guardian. It informed of her father's death when his helicopter crashed. "So, the bastard is dead. I hope he burns in hell." Then she thought, *I had better give old man Peters a visit and see what the bastard left me.*

Abbey stared out of the window. Men in suits carrying briefcases scurried past, frightened of being late for work. Cars searching for a parking place came and went. A motorbike raced past, leaving a plume of exhaust in its wake.

\*\*\*

At noon, Abbey changed and left her flat. Emerging from the underground, a snack and a coffee in a sandwich bar sated her immediate needs. With long strides, she strolled along a cobbled street. The brass plate on the wall of the building named **Peters and Hardgrave, Solicitors.**

On entering the building, Abbey stood in front of the receptionist's window and waited.

The well-dressed mature woman lifted her head and smiled. "Can I help you?"

"I must see Mr Gregory Peters."

"Please may I have your name?"

2

"Abbey Lane."

"One moment, please." She made a telephone call. "Mr Peters will see you. Take the lift to the top floor, his office is right in front of you."

Abbey shrugged. "I know."

The old lift, a dark and creaky thing, moved at a snail's pace. The scent of wax polish contaminated the air.

When it shuddered to a halt, Abbey stepped out and onto the carpeted hall. On the door opposite, she knocked and entered. "Good Morning."

He lifted his eyes from a document, gave her an appraising look and gestured with his right hand towards a seat. She chose the chair nearest the desk. With her hands resting in her lap, she waited.

Peters' mahogany desk, overflowing with coloured folders, dominated the room. In her eyes, he was — calm, cold, polite, and wearing his usual expensive dark blue suit. A pair of black-rimmed glasses magnified his eyes.

She let her eyelids close for a moment.

He lifted his head and peered across the top of his glasses. "Good morning, Miss Lane. I see you dressed in black, appropriate, but as you never met your father unnecessary. I cannot help but notice the dark rings under your eyes. I guess you've been partying with your student friends." He paused as if thinking. "Would you like a glass of water? I have still and sparkling."

"No, thank you. I'm fine."

His face creased as he stroked his forehead. He glanced at the paperwork in his right hand and then lifted his head. "As you well know, your late father's lawyers gave instructions to this firm for your nurture. This we have undertaken. However, his will makes no provision for you." He fixed his eyes on Abbey, waiting for her reply.

Frustration welled up in her as she struggled to come to terms with what he said. "He was lucky. One moment high in the air, and in a flash, he was nothing. Unlike thousands, he didn't

3

suffer. Let's face it, I was a mistake he wanted to forget. I'm no longer a child. I grew up a long time ago; I did not have a choice. I've always described myself as a cut flower, no roots. To you and the world, I'm vibrant, intelligent and need for nothing. You have no idea what it was like for me at school. Other girls often spoke of their parents. Holiday periods were the worst. At the end of every term, I had to wait for someone I didn't know to collect me. They would take me home or to a hotel for a so-called holiday. In my entire life, not a birthday or Christmas card, nothing. I'm glad he's dead."

Peters gaped in astonishment at her outburst. Nothing she said was new but hearing it from her lips moved him. "I can't say I understand, but after talking with my partners, I need a decision from you. Your Chelsea flat and Mini Cooper are in fact owned by this firm."

She lifted a stray strand of blonde hair and pushed it behind her ear. "What does that mean for me?"

He shrugged. "All I know is you are the result of a casual liaison, and your mother died giving you life."

"What was he like?"

"I know nothing except what I have read in the newspapers. This partnership received its instructions from New York. When we needed funds, we sent a letter. We never asked questions."

"So I was a line in the accounts."

"Not exactly but we all need to know who we are and where we are from."

"Don't tell me he cared. That man never loved me as a father. I doubt if he ever noticed what it cost. Out of mind and out of sight. He abandoned me and never gave a toss."

"It's okay to be angry with your father, but please control yourself in my office."

"It makes no difference. That bastard is history."

For a moment, they sat in silence.

From a right-hand drawer, Peters removed a document. "I advise you to read this."

Her hand shook as she took the sheet. "I always read every word before I sign anything."

He nodded. "I would always urge you to do so."

She bit her lower lip as she pondered the proposal. "This binds my hands. I get the flat, car and a hundred grand but relinquish any further claim on my father's estate."

"Correct."

"What if I refuse to sign?"

Peters closed his eyes for a moment. "As you progress through your life, you will reach a fork in the road. You have to make a decision, left or right. The choice is yours. In this instance, if you do not sign, you will receive a notice to vacate and return the car to this firm."

She rolled her eyes. "Could I buy the car?"

"I'm guided by their instructions."

Her eyes met his. "I see, but if I contest his will?"

Peters stretched his arms down the side of his chair. "You must decide, and I warrant there's a lawyer in New York who would take your case on a no-win, no-fee contract. However, your father's legal team would stretch this out ad infinitum. In the intervening time, where would you live? From what I know, a one-roomed apartment in London is expensive. And you could lose."

"I need to think it over."

"I need an answer by tomorrow morning." A smile filled his face when she asked to borrow his pen." He handed her his gold fountain pen. "Keep it as a reminder of the day your world changed."

She grimaced and signed the sheet. "When do I get the money?"

He returned the single sheet to the drawer it came from and removed a cheque. His deep voice was all business. "Please sign the attached receipt and listen. As from the end of this month, the property and car are yours. Do you understand?"

"How did you know I'd sign?"

"You didn't have much choice. But you never answered my question."

Her heart pounded. "Of course, I understand, and I'll need to look for a fucking job." She stood and marched towards the door. "Don't worry, I can look after myself. Thanks for everything. See you around."

"I recommend you get some sleep."

A soft sigh escaped her lips as if her mind needed time to process her thoughts. "This morning, I tried to imagine my father. I couldn't."

He lifted a sheaf of papers and pushed them into a folder. "If you need help with anything, call me. You have my private number."

On her way home, she tripped on the outstretched legs of a homeless man half-asleep on the pavement. "Sorry, I was miles away."

The man did not speak. The harshness of life on the street had taught him to keep quiet.

"How's it going?" she asked as she sat next to him.

He turned his head towards her. "Could be better but then it could be worse."

"What do you mean? What could be worse than this?"

He coughed. "It could be raining."

She laughed. "Sorry, I didn't mean to laugh. If I gave you a couple of pounds, what would you do?"

"Buy something to eat."

"Do you have a name?"

"Bob."

"How about I took you to a cafe and bought you a meal?"

"They don't let the likes of us inside."

A woman passed dragging a young child who asked, "Mummy, why is that lady sitting with that man?"

Abbey watched the mother and child as they walked on. "I've had a shit day, my fucking father died." She reached into her pocket, removing a leather purse. From the inside, she took two crisp notes. "Take this, and I hope life improves for you. Buy a lottery ticket; you never know, your luck might change."

"Sorry about your dad."

She shoved the notes in his hand and stood. "Hope the rain holds off."

Bob stared at the two twenty-pound notes and hesitated a moment. "Are you sure you haven't made a mistake?"

Bob and Abbey exchanged glances. "I don't make mistakes."

She stopped at the next corner shop. Fifteen minutes later, she entered her flat, dumped her coat and bag on the floor. The milk she put in the fridge and with her free hand switched on the percolator. With a steaming cup in one hand, she turned on her laptop as she sipped the dark brown liquid.

Not one of her emails required an answer. Weary, she snuggled into the comfort of the cushions on her sofa, and let her mind wander. She experienced a sense of freedom, as if on a giant helter-skelter. Her thoughts turned to mundane things. *The way I waste money, and with my university fees increasing, this flat will have to go. When Brian marries me, we can live at his place.*

The sounds and images of her life came and went as she tried to cling to those she loved. The face of her first lover as he fumbled with her blouse made her smile. The sound of a car's horn outside spoiled the moment. Then she recalled her chat with Jacob Spink on how to make money.

# Two

For the first time in a week, it was not raining. Streaks of cloud scudded across the London sky and the mid-morning sun gave warmth. At first glance, the old red brick structure appeared derelict. Since Jacob's first viewing a rainbow of graffiti now enveloped the whole facade. The new sign bolted on the wall read, 'Under Renovation'.

Jacob Spink clambered out of the taxi, turned and paid the driver. Dressed in a faded blue denim outfit covered by a well-worn, fur-lined, black parka he searched for a set of keys.

Visions of a prosperous future filled his mind as the padlock on the main door sprung open. On entering, he turned, closed and slammed the bottom and top bolts home. Stray shafts of light exploded through slits in the steel security shutters.

He flicked the light switch, but nothing happened. In the gloom, he coughed as his feet disturbed thick layers of dust. Advertising pamphlets littered the floor. On the worn wooden counter, three mugs encrusted with green mould rested. After months of searching, he had found the owner living in a retirement home. The old man may have been ancient, but he was no fool. He bargained long and hard, adamant a developer wanted to build a block of flats on the site. In the end, he agreed Jacob could rent for one year.

This grim building was to be his new home. Developed as an underground station entrance, and located next to a lorry-park. The old man's newsagents had made a living.

Jacob lifted the trap door behind the counter. With the light from his torch, he descended the staircase. A musty, sweet smell filled the still air. One broken lamp hung from the ceiling. In the dim light, he saw a room trapped in time. Broken furniture littered

8

the floor. The works of spiders hung as filthy rags from the ceiling. To his left, a larger room with one narrow shuttered window contained piles of rubbish. To his right and along the passage was a kitchen. An electric hob and refrigerator nestled against one wall. Next to this, a bathroom, containing a rusty cast-iron bath with lion's feet. A cracked wash-hand basin and a dirty toilet completed the installation. The beam of his torch shone on a rust-caked steel door. From his jacket, he removed a copy of the original plans. As far as he could determine a section of tunnel and platform still existed behind the door.

On returning to the central room, he plonked his frame into a sagging armchair and lit a cigarette. "With a few alterations, this will be perfect."

He had two sets of keys but needed two more for his team. Tomorrow, his builder would start to refurbish the basement

\*\*\*

Six weeks later, the whiff of fresh paint still lingered. Seated in an expensive black leather chair, Jacob turned on the VDU (Visual Display Unit). "They can wait until I'm ready." On the screen, he studied the faces of Abbey Lane, Tyler Pettit, and Michael Sinclair.

Abbey was the eye-catching and clever one, a classic spoilt brat who aroused his desires. He knew she would question everything.

Tyler was a mummy's boy. She still chose his clothes, and it showed. However, computers were his passion. Well into his second year, he could repair a mainframe blindfolded. The good news was his family had limited funds, and he needed money to complete his degree.

Michael was a handsome boy with the body of an athlete. There were solid muscles under his shirt and not from just working out. Women loved the mischievous way his sandy hair flopped over his eyes. His ability to test algorithms faster than most could understand them gave him an edge.

Jacob turned up the volume and listened to their chatter. After five minutes, he clambered up the stairs and unlocked the door. When they were inside, Jacob slid the top and bottom sliding bolts across. "Follow me."

Soft white lighting lit the basement room. Four forty-inch flat-screen monitors hung from its walls. Back-up equipment, electronic meters, and UPS machines blinked and flickered.

"What do you think?" asked Jacob.

Abbey's eyes twinkled as she toyed with her keyboard. Although the youngest of the four there, she maintained a degree of common sense. In a clear voice, she asked, "Not exactly the Ritz but you get full marks for the equipment. Out of interest, what are you going to do with the shop?"

Jacob frowned. "Leave it. It's of no immediate use. The local yobs have fun painting graffiti on the exterior walls."

Abbey flicked back her blonde hair from her face. With an expressionless stare, she asked, "Before we start playing, how secure is the network?" She waved her right hand. "And who paid for this?"

Jacob's face glowed with self-confidence. "Ours is a pact of convenience. Between us, we have written and developed a programme that will skim bank accounts. I trialled it and paid my builder."

"It's polite to ask, "said Tyler

"Why?"

Michael jumped in. "Who gives a shit? When do we start?".

"I needed the money," said Jacob. "If I say I'm sorry it doesn't change anything? Anyway, there's no defence to our electronic worm. Two types of bank exist, those we have yet to hack and those who don't know we've stolen their money."

Michael spun in his chair. "One thing we can guarantee is you'll create a reason even if there isn't one."

Abbey changed the subject. "What about system security?"

"I am the best there is in computer program technology and superior to you. Don't glare at me like a demented moron. You know you can't do better. It's not possible to track us as the internet protocol sees our location as one of many countries. Today it could be Afghanistan and tomorrow Israel. This system is idiot-proof, and tomorrow we make money."

"Are you going to live here?" asked Michael.

"You'd better believe it. This is my kingdom, and my power is here."

Abbey wrinkled her brow as she glanced at her watch. "Time I was gone. Have a hot date tonight."

"Anyone we know?" asked Tyler.

"I doubt it, he's an investment banker. Not your type and he's going to divorce his wife and marry me."

"A married man with money," said Tyler.

"What I've got, he can't get enough of. I've one life, and I mean to make the most of it. I don't come cheap." She stood, made her way to the shop and waited. "Jacob, are you going to lock the door?"

An abrupt, "Of course," vibrated up the stair.

The three men climbed the stairs. Abbey, followed by Tyler and Michael, strolled out. They smiled as Jacob slammed the bolts home.

"You would think it's Fort Knox," said Tyler.

"I must admit, he's as mad as the proverbial hatter, but I need the money," said Michael. "See you tomorrow. Have a good night, and be careful."

She grinned. "I promise I'll be terrific."

The two men laughed.

***

The following afternoon, Abbey, Tyler and Michael joined Jacob.

Jacob cracked his knuckles. "Are you ready?"

"Get on with it," said Tyler.

"On my command, five, four, three, two, one. Let's make money."

At once, fingers rattled keyboards.

11

Abbey watched many algorithms stream across the screen. She held her breath until **access granted** flashed. With her right-hand middle finger, she jabbed a key. Her eyes glowed, and a broad smile blossomed on her face.

"Five thousand, two hundred, and three," she shouted.

"One thousand," said Tyler.

"Five hundred," said Michael.

"I won," said Jacob. "Ten thousand."

"We agreed on equal shares," said Abbey. "That's four thousand apiece; Jacob can keep the odd change as operational costs."

They nodded in agreement.

"Pity we can't hit them harder for longer," muttered Tyler.

Jacob leaned back in his chair and churched his fingers. "Do that, and we go to jail. We are time-limited. Our worm enters their system and exits without a trace. I don't know about you three, but I can live on four thousand a day."

Abbey swivelled her chair. "At four grand a day I won't need to look for a job."

"We must find a way to increase our take," said Tyler.

"I've been working on something, but you must understand, small risk, small profit. Big risk, big profit, but with a calculated risk, you can hit the jackpot," said Jacob.

The three of them turned and faced Jacob. When he opened his mouth, there was no mistaking his South African accent. Whatever game he played, he was not accustomed to losing. He had the outer shell of two races; light-skinned but with African features. His clothes were casual but so perfect they could have been new.

There was a moment of unusual silence.

"Are you going to tell us, or do we have to guess?" asked Abbey with a faint smile. "Or are you going to pull a rabbit from the screen?"

His eyes narrowed, which made her uneasy. "All it takes is conviction, courage and confidence." He held up his notebook. "While you lot act as students I've been digging and snooping."

Tyler started coughing.

"Spit it out," said Michael.

"As you know, I often trade information on the dark-net where my talents are appreciated. I can find, track and alter most computer programmes. Digital portals are my speciality.

The UK and other countries use ICBMs as a deterrent. My idea is we hack into the launch programme and fire one. I've even chosen a target." He picked up and opened his notebook. "There's Palmyra Atoll, uninhabited and a thousand miles from anywhere. The US built an airstrip during the war, but it's abandoned."

Abbey's eyes flashed with anger, much like lightning on a pitch-black night. "You have a talent, but you're a fucking lunatic. Skimming from the banks is fun, and it serves them right for being so defenceless. This is plain fucking stupid. I'm out of here before you fuck up and armed police kick in the doors."

"What are you proposing?" asked Michael

"The world belongs to the strong," said Jacob. "Every missile control centre has a dozen basic computers attached to their network. I found one for checking vehicles connected to a missile launch facility in Siberia. I exploited their weakness and discovered a way to bypass the launch codes. The missile programmes are old technology. My problem is combining my programme into the fire and control systems. Once inside, I have remote access. The good news is when you are into one system, the rest are similar. Name me a country with missiles, and I'll fire one."

"How about India?" said Michael.

"Okay. The show begins at ten tomorrow morning." His lips moved, but his eyes never left the screen as his fingers worked his keyboard. "Abbey, you can hack into a weather satellite for the east coast of northern India."

13

Anger flickered in her eyes. Clenching her fists, she said nothing. Her face filled with suppressed rage until the flood gates opened. She snapped. "I want nothing to do with this. If you want a weather forecast. Do it yourself."

Agitated, Tyler ran his fingers through his hair. He opened and closed his mouth, but nothing came out. With a shrug, he glanced at Jacob. "I'm leaving."

Jacob tossed his head back and laughed. "I'm a genius, but then you know that. Never forget there's my subconscious mind with its high ideals. I want to guarantee the survival of you and me. So yes, I want to fight the system. I guess my idea makes me the chosen one. Am I ashamed? Not at all. Life's cruel. Get over it. As I said, the show starts at ten, with or without you."

"There's an unpleasant smell in here, and I want to throw up," said Abbey. "Are you two coming?"

"Sometimes we make bad choices for the best of reasons," said Michael. "This isn't one of them. I'm on my way."

As the three left, the rattle of tapping of keys filled the room.

"Do you think he can break into their defence systems?" asked Michael.

Abbey shrugged. "Anything is possible. Last year a fourteen-year-old hacked into the Pentagon. One thing is certain, if anyone can, he can and will."

# *Three*

Jacob sipped from a mug of cold coffee. To those who did not know him the crow's feet around his eyes made him appear older.

Abbey, Michael and Tyler approached the shop door. With a fixed smile on her face, she punched a button on her mobile.

Seated at Abbey's desk, Jacob closed his eyes and swore in Afrikaans. The last thing he needed was those three. His fingers raced across the keyboard. Finished, he removed a portable drive from her laptop and slipped it into his shirt pocket. One quick glance assured him everything was as she had left it. Moments later, he charged up the stairs.

A grin filled Jacob's face as he opened the main door. "You came to see a genius at work."

Abbey stared at him with contempt. "I'm here to see if you've come to your senses."

"Fine," said Jacob.

The three of them followed Jacob and descended into his empire. In seconds, each of them sat in front of their keyboards.

Jacob let his eyes skate over her shapely body as he dissected her pluses and minuses. Her black designer bag, which hung from the back of her chair, caught his attention. Its colour matched her lipstick.

She turned and smiled. "Have you given what you said last night any thought?"

He gazed at her with malice. "You could humour me."

"I question your thinking."

Jacob's brow twisted in thought as he glared at her. "You're wrong, Abbey. If I can launch a missile, it will force our government and the rest of the world to immobilise. No missiles, no nuclear holocaust., for the first time, world peace."

"If you believe that, you're raving. Those in charge will create a bigger stick to beat people with."

Jacob stood and sidled to where Abbey sat and placed his hands on the back of her chair. "The shock of an outsider being able to launch an ICBM will put the brakes on missile production." When he moved his hands, her bag dropped to the floor and burst open. "Sorry." He picked up the bag, slipping the memory stick inside.

Abbey grabbed the bag, retrieved its contents, stood and turned to the others. "I don't know about you two, but I'm out of here."

"Don't come back."

"I don't need this shit. You're a fucking idiot."

There was stunned silence as she headed for the stairs.

Tyler followed her. "Looks like I'll have to find a job."

"You and me both," she replied.

When the main door closed, Tyler said, "You know he'll try."

As they walked from the shop, she said, "There's a fanatical flaw in his character. He's dangerous."

\*\*\*

With a dry smile, Jacob said to Michael. "Find me a weather satellite over northern India."

Without answering, Michael punched the keys, loaded one of his favourite zombie programmes, and waited. "I have a great view of the east coast and no clouds."

"Michael, watch the screen." Jacob pressed one key.

"So far, nothing."

"You must be blind." Jacob pushed him out of the way and stared at the screen. "This can't be happening."

Michael shook his head. "Maybe you're not as good as you think."

16

"What are you saying?"

"Let me offer you a piece of advice."

"You're a student computer engineer. What guidance can you give me?"

Michael smiled. "I suggest you engage your brain before operating mouth."

"You doubt my skill."

"You'd better believe it. Next time make sure you can do it and don't fuck up. I'm off."

Jacob grimaced when Michael left. On bolting the main door, he returned to his desk.

# *Four*

Abbey placed her supper of roast beef sandwiches on a tray and carried it into the living room. She sat on the couch, placing the food alongside. While eating, she read her presentation for the next day. Happy, the folder slotted into her workbag and tired, she made her way to bed.

\*\*\*

Michael raced along the corridor after Abbey. As she made her way to the lecture room, she moved with confidence. When he caught up with her, they laughed at Jacobs's failure to launch a missile.

"You know he won't stop trying."

"I agree. Jacob believes in himself."

"I'm in here," said Abbey, stopping at lecture room three.

"Number six for me," said Michael. "Are you around later?"

Abbey nodded. "Why?"

"Tyler thought the three of us could go for a drink."

"Tyler, or you?"

He shrugged. "To be fair I suggest the drink."

"Why?"

"The future. Do we need Jacob?"

She stopped, tilted her head to one side and then delivered her answer. "Jacob set up the programme. Somewhere in there will be his control steps. Leave it with me, and I'll get back to you. Must go."

He watched as she entered the lecture room and wished.

\*\*\*

18

Abbey awoke from a disturbed night's sleep, rolled over and turned on her radio. From half-asleep to wide-awake took less than a second as the newsflash registered.

She tried to contact Jacob, but each time her calls diverted straight to his voice mail. Abbey shrugged when she discovered the main door to the shop unlocked. Warily she entered. The hatch to the basement was open, and the clatter of fingers operating a keyboard eased her mind. She closed and bolted the main door. Tense, she reached the bottom of the stairs, digital algorithms raced across four screens. A flood of horror gushed through her. "Jacob, what the fuck are you doing?"

He gave a manic chuckle as he lifted his head. His eyes gleamed. "At this moment, I'm into a USAF Base, 450 nuclear missiles are mine to operate. They built these places in the sixties, and much of the equipment is original. Designed to be secure. Then one day a telephone engineer installed fibre optics. To make matters worse, the idiots installed the backup to a PC. You're familiar with the domino effect, well join that to a cyber cascade and you have World War Three."

Abbey tried to control her voice. "You're deranged. If your data falls into the wrong hands, a ton of shit will hit the fan, and I don't want to be under it."

He grinned as he looked at her. "I'm a genius. I can save the world from itself. I'm shaking the trees to discover what falls out."

"You're fucking mad."

Jacob snapped. "You're jealous."

She shook her head. "Why would I be jealous of a dickhead. Delete the program."

"He held up his hands as a signal of truce. It's a matter of pride. I use a Ministry of Defence server to direct my traffic, and everything is password protected."

"I can crack passwords in my sleep. What's so different about yours?"

19

He laughed. "I've hidden them where the sun doesn't shine." He savoured the moment.

She stared long and hard at him. "Be careful, search programmes advance each day. Tomorrow might be the day when the world finds you. Nothing is foolproof."

"I haven't told you the best bit."

She looked at him quizzically. "Tell me."

"I can stop those missiles from ever launching."

She attempted to make some sense of his actions. "I'd sooner you did nothing. I'm out of here."

Fearful but not intimidated, she left. Somehow, she must inform the right people. They could stop this.

The day was bright, sunny, but cold and she kept moving to keep warm. For no reason, she entered a park and found an empty seat by the lake. Her mind fought with itself. A mother and a small child dressed in pink played on the grass. The child staggered a few steps before falling on her well-padded bottom. Part of the game was to clap and squeal before she rolled over and got up again. She was black and cute. Her mother watched over her. The girl giggled and waved her arms, but her mother waited until she wobbled to her.

Abbey smiled, aware she needed these reminders. Burkes famous phrase came to mind. For evil to exist, it only takes good people to do nothing. With her catch-22 unanswered, she stood and left.

Today the slightest irritation made her want to vomit. She could not even fill up her Mini with petrol without the fumes making her wretch and heave. How could anything so natural feel so bad? It was worse than gastric flu, at least with the flu you knew it would soon end. This would go on for another seven months.

Abbey closed her eyes but could not relax; she needed an answer to her question. Jacob filled her head as she texted Mr Peters. "I need your advice."

20

She waited, changed into her pyjamas, made a hot chocolate, turned on the television, flicked to the news channel and lay on the couch. The news reported that the Indian Army was investigating the unplanned launch of one of its missiles. The telephone rang, dragging her from a snooze. She reached over and lifted her mobile. "Mr Peters."

"How did you know it was me?"

"You have always used a telephone. My friends use mobiles."

"I'm a simple man, but you are no longer my responsibility."

"You said if I needed help to call you."

"I did, didn't I? How can I help?"

"An associate of mine has written a computer programme that has the potential to harm millions of people."

"Okay, but you should tell this to the police."

"I can't."

"Why?"

"I don't suppose you noticed, but I've taken nothing from my account lately."

"I did but then why would I worry?"

"Ever heard of skimming?"

"It's theft."

"Well a few of us geeks have perfected a programme that skims bank accounts, and I'd prefer if the world didn't find out. One of my associates has conceived Armageddon, and I need to inform the right people."

"Can I ask? Are you high on drugs?"

"I don't do drugs."

"This friend, does he keep copies of his programme? Can you get hold of them?"

"No."

"Couldn't you delete it or something?"

"If I had known, yes, but I didn't."

"Leave this with me. Give me time." The line went dead.

21

The wait was painful and endless, her hands shook, head ached. When her mobile rang, she let it ring again, scared to answer the call. Then she did. "Yes."

"It's Peters. There's a Commander William Haliwell on his way to your flat. I don't think he believed me when I told him your story."

If he doesn't, kiss your arse goodbye."

"Miss Abbey, you always have a way with words."

"I hope so." She turned her head as the rapping on the door broke her train of thought. "Must go. Someone at the door."

"Abbey, just tell Haliwell the truth. He's a good man."

She ended the call, strolled to the door, peered through the spy hole and saw a strange man. "Who is it?"

"Commander Haliwell, Scotland Yard."

"You'll have to wait." In minutes, Abbey, wearing an old brown dressing gown, eased open the door until the security chain tightened. "Can I see your ID?" She took the warrant card from his hand, gazed at the photo, and then back at him. "Metropolitan Police–Counter-Terrorism." She passed his card back, shut and removed the security chain and motioned for him to enter. A shiver passed through her as if someone had walked over her grave. She closed and locked the door.

He was taller than she expected. The top of her head reached his shoulders. "My lawyer told me you were on your way, but I didn't expect the top brass."

The well-built, middle-aged man wore an immaculate pinstriped suit, white shirt but no tie. With the look of a man working unsociable hours, he slumped into the one armchair.

He stared at the pale-faced young woman in front of him. "Miss Lane, I'm a professional, and we need to talk. From what I know, I'm here to drag you out of the shit. Tell me what you told my old friend Gregory Peters."

22

She levelled her eyes at a man who possessed a harsh coldness in his gaze. "I'm not scared, I'm fucking petrified. Who knows what a mad man will do just because he can."

He leaned forward, his hands clasped in his lap. "Are you wasting my time?"

She made no effort to disguise her annoyance. "What do you mean? I know he launched an ICBM from the east coast of India."

Haliwell grimaced as he shot forward in his chair. "Jesus fucking Christ, what's his address."

Abbey told him.

He pressed a key on his mobile. "Haliwell, encrypt this number and call me." He waited a few seconds and answered before it completed one beat of its ring tone. "Code-Gold." He gave the address. "I need an armed squad and total lockdown. We are not dealing with teenage terrorists, this man's an educated maniac. Silent mode to apply. Track my mobile, I'm on my way." He pointed. "You, come with me."

"Why?"

"Because I say so."

"Can I get dressed?"

His eyes lowered. "Sorry, wasn't thinking."

"Are you married?" She shouted as her bedroom door slammed shut.

From the floor, she grabbed her well-worn blue jeans with holes in the knees. Her wardrobe provided a thick Arran sweater and an expensive black leather jacket. A pair of black Doc Martens slid over her white socks.

As she opened the door, he grabbed her arm and dragged her out of the flat to the waiting car. "Get in and shut up." He told the uniformed driver the address. "If you burn rubber, I'll not complain. Turn off your siren. The clock's ticking, and I want to catch this idiot."

"Yes, in answer to your question. My wife is always on time when we go out. Your friend, does he have a name?" Haliwell asked casually.

Abbey laughed as the car sped around a corner and she gripped the back of the seat in front. "Jacob Spink."

Seated in the rear of the Range Rover she could hardly hear the power of the engine. They stopped at a set of traffic lights but the instant they changed to green, the unsmiling driver brushed the accelerator and the car leapt forward.

***

"Stop," Abbey shouted.

"Do it," said Haliwell.

Before they had time to exit the car, two grey-painted personnel carriers stopped millimetres behind them. Clad in grey body armour, and carrying a machine pistol, one man jumped from the driver's cab to the pavement. As if he had plenty of time, he sauntered to the front of the car. "Inspector Madden, Sir. What are your orders?"

As his feet touched the pavement, Haliwell pointed at what appeared to be a derelict building. Its front, covered in colourful graffiti and steel shutters sealed both windows. The street lamps gave a sinister light as they flickered and buzzed.

"That is your objective. Direct your team to lock down the entire area tighter than a duck's arse and the first man to make a sound will be directing traffic for life. My friend and I will try the simple approach."

The inspector's eyebrows arched. "And that is, Sir?"

Haliwell glanced at the building; his stomach rumbled, reminding him he had not eaten since breakfast. "The first rule of diplomacy. Talk in a whisper but carry a big stick." He pointed. "You, give me two Glock 17s." He shoved one behind his back and into his belt, the other into his trouser pocket. "Inspector, tell me when your men are in position."

24

In silence, the area buzzed with activity as armed officers took their positions.

For a few minutes, he stood and did what he did best. Unhurried, his eyes roamed the area; missing nothing as armed men dressed in grey uniforms took their positions.

He turned and spoke to Abbey. "Tell me everything about Spink."

She thought for a moment. "Jacob is from South Africa, twenty-five and weird. He has a white father and a black mother who separated a few years back. I understand he has a first in mathematics and is studying for his Masters in computer programming."

"How did you meet?"

"He offered to help a few of us with our assignments."

"Have you slept with him?"

"Is that important?"

"Everything is. I'm attempting to build a profile of a man I may have to kill. I don't want to, but sometimes there isn't a choice."

"No, I haven't. Now that you ask, I've never ever thought of him sexually. And before you dare ask the next question, I'm not a virgin, but I'm choosy with whom I have sex. He's a bit of a dick-head."

Haliwell's face turned red, acknowledging a line he should not have crossed. His mobile rang, and he glanced at the screen. "Good evening, Gov."

"I'm told by a member of my junior staff that two PCs full of armed men and women, left the yard twenty minutes ago. Be polite and tell me why?"

"Mam, the rogue missile fired from the east coast of India. I have a lead on who overrode the safety protocols. It's a mathematics genius studying programming. He cracked the system."

"The Pentagon did it ages ago. Why do you think so many of North Korea's missiles failed? And I worry about what crap is on

25

Face book. Haliwell, you can consider this a mission briefing. Don't kill the bastard. We need to know how and why. A bullet in the leg usually stops them."

"There are always risks, mam."

"That's why I never sleep well at night, Haliwell." The line went dead.

"We are ready, Sir," said the inspector.

"Right, young lady, time to make a move."

She shrugged. "Please don't shoot Jacob. He's an oddball but doesn't deserve to die."

Haliwell raised his eyebrows. "He has two choices; if he chooses the wrong one, I put a bullet right between his eyes. Do you know there are those out there in the community who would rather ignore things like this and simply hope it goes away? Right you lead. The inspector and I will follow."

At the shop's entrance, Abbey used her mobile to contact Jacob. She listened as his voicemail activated. She tried again to no avail. With her fist, she pounded on the door.

\*\*\*

Jacob, smoking a cigarette, listened to his phone ring and continued punching his keyboard. A pot of instant chicken noodles steamed on his desk. As was his way he pressed F12 on his keyboard and Abbey, along with two men, one wearing body armour, appeared on his screen. "You bitch." He grinned from ear to ear as he pressed several keys in quick succession. At once, four screens displayed the same message.

\*\*\*

Haliwell nodded to the inspector who signalled to one of his men. A few seconds later, a constable arrived carrying his Big Red Key.

"Open it," said Haliwell.

"Stand back, Sirs." The man moved forward, swung the Big Key, and struck the door once, splitting the wood around the lock and two bolts. On one hinge, it swung open.

Haliwell was an officer often misjudged by his team. As a thinker, he calculated every move. His adversary in this instance was not a terrorist. With his right hand, he drew his Glock and made sure the safety was on. They stood motionless, listening. He glanced at the inspector "You first." He pointed, "Abbey, stay outside."

Abbey sighed and said in a loud voice. "There's a trap door behind the counter."

"Found it," said the inspector.

To be on the safe side, the inspector lifted the cover towards him. Once vertical, he shouted, "Jacob Spink, Armed Police. Do not make any sudden moves. Please climb the stairs with your hands behind your head." He waited for a reply.

Haliwell nodded to the inspector. "Use two stun grenades. Jacob, this is your last chance."

From his belt, the inspector pulled two grenades, removed the pins and dropped them through the opening.

They detonated as the trapdoor shut; the shockwave shuddered through the walls. Dust fell in a fine mist, clouding the room

The inspector coughed. "If anyone's down there, they're unconscious."

\*\*\*

Cursing Abbey, Jacob switched on his battery-operated headlamp. The white beam lit a long, brick-built tunnel.

When the builders removed and dumped every carpet in the skip, Jacob saw the metal cover and gave it little thought. Later, curiosity got the better of him, and he explored the tunnel workings from end to end. When he found an exit, the secret stayed with him.

The air smelt damp. Walking at a fast pace, he swept the beam from side to side. A thought bothered him; if he dropped his torch, he would be lost. Sweat dripped into his eyes as he gripped the chrome-plated shaft. Forty minutes later, the tunnel forked. Continuing left for a further three hundred metres, he stopped and climbed a metal ladder, its rungs set into the wall. On reaching the top, he eased the cover off its housing, clambered out and with his foot slid the cover back. Seething, he left the school playground and crossed a busy road. Hungry from his exertions, he entered MacDonalds. With a triple cheeseburger in his right hand, he seated himself in a far corner. While eating, he gave thought to his future. He wiped his hands on the paper serviette and left. In minutes, he made his way through the back doubles until, gazing in disbelief, he saw the armed police. Like a ghost, he withdrew into the shadows and waited. He checked his watch, time was against him, and he had a score to settle.

***

Haliwell grinned. "Inspector, rank has its privilege, and as you're wearing armour, you can go first."

"Thank you, Sir" He lifted the trap door and roared. "Armed police, make no sudden moves." One-step at a time he descended. As his feet touched the floor, he sidled to the right and stopped when he struck a chair. His eyes scanned the empty room. "The bird's flown."

Haliwell rubbed his chin. "Abbey, where's he gone?"

# Five

Abbey stood close to Haliwell, beads of sweat trickled down her spine. "Shit, there's a door in the bathroom."

Haliwell glared at the inspector. "You heard her. Go find."

The inspector shouted to his men to follow as he raced away. Moments later, he returned. "It's rusted solid; you'd need a JCB to open it." He lifted the noodles. "These are warm. Pound to a penny he's still here."

Haliwell descended the stairs and gave a casual glance at the banks of screens. "Cosy." A question formed in his mind. *Which one is his?*

Abbey anticipated his question and pointed. "It's still powered up, shift the mouse."

Haliwell shifted the red mouse to one side. Four monitors came to life. "Inspector, take a gander at this. He saw us coming."

"Hidden cameras. This guy's not stupid."

The screens flashed and displayed a message. *Deny everything and touch nothing.* The skull and crossed bones appeared. Two minutes later pictures of the first atomic bomb tests on Christmas Island flipped on and off, and the National Anthem played in the background. After five minutes, it reverted to the message.

Abbey rolled her eyes. "Don't touch the keyboard. He'll have set traps."

Haliwell nodded. "I'm not that stupid, but where is he?"

"There is no way out," said the inspector. "I guarantee this place was sealed tight."

Haliwell stared at the inspector. "If you're right, he's still here. Rip this place apart. God knows what he's done."

"God might know, Sir, but I'm sure I don't." He shouted up the stairs, "Sergeant."

"Sir."

"Have your men search this place. There's a lunatic in here, and we need to find him." Four grey-clad men wearing body armour descended the stairs.

"Where do you want us to start, Sir?" asked the sergeant.

"Check the bathroom and work your way back. I'll start in the bedroom."

The men left as the inspector strode into the bedroom. He banged the walls, studied the ceiling, checking for anything out of the ordinary. He jumped on the carpet and peered under the bed. The forty-watt ceiling light was useless. He left and returned with a torch, the lack of fluff under the bed made him curious. Then he saw something that focused his attention. With a heave, he lifted the bed and leant it against the wall. His jaw dropped when he saw the open manhole. "Bloody hell. This wasn't on the schematic... Boss."

"What?" asked Haliwell. He stepped forward for a better view and both men stared into the deep, dark shaft. "Have your men investigate where it leads."

The inspector nodded. "Yes, Sir."

Haliwell waited until two men entered the shaft and vanished into the dark. "Tell me the moment they find something. I'll contact the Yard and arrange to have Jacob Spink's photo and description circulated. I'll also demand the attendance of our computer geeks to check this lot."

The inspector listened on his radio to his men as they traversed the tunnel.

***

One-hour later two technical specialists from GCHQ arrived. With care, they disconnected each PC and removed the hard drives.

"What's your plan?" asked Haliwell.

The woman, who appeared youthful enough to be a student, lifted her head. She cleared her throat. "We take these back to our secure workshop and analyse the content."

"What do you hope to find?"

"Out there it's the wild west of hacking these days. A ten-year-old with a laptop can do it. This cowboy will have disguised his digital fingerprint and encrypted the programme, but we have the tools to bypass most things. For the moment, we can assume he penetrated missile sites. We have to find out if this nerd got lucky or he located an open door."

Haliwell ran his hand through his hair. "Rather you than me. It takes me ten minutes to send an email."

She smiled. "We get paid for our ability. Our problem is that it's almost impossible to keep up with the pace of technological change. Everything is vulnerable to attack. I read a government report last week. On their probability scale it appeared that the chance of anyone hacking into an ICBM recorded zero."

"Can you delete his programme?" Abbey asked.

Her eyes darted towards her. "I need to get into his mind and think as he does. Anything you can tell us might be useful?"

Abbey shrugged. "He created massive algorithms in his sleep. I can tell you he saved nothing to those drives. He uses proxy servers and the cloud. He protected everything with convoluted passwords. And before you ask, I don't know what they are."

The older technician dropped his tools into his bag. "Kathy, I've finished. It's time we returned to our dungeon and take this idiot out of the system."

Haliwell caught his gaze. "Can you?"

His eyes locked onto Haliwell. "We'll work on the problem, but if we can't, the shit hits the fan, and we're in more danger than you think."

# *Six*

Haliwell turned and faced Abbey. "You, go home, get some rest but make sure you and your classmates are in my office with your passports at nine tomorrow morning or else."

Indignant, she faced him, her arms crossed. "Do you expect me to find my own way home?"

Haliwell grinned. "Yes."

"So much for the public helping the police. Where's your office."

"New Scotland Yard." He fumbled and retrieved a card from his jacket pocket. "Show this at the main desk, and they'll escort you."

"And if I don't turn up?"

His eyes sparkled. "I'll have you arrested."

She shrugged. "An interesting point but first you prove I've stolen something. I never told Peters which bank."

"Abbey, shut up. I can hold you on causing a public disturbance by farting in a lift. My people can probe your bank accounts. Believe me when I say I have the power to direct judges. It may not be kosher, but then I don't give a shit."

She laughed as she climbed the stairs to the shop. "See you tomorrow and I'll make sure the others come with me."

"I suggest you do." The calmness in his voice made her smile.

\*\*\*

A shout came from the tunnel entrance shaft. The thump of boots on metal rungs told the inspector his men were returning. He helped both into the bedroom. "Find anything?"

The sweat on their brows sparkled in the light. "After a few false starts we discovered the ladder Spink used to climb to the surface. It led to a school playground," said the senior constable.

"Go and wait in the wagon."

The inspector gave Haliwell the news.

He shrugged. "I'm not surprised. Leave two men here until the local plod arrive. Tomorrow is another day."

With the building secure, Haliwell and the inspector left.

***

As Abbey approached the closest bus stop, she saw Jacob. His movements were stiff as he emerged from behind the bushes and into the gloom.

A wicked smile played on his lips, and his eyes had the look of annoyance. "Well if it isn't the telltale."

She glared straight at him as fear-drenched her. The fingers of her right hand gripped her house keys.

He took a step forward shoving his face close to hers. "You have something of mine. Give it to me, or I'll take it."

Abbey's shoulders stiffened as she stared straight at Jacob. "The police are searching for you. Fuck off before I scream."

His voice rose. "I watched your friends leave. So what do we do now?" He had expected panic. She was tougher than he had imagined.

As if she had read his thoughts, she sliced his face with her right hand and ran.

He staggered, shocked but recovered and raced after her.

She charged across the road and into the shadows of a building site.

Blood dripped from his wound as he followed.

Abbey was halfway through the rows of half-built buildings when she heard him roar. "I'm going to kill you but first I'll fuck you."

She ran fast, turning right into a passage between two houses. The narrow gap between a worker's hut and a wall gave her

33

hope. Desperate, she dragged her frame in, dropped to the ground and prayed.

He ran past, but then stopped. Her stomach heaved, and bile dribbled from her mouth.

Tense, she waited and listened to his foul-mouthed curses. Shouting her name, his voice faded in the distance.

For an age, she did not move. Making as little sound as possible, she crawled out and into the open and vomited. Wiping her mouth with her sleeve, she checked in every direction before taking her first steps. She moved silently and kept to the shadows until she reached the back of the site. Here loose fencing made it easy for her to return to the solid surface of the road. There was no one about. Wary, she walked at a fast pace and in a few minutes came to a wide road and started along. As the distance between her and the building site increased, her pulse rate decreased.

*\*\*\**

Jacob tasted blood on his lips as he made his way towards his hotel. At an all-night chemist, he stopped and let the man treat his wound.

"You need stitches," said the chemist.

"I'll go tomorrow," said Jacob. "How much do I owe you?"

"Bandages, dressings, a bottle of antiseptic. That's eight pounds please."

Jacob took out his wallet and removed a twenty-pound note. "Keep the change. Thank you for your help." He lifted his small case and left.

The man watched as he vanished into the dark.

*\*\*\**

The George, a converted warehouse with twenty-five bedrooms, was his secret place. From his window, there was a view of a debris-filled canal. At night, residents kept their windows closed to keep out the smell.

While walking, Jacob's mood changed. He needed someone to take his mind off that bitch, and he knew where to find her.

As he approached a narrow, cobbled lane, a slim young woman dressed in thigh length black leather boots, red leather skirt and jacket stepped out of the shadows. "Need some company, darling?"

"Jesus Christ, Wendy, you scared the shit out of me. What I need is the use of your body."

She shook her head. "By the look of your face, you need a doctor."

"Look, are you working? If you're not, I'll go elsewhere."

"Two hundred pound and the before you fuck me, money up front."

He laughed as he withdrew his wallet. "Two hundred."

She grabbed the money and counted every note. "What are we waiting for? Same place as usual?"

The night manager at the George smiled when Jacob and Wendy entered. He knew who and what she was but this guest paid a month in advance for the room. What he did behind a closed door was not his business.

\*\*\*

With Jacob's needs sated, she rolled off the bed and grabbed her dress.

"Next time it'll cost you double to bugger me."

He laughed. "You'll take my money whatever I do. You're a whore."

"Fuck you." She slipped on her shoes, grabbed her coat and left.

He watched the door close before sliding off the bed. To prevent unwelcome visitors, he removed a wooden wedge from his case and shoved the thin edge under the door. His mind went into overdrive as he set the alarm on his mobile for an early start. While relaxing on his bed, he talked to himself and worked out an escape route. Overcome by tiredness, he yawned, closed his eyes and fell into a deep sleep.

\*\*\*

As she strolled along the road, Abbey cursed aloud. A thought struck her, *Jacob would never give up.*

On entering her flat, she tossed her coat over a chair. From a cabinet, she took a half-full bottle of gin into the bedroom. Removing the screw cap, she gulped a couple of mouthfuls and seated herself. She closed her eyes for a moment as her mind wondered. *What is happening to me? So far, I have lived a life of self-indulgent pleasure. Money has never been a problem and men wanted me.*

As she swallowed the last of the gin, she undressed and collapsed onto the bed. As the mattress sprung back, her handbag tumbled to the floor. Sleep did not come. Every idea, urge and episode from the day played on her mind. Each moment demanded scrutiny. *I can't stop Jacob any more than Canute can stop the tides. What happens, happens, it's my fate. My life is a sham, I never had to worry, but I would never wish it away. Change is coming. It has no choice. If I swim against the tide, I'll drown. Change or die, isn't that what people tell you.*

Worn out, her brain finally dragged her into the abyss of sleep.

Her eyes opened at six the next morning. With a pounding head and a foul taste in her mouth, she remembered finishing the bottle of gin. It hurt to move. Thankfully, she had drawn the curtains, bright light always made her feel worse. She curled under the duvet and closed her eyes.

At seven, she fell out of bed, kicked her handbag and swore when its contents scattered across the floor. Leaving the mess, she showered, put on her bathrobe and sat in front of her laptop. With deliberation, she hacked into Bank of Scotland's system and with bloodshot eyes glued to the clock on the wall activated her program. **ACCESS DENIED** flashed on her screen. "Shit, shit, shit."

Frustrated, Abbey stared at the screen. Grim-faced she leaned back in her chair and checked her bank account. One hundred and seventy-one thousand pounds was enough for her to live in comfort. Undecided what to do next, she sat next to the window. Then she remembered her handbag. Returning to the bedroom she bent to retrieve her bits and pieces, her head spun as she gathered all she could see.

*** 

At three in the morning, Jacob awoke, rinsed his bloody face and dressed. At speed, he checked the room. The drawers were empty, the bathroom clean and no waste in the basket. With his suitcase in one hand and a shoulder bag containing his laptop slung over his shoulder, he gave the room one final glance and closed the door. In silence, he strolled along the corridor. He paused, checked for an intruder alarm before opening an emergency exit and descended the fire escape. A heavy mist cloaked the surroundings in a white veil. The orange glow from streetlights barely penetrated the haze. On reaching the ground, he shivered.

At a steady pace, he walked across Blackfriars Bridge. He grimaced at the sight of a man wearing a shabby black coat that dragged on the ground. *Don't look at him. Keep moving.*

Jacob slowed and acted as if he were checking something. As he started walking again, he glimpsed the man's face hidden behind a tangled mop of hair.

The stranger's hand grabbed his shoulder. "Give me your fucking wallet."

Jacob went to run.

A humourless smile creased the man's lips as the blade of a carving knife reflected the dull glow of the streetlights. "Give me your fucking wallet, arsehole, or I'll cut your heart out."

Jacob's pulse raced as he forced a smile. He stopped, placed his suitcase on the ground and reached inside his coat. The stench of body odour and meths hit his senses. He turned away and retched.

The man grabbed a fistful of Jacob's coat. "Stand fucking still."

Jacob tripped on his case and stumbled. The blade entered under his ribs. For a split second, he did not believe what was

37

happening. Confused, he doubled up, his face twisted, and his legs buckled.

"I told you not to fucking move."

Pain wracked his body as his attacker twisted the blade free. In his final moments, the last signals from Jacob's brain made his legs twitch.

The man bent over and robbed him of his wallet. The laptop he glanced at before it disappeared into the Thames. He lifted the suitcase and ran.

Ten minutes later a patrolling police car saw Jacob's body and stopped.

The police officer jumped out and shone his torch on the man who lay on his side, three feet from the parapet. "Sorry, mate, but you can't sleep here." As he nudged the body with his foot, he saw the pool of thickening blood. With two fingers placed on the man's neck, he checked for a pulse. This was his first dead body.

He shrugged and returned to the car. "This one's for you, Sarge. He's dead."

The sergeant turned off the engine. "And I wanted a quiet night. Touch nothing and tape off the area. I'll contact the station. We need a Scene of Crime Officer and forensics."

The constable opened the boot, removed a roll of blue and white tape, and created a temporary cordon.

***

Haliwell opened his eyes from a fitful sleep. His dream of the world erupting into a nuclear storm scared him. When he checked the time, the truth was obvious. Weary, he had laid-back in his office armchair. Dressed and still wearing his shoes, he grunted. Cramp hit his left leg as he stretched, and forced his aching body erect. With a shrug, he thought, *why didn't I go home?* Then he remembered the world could soon end. He checked his phone, no messages. From his bottom drawer, he removed his washing gear and a towel. He grinned, the world can end after I've had a shower. He stretched again and yawned. Half asleep, he staggered along the corridor, into the communal shower, set the thermostat, and turned on the hot water. The heat relaxed him, and he stayed for longer than he should have. Refreshed, he left the cubicle and dried himself with his white cotton towel. He had much to ponder. His office clock showed seven thirty. "Breakfast," he muttered.

Still deep in thought he entered the cafeteria, grabbed a carton of milk and bowl of Weetabix from the self-service section. Requiring solitude, he searched for an empty table. After eating and two cups of black tea, he returned to his office.

Haliwell looked at his watch. Time to engage brain. For a minute or two, he stared out of his one window with a view over the city. Ready for his meeting, he went back to his desk and made a few notes on his pad. On the dot of nine, his secretary knocked and entered. "Abbey Lane and two young men to see you, Sir."

"Thanks, Annie."

"Tea or coffee, Sir?"

His face widened to a grin. "Yes please. I'll have an extra strong black coffee."

She nodded, opened the door and guided Abbey and her associates into the room.

As they entered, Haliwell made a gesture with his right hand towards the three chairs in front of his desk. "Abbey, in the centre. You two if you can make a decision." His eyes never left the men. "Her I know. You two, name, date of birth and address?"

"Michael Sinclair, August 8, ninety-eight. LSE. I survive in a bedsit."

Haliwell closed his eyes and shouted. "I asked for your address."

Michael jumped. "Fourteen Duke Street, room number five."

"Now that wasn't difficult." He pointed at Tyler. "You?"

"Tyler Pettit, July 10, ninety-seven, LSE. Twenty-four Abercrombie Crescent. I live with my mum."

As they spoke, Haliwell studied their body language. From experience, he knew they were scared shitless and telling the truth. "I hate to tell you, but your pal Jacob has dropped you in deep, smelly shit. Abbey gets a gold star and for the moment a get-out-of-jail-free-card. I haven't decided what to do with you two. Tell me everything you know about Jacob Spink."

Michael and Tyler more or less repeated Abbey's story.

"According to the South African police, your friend is antisocial, has no criminal record, and does not belong to any terrorist organisation. He does have a talent for quantum physics and writing computer programmes. The LSE said he was strange but not stupid. He caught you three on one hook, but he didn't need you."

Haliwell raised both eyebrows as he rapped his fingers on the desktop. "Somewhere he left his digital signature. And I doubt if he can survive without using the net. GCHQ will find it, and we'll catch him." He gave a dark smile. "You may go, but as you're under investigation, I'll take your passports. Take note, my officers will keep an eye on your every move."

"This is madness," Haliwell muttered as the trio left. He lifted the telephone and punched in an internal number.

"Inspector Thomas, Sir."

"Any news on our man?"

"Not yet but those downstairs have circulated his photo and description to airports, stations and ports. I reckon we'll have him by the end of the day."

"We should be so lucky."

He ended the call and shouted, "Annie, you forgot my coffee. I'm going upstairs to see the boss, but I need caffeine."

Annie entered carrying a steaming cup of coffee and a cream cake. "I didn't forget, and the cake is on the house."

Haliwell grinned. "I know. None of the women in my life ever forgets. Most enjoyed reminding me of my sins."

"You never sinned, Sir."

"Believe me, I was young once."

***

At the end of a corridor, was a quiet zone. Four comfortable looking armchairs and two small tables filled the space. A neat pile of out-of-date magazines rested on one table. In one corner, a percolator bubbled away as it turned expensive coffee into sludge. This sanctuary from the rest of the building was empty. Haliwell poured himself another cup of the hot brew and seated himself in an armchair. As he sipped, his jumbled thoughts slotted into place. *Oh, how I wish I could sit here in peace and quiet for an hour or two.* He shook his head and drained the dregs from his cup.

Three minutes later Haliwell entered a large plush office. With it being on the top level, the windows stretched from the floor to the ceiling. For a moment, he gazed at the panoramic view of London.

Wearing his perfect charcoal grey suit, Deputy Assistant Commissioner Arthur Robbins was an officer with forty years' experience. Dark rings akin to Haliwell's surrounded his eyes. His face lifted as the Commander entered. "You have good news?"

Haliwell was tempted to say something witty but grabbed a chair and seated himself in front of a polished desk covered in files. "No, Sir. We lost our suspect and GCHQ are quiet. I'm here to recommend our next course of action. It's time to inform the government."

The deputy assistant leaned back in his swivel chair, turned and gazed out of the window. "How long do you think we have?"

"I've no idea, Sir. I was hoping for a breakthrough from GCHQ."

"Are you tired?"

"No, Sir."

The chair spun back as he faced Haliwell. "I am. I'm tired of budget cuts. Tired at the lack of staff, Isis, and the rest of them. They don't give up trying to disrupt this city and those in power want their pound of flesh."

"I know. With the hours I'm keeping, the only reason my wife doesn't think I'm having an affair is she tells me I'm past my sell-by-date."

"In fairness, at the end of the day, no one gives a shit, so long as it doesn't involve them. I'll take this to the top, so standby for a Cobra meeting. Write a few notes, so you don't have to think. You know the drill and make sure you're prepared for at least one idiot to ask a stupid question."

Haliwell stood ready to leave. "I understand there's a white paper on this which states it cannot happen."

"Governments will always avoid the issue if they don't know the answer. Can I recommend you go home and change? Wear something less creased. Must look your best for the PM."

"Sir." Haliwell smiled, left and made his way back to his office.

From his desk drawer, he removed his Audi S8 keys. As he left, he muttered, "Annie, I'm going home to change my suit."

# *Seven*

Arthur Robbins, Deputy Assistant Police Commissioner, leant forward and tapped his driver on the shoulder. "Change of venue, SIS (Secret Intelligence Service) Building."

The female driver nodded as she drove the black three-litre Range Rover out of the underground car park.

"I thought we were attending a Cabinet Office Briefing," said Haliwell.

Arthur hesitated. "Need to know."

The car stopped at the main entrance of SIS. The two men exited the vehicle and entered the building. The armed guard motioned for them to wait. When he was ready, they passed through the metal detector arch.

At reception, a petite, but hard-faced woman, checked their identity cards against the visitor register. Without raising her eyes, she handed the cards back, pressed a button on her console. In moments, an armed officer escorted them to a lift, let them enter and pressed an unmarked button. The doors closed and the unit descended until the green LED indicator started flashing. The unit's speed of descent gave no idea of distance travelled but it had taken more than ten seconds.

The doors opened, and as the two men traversed the corridor, two armed guards fell in behind. They followed until they reached the operations room. Inside, twenty people, a few wearing uniform, encircled a polished and long oval table. On one wall, a giant screen remained blank.

Haliwell recognised the government ministers and the heads of the armed forces. Others he was sure he had seen before but could not remember where. He and Arthur seated themselves.

43

Minutes later, the Prime Minister entered, followed by her secretary. She stood and rested both her hands on the table. "Good morning. Thank you for attending this meeting. I know you are busy." She seated herself.

The Prime Minister's secretary nodded, and the lights dimmed. The screen on the wall flickered into life. In silence, everyone watched as an ICBM launched from its silo. When the missile dived into the sea, the lights brightened. There were nods and murmurs from around the table. She placed both her hands, palms down, on the polished tabletop. "Before I open this meeting, no notes and everything said here remains here. The media believe they know as much as we do, and it must remain that way. This morning, India's Prime Minister informed me that this launch was not authorised. My own ministers tell me this cannot happen. However, I am informed our Assistant Commissioner Robbins disagrees."

Arthur stood. "Prime Minister, Commander Haliwell is the officer in charge and has the facts. I bow to his knowledge."

Halliwell stood and opened the file in front of him. He paused, glancing at those seated around the table. "Prime Minister, ladies and gentlemen, I have questioned three students concerning the launch of the alleged rogue Indian missile. They confirm that a fellow student, Jacob Spink, deliberately hacked and launched the missile. Thank God, it fell into the sea and did not damage anything or anyone. I believe he has access to other missile sites."

Across the table, a grey-haired man spoke. "Commander, are you telling us that this man bypassed the top-secret system of launch codes?"

Behind his back, Haliwell clenched his fists. "I am, Sir."

To his left, a large bull of a man spoke. "Are your sources reliable?"

Haliwell glanced at his notes before answering. "Absolutely, Sir."

"Commander."

"Yes, Prime Minister."

"Tell me the worst-case scenario and your recommendations?"

Haliwell grimaced. "Prime Minister, in a short space of time the world has changed. Computers, networks, cyber space and Star Wars technology confuse me. As I understand, our missile systems are questionable. Jacob Spink, a student, has infected them with a worm or virus. If not detained and his operating programme destroyed, this man can launch another missile. As I'm not an internet or missile expert, I'll leave the advice of what to do to those who know. For the moment, I would suggest we contain and control this situation and refrain from informing the media."

The Prime Minister gave the nod. "Admiral."

A tall man in his late fifties stood. "Prime Minister. Before this meeting, I discussed the Commander's scenario with my people. They are experts in missile technology. I understand there's no possibility of our missile safety systems and launch protocols being compromised."

Haliwell gave a dry smile, said nothing and leaned back in his chair.

The conversation shifted from negative to positive. A few of those present stated an unauthorised person or persons could not gain access to British missiles.

After two hours of discussion, the Prime Minister interceded. "Commander Haliwell, I am grateful for your frankness, it's something that's in short supply these days. I leave this enquiry within your department. The Defence Minister will order an in-depth investigation into our own missile systems. Until there is proof of interference, nothing will change. However, I do agree with the Commander. There will be a time to inform others, but this is not it."

Haliwell flushed with exasperation.

Arthur nudged him. "Ready?"

With others, they waited in the passage until the Prime Minister departed. Even then, the lift only took four persons.

Thirty minutes later, they were on their way back to Scotland Yard.

"You know when the shit hits the fan, we'll be up to our arses in hungry crocodiles. Find this Jacob Spink," said Arthur.

"We've done everything we can, Sir. If he's found a bolthole to hide in, we stand no chance.

"I want good news, not a verbal report on how you're wasting time. Someone must know something."

"He was a loner, no real friends and no significant other."

The car entered the basement car park and stopped by the lift. "Be a good man. Keep me apprised at all times."

"Yes, Sir." *Three bags fucking full.*

\*\*\*

Around midday, John Newton stirred, reached for his bottle of cheap wine and remembered the suitcase. Today he was lucky it still lay beside his mattress. Black bin-liners stuffed with his belongings surrounded him.

With the kitchen knife caked in dried blood, he forced the locks and unzipped the top section. Trousers, underwear, open-necked shirts, unfashionable suit and jumpers filled the space.

He opened the bottom half and grinned. His dirty hands grabbed the digital camera and a watch. These he could sell. He lifted a white dressing gown and found a large padded envelope. He weighed it in his right hand. In seconds, the blade of his knife tore into the paper, and the contents fell into his lap. His eyes bulged, and with a loud roar, he screamed, "Holy shit. I can get high forever."

A shadow drifted across the entrance to his lair. "Are you having a fit or something?" asked a gruff voice.

He lifted and tossed half a brick at the shadow. "Fuck off."

His hands shook as he checked one of the plastic-coated packets. *These can't be real.* He pulled three of the ten-pound notes

46

from the package. They had the smell of new money, and they were plastic. *Tonight I stay in a hotel.* He glanced at the clothes. *They might even be my size.* From the case, he removed trousers, a shirt and a jumper and checked the sizes. They were larger than he usually wore but not a problem. While scratching his nose, he saw his grime-covered hands. "Shit, I need a wash. Mungo's here I come."

***

Forty minutes later, John Newton arrived at St Mungo's homeless shelter. He clutched the case in his right hand as he strolled into the building. The stench of bleach invaded his nose.

The middle-aged man seated behind a desk lifted his head and smiled. "Sorry, mate, we're full for tonight, try the Salvation Army, you might get lucky."

"I don't want a bed, but this guy offered me a job, and I need a shower before I meet him. Night watchman, warm office and it pays ok. Please, Mister. Tell you what; he gave me a few quid to buy some decent clothes. I'll give you twenty for the use of bath and a razor."

The man held out his right hand. "Show me the money."

John pulled a roll of notes from his pocket, peeled off two and handed them over.

"You know where the bathrooms are. Razors are in the cupboard. The cleaner has just finished. Don't make a mess."

"Thanks, you've saved my life." He lifted the case and strolled to the bathroom.

It was as he remembered, functional, bare of any frills or unnecessary comforts, and it was clean. An old mirror glued to the far wall sparkled in the light from the window. White towels lay in a neatly folded pile on a wooden bench in the corner.

His thoughts drifted. I could murder a drink. He half-filled the bath, dumped his clothes on the floor and lowered his scrawny frame into the clear water. His mind swirled, as if in another world.

***

47

Ted Harper stared at the ten-pound notes. Those who begged on the streets always arrived with a pocketful of copper coins mixed with a few ten pence pieces, never a roll of new money. Twenty pounds would buy booze, cigarettes or drugs, never a bath. He lifted the telephone and contacted the police.

Two plain-clothes police officers arrived minutes later.

"That was fast," said Ted.

"We stopped along the road to buy and eat our sandwiches." The older of the two held out his warrant card. "Detective Sergeant Wilson and Detective Constable Silver. Where's this man with a bundle of tenners?"

"Having a bath."

"We'll wait. Any chance of a cup of tea?" asked Wilson.

"I'll ring the kitchen," said Ted.

Three mugs of tea arrived as the men chatted.

Twenty minutes later, John waltzed through the passage door. "I left my old clothes on the floor. You can do what you like with them."

"Smart," said Wilson. "Come into some money?"

"Backed the winner on the three-thirty at Kempton Park."

"National Hunt," said Silver. "My horse is still running."

"Can't win them all."

"Nor can you," said Silver. "The last race at Kempton was ten days ago on the flat."

John shrugged. "Made a mistake. That's not a crime."

"He told me he received an advance from a potential employer," said Ted.

"You heard me wrong."

"Just to let you know and before you answer, I'm Detective Sergeant Wilson." He held up his warrant card. "What's your name and where did you get the money?"

"John Newton. I found it."

"Where?"

"Beside me, when I woke up."

48

Wilson always considered himself a great judge of character when he interviewed suspects. His reason did not fail him with this man. "You want me to believe someone placed a large sum of money for you to find in your shit hole. Let me tell you I have never believed in Father Christmas or fairies. You can do this the easy or hard way. Silver, collect his old clothes while I escort our friend to the car. Ted, you are my witness."

He turned to John. "Sir. You do not have to say anything. But it may harm your defence if you do not mention when questioned something which you later rely on in court. Anything you do say may be given in evidence."

John stared at him in silence.

Wilson picked up the case and gripped John's arm with his free hand. "You're in the back."

Silver returned and placed John's old clothes into an evidence bag. This he dropped with the suitcase into the boot. He slammed it shut and jumped into the passenger seat.

John closed his eyes. Wilson guided the unmarked Astra through the busy streets of London. Twenty minutes later, the car entered the Metropolitan Police underground car park.

Wilson and Silver escorted their suspect into the building towards the custody sergeant. With their man logged, they placed him in an interview room with no windows.

Wilson sat on the edge of the table and smiled. "Anything you want to say before we have your clothes tested?"

"Why do you want to test my clothes?"

"You'd be amazed at what we discover from people's clothes. I bet you were wearing them when you stole the money."

John shrugged. "Suit yourself."

Silver, carrying the evidence bag, vanished for a few minutes before rejoining them.

Wilson pointed to a chair. "You can sit or stand, I don't care."

John pulled a chair out from the table and seated himself. "I want a lawyer sitting next to me before I answer your questions."

Wilson spread his hands. "Silver, when we finish chatting, get this man a brief."

John puffed out his cheeks. "Any chance of a cigarette?"

Wilson pointed at a no smoking sign. "Tell me, where did the money come from?"

"How the hell do I know? Last night I was out of it on Meths and coke. The suitcase was next to me this morning. I forced it open and found the money."

"Shall we peek inside and see if we can find its owner.?

"Not my decision, is it?"

Wilson grinned and pressed a button, which switched on the video machine. "Did you force both these locks?"

John folded his arms. "No, I used the power of my mind."

Wilson nodded to the uniformed police officer. "Please list each item as I remove them from the case."

"Hey, Clouseau, I found the case, and you can't prove I didn't."

"Shut it. You don't ask questions. You do as you're told." A knock interrupted them. Silver opened the door. "Someone wants to talk to you, Boss."

"It had better be important."

Wilson closed the door behind him.

"We will wait until my colleague returns. How did you end up homeless?"

At that moment, the door opened. Silver stood back while another man and Wilson entered. "My name is Chief Inspector Raymond Paris. You do not have to say anything, but it may harm your defence if you do not mention when questioned something which you later rely on in court. Anything you do say may be given in evidence."

"I've already cautioned him. What's the score, Sir?"

50

"It's your lucky day, Wilson. This man left a blood-covered knife under his sleeping bag. The blood type is the same as a man found on Blackfriars Bridge last night. Charge him with the murder of Jacob Spink."

"That name sounds familiar," said Silver.

"Why?" asked Wilson.

Silver pondered for a moment or two. "The terrorist squad want him stopped if he tries to leave the country."

"Well he's in the mortuary freezer," said Paris. "I thought it was a straight forward mugging. Those upstairs will be feasting on my balls when I tell them he's dead. Lock this one in a cell and don't let him see or talk to anyone and I mean anyone. I'm going upstairs."

# *Eight*

John Newton stared at the three grim-faced police officers. "Why's no one asking questions? And what's with this terrorist thing?" The interview room door opened, and an older man entered.

"Newton, I'm Commander Haliwell. My security team will take you from here to a safe house. Your nominated solicitor is aware that you're now a terrorist suspect. Sergeant, please go and collect a one-piece coverall for our guest."

Wilson nodded and left.

"Don't give me that shit. You know I'm not a fucking terrorist. My name is John Newton, and that makes me somebody. I have rights."

"You should have studied law," said Haliwell. "I can and will hold you for fourteen days. You have the information I need, and you will give it to me. Where's the laptop?"

"What the fuck do I know?"

"Get that addled brain of yours working, or you might find you're put away for a long time on a charge of murder."

Sergeant Wilson returned with a white coverall and flung it at Newton. "Strip and put that on." Silver placed his borrowed clothes into an evidence bag."

As he undressed, John gazed at the men. "I bet you lot get a hard-on watching this. You can give me a blow job or if you like, play with my balls."

"Shut it," said Wilson. "Hold your arms out."

"Why?"

"Do it."

John pushed out his arms and a set of handcuffs clamped onto his wrists.

When Silver pulled open the door. Four armed police officers stood, waiting.

"Hood," said Haliwell.

"My pleasure, Sir," said Wilson as he covered Newton's head.

Two armed men ushered Newton out of the room and along a corridor to the lift. As he sensed the lift descending, he asked, "Where are we going?"

"You'll find out when we get there, but I can tell you it's a no smoking and a no drinking venue. You are going to become as dry as the Sahara."

"No problem, Sherlock. I can do that in my sleep."

Haliwell laughed. "Who mentioned sleep?"

The buzzer operated, and the doors opened.

Still holding his arms, two men pushed him into the rear seat of a car. One fastened his seat belt.

Haliwell settled into the passenger seat while two of his team sat alongside Newton.

"You know where," said Haliwell to the driver.

"Yes, Sir."

*** 

John sat between two silent men. He needed a fix and his hands shook. "You can't do this. Stop the fucking car. Let me out."

Everyone laughed.

With little traffic, the driver sped along the narrow country roads. Tall Pine trees on either side obscured the sun.

Fifty minutes later, the vehicle took a hard left, forcing John to lean on the man next to him. He jumped as stones struck and rattled the underside of the car.

The winding road led to a three-hundred-year-old building. The gruesome structure came into the driver's vision. On three sides, rows of Silver Birch swayed in the cold autumn wind shielding the grey-stone walls from prying eyes. The car passed a marble fountain, unused and dry. Dead leaves filled the once ornate

53

fishpond. Those locals who ventured near understood the building was a private clinic.

The driver followed the track and stopped outside a two-storey granite-faced building. Two men grabbed John and hauled him from the car and into the building.

"Take him to the backroom," said a short, plump man.

Haliwell spoke as he entered. "Is everything ready?"

"The beds have clean sheets, and the kitchen cupboards contain enough food for an army. The interrogation room is as you requested."

The two officers forced John onto a wooden chair and removed the hood.

He gazed around the empty white, painted space. A thought crossed his mind as he realised this was his prison.

"This is your own private room. Shout, scream or cry, no one will hear you. No one, apart from my team, knows you're here. When I allow you to sleep, my men will give you a mattress, piss on it, and you lose the privilege." He glanced at his Rolex. "It's late, and I'm tired. Tomorrow I need answers and you will supply them."

John sneered. "Don't suppose you have any cigarettes."

Haliwell nodded to one of his men. "Let him have one but no matches."

John snorted. "Bastard." He gazed at the bare walls, nothing, not even a crack in the paintwork, disturbed the smooth plaster. High and beyond any hope of reaching, two floodlights lit the space. Not even a shadow broke the stark whiteness. He wondered if they ever went out.

John lay on the mattress, his hands shook and his mouth parched. The fear of the unknown scared the hell out of him. His drug-damaged mind wandered. His vision travelled into the corners of the room. The walls appeared to meet at ninety degrees, but then they moved. He shook his head, and they drifted back into position.

"You don't frighten me," he shouted. "I know people."

His withdrawal symptoms ebbed and flowed. Stabs of pure pain rocketed through his nervous system. *They want me to scream, but I won't.* Shaking, he curled into a tight ball, closed his eyes and fought the devil burning his brain.

Early the next morning he screamed for hours. The pain in his stomach, legs and spine erupted in waves. "I know you're watching. Give me a fucking fix. Please, one to ease the pain. I promise I'll not ask for another."

***

"How long before we help him?" asked a male nurse.

Haliwell turned on his chair. "Another twenty-four hours at least. When I'm ready, we give him a lifesaver. With luck, he'll remember what he did with that laptop. I'm heading back to my office. Don't let him die. See you tomorrow."

The nurse returned his gaze to the monitor. "I might need to use a straight jacket. He'll start banging his head next to kill the pain."

"Do what you must, but I need him breathing."

"No problem, Sir."

***

The monitor showed John curled into a ball. The nurse returned to reading his book. As he glanced at the screen, John vomited a greenish-yellow liquid.

"That's all I need. Harry, the fucker's thrown up." The two male nurses entered the room. Harry carried a straight jacket.

"Arms out, Jonny boy. Believe me; this is for your own safety."

Blank, bloodshot eyes stared at Harry. "Fuck off."

"You're not going to die. Well, not yet."

With practised efficiency, one man pulled John's arms into the air. In one swift movement, Harry fitted the canvas jacket, and in seconds, their patient lay secure.

One nurse nudged him with his foot. "The boss says you can have something tomorrow if you tell him what you did with the laptop."

John lost all hope of a life without pain.

"One good fix and you will tell us everything. For the moment, I'll let you have a drink of water. It'll make your mouth taste better, but the mattress goes. We need to have it washed."

"Fuck off, bastard."

The man placed a plastic water bottle on the floor, and pulled the mattress clear.

John struggled to his feet and charged at the wall.

The nurse's hand shot out and grabbed him. "Go get the restraints for his feet. The governor wants him in one piece."

John kicked out, but the man's grip never faltered.

"Bad move. Now I have to feed you."

Harry returned and bound John's legs with wide leather straps so that he could not stand.

"I have rights," screamed John.

The nurse pushed him onto the floor. "You left your rights at the door. You're terrorist scum. You lost any right to live when you changed sides. Tell the man what he wants to know and just maybe you'll survive."

"You can't do this."

Harry laughed. "We have and who are you going to tell? One quick injection and you'll be food for insects. The coroner's report will say death from a drug overdose. Now shut the fuck up or I'll gag you."

For the next thirty-six hours, the nurse gave John two codeine tablets, three times a day, mixed in with his food. To keep him quiet he was gagged.

Haliwell returned, dropped his briefcase on the floor. He faced the two men monitoring John. "Strap him in the chair. Do not remove the straight jacket and turn the camera towards the ceiling."

"Yes, boss," said the nurse.

Ten minutes later, John sat, secured to a heavy wooden chair, its four legs bolted to the floor.

Haliwell entered carrying a white plastic chair which he placed one metre in front of John. Before he sat, he removed the gag. "That goes back on if you scream or shout. Understood?"

John nodded.

Now I don't have a lot of time. I want answers right now, or I walk away."

John lifted his head. "You can't do this."

"I have and you can't stop me." Haliwell stood and lifted his chair.

"You can ask me questions, but I don't remember stabbing anyone."

"I never said you stabbed him. The laptop, who did you sell it too?"

"This is so funny."

"Care to elaborate."

"Since I became an addict, I promised myself I'd get clean. You are doing me a favour, and now that it's happening I find life is boring, and the only thing I can think of is the next fix."

"The laptop. Where is it?"

"I don't know."

Haliwell stood and strolled out of the room.

John screamed, "I don't fucking know or care."

Three minutes later, Haliwell returned with the nurse. "Inject that piece of human debris."

The nurse tapped the hypodermic to remove any air. With John's bare right foot tight between his legs, he injected the contents into a pulsing vein.

"Give him a couple of minutes and you can go," said Haliwell to the nurse. As he watched the pain fall from John's eyes, he smiled.

"That's good stuff. What is it?"

"I've no idea. Harry calls it his concoction."

57

John's eyes bored deep into Haliwell's as if trying to read his mind. "Cold turkey made me hate myself for the things I've done. Today I hate you too. Since I don't give myself respect, you can fuck my arse. I don't care. For me, everything is black or white, but never right or wrong. At this moment, you're a person to make my next fix possible. Property is something I can sell. It's another form of money. The thief always wins. My life between each fix is a nightmare of wild activity, but every hit is a winner."

Haliwell waited for John to hit a high. "Why did you murder that man, John?"

"I needed money, and I didn't kill him."

"The blood on your knife says you did."

"He fell onto the blade."

"So. it was an accident?"

"Black and white. An accident."

"Where's the laptop?"

"In the fucking river. You don't get much for a crappy laptop these days. Mobile phones are better."

"Are you sure?"

"I just fucking told you where it is. Are you so old you're deaf or just fucking stupid?"

"No, John. I'm going now. The nurse will take care of you. Sleep well."

"Another concoction would be great."

Haliwell stood and lifted his chair. "I'll see what I can do."

"You do that."

On his return to the office, Haliwell let out a long breath. "Let him dry out and make sure he's in good condition for his trial. When we recover the laptop, I'll be back to charge him with the murder of Jacob Spink."

"Good hunting," said the nurse.

58

# Nine

Abbey attempted five times to contact her lover Brian, but every time his mobile went straight to voice mail. She texted *must see you. I am pregnant Luv U.*

His reply came late in the afternoon. *My flat at eight.*

She gathered her things and began the journey she had embarked on so many times. Once a week she and Brian would meet, make love, go out for a meal, return, and make love again.

The evening rush on the underground was building as she descended to the platform. Two minutes later, she boarded a train and stood next to the doors. As the carriage shuddered and the wheels screeched, thoughts of the future with Brian filled her mind.

At Rickmansworth, she alighted and made her way to his place. As she opened the door, she thought of her three bed-roomed flat and decided it might be better to live there. Being early, she made a cup of coffee, seated herself on the settee and waited.

Worried she checked the time. Ten past eight. He was late.

She used the remote to turn on the television and watched the news. Fed up with the problems of the world, she stood and paced from one side of the room to the other.

The ITV ten o'clock news ended as Brian lurched through the main door. She ran to him expecting an apology but instead whisky fumes belched from his grim lips. Almost robotically, he staggered a few paces. With a loud groan, he fell on his knees and vomited. Second-hand whisky fumes filled the room. His eyes turned towards her. "What the fuck are you looking at?"

Never had she seen him like this. Her dreams died as revulsion took their place.

He tried to stand but collapsed on the carpet with a crashing thud.

She moved to help him.

"Don't fucking touch me. Tell me how much and I'll pay for an abortion."

The shock of his words registered on her face before she could hide it.

He raised his eyes to meet hers so she would know. "To me, you're something to fuck when it's raining."

Words jumped from her mouth. "You said you loved me and we were soul mates."

"You weren't fucking pregnant then." His right hand grabbed her skirt, dragged her to the floor. He slapped her hard across the face. She stifled a scream. Gripping the edge of the table and bookcase, he pulled himself to standing and staggered towards the bedroom.

On her hands and knees, she followed.

As she moved to steady him, he shoved her away. "Touch me again, and the next will be between the eyes."

"I care what happens to you. I love you."

"It's not love because you say it is. You were my bit on the side and once a week a pretty good fuck."

Abbey's heart skipped. "You promised you would leave your wife."

He wiped his mouth. "And you believed that shit. Every Friday night Casanova uses that line before he goes home to his wife. For fuck's sake, you're a spoilt rich kid. Get a life." With eyes closed, he curled into the foetal position.

Holding her cheek, tears dripped from her eyes. In a distressed state, she dragged herself upright. Loud snoring told her he was no longer a threat. In the bathroom, she bathed her face with cold water. In her naivety, she had believed their bond was unbreakable. Tears blurred her vision as she collected her things. For the hell of it, she left the main door wide open. His keys she tossed into a nearby drain.

Fresh air recharged her thoughts, and with each stride, her mind cleared and she became more determined. The physical distance between them created an emotional chasm.

Brian had used her to satisfy his ego. Aware her love was never reciprocated, more tears formed. As she walked, her hair fluttered in the light breeze. The death of her father changed everything. Her pleasure-seeking life was over. Tonight she was another pregnant single girl in London. Determined, she steeled herself to think of her child. Something she could mould, build, direct. Tonight, she was a woman with a future and Brian was history.

***

Haliwell stretched his legs as he relaxed in the leather-clad rear seat. His driver remained silent as he coped with the problematic city roads. He had long ago stopped commenting on the traffic. Haliwell flipped through his notes. The events of the last three days might be promising. No further missiles had launched. Mentally, he summed up the situation. They had been lucky; the death of Spink may have prevented a nuclear disaster.

Once he had the laptop, it would be over. He grimaced, the Thames was a fast and dirty river, it could be anywhere within a hundred metres dependant on the tide. The services of the police diving team were vital in finding the laptop. Although the river was at its cleanest in decades, how much could a diver see if he disturbed the sludge on the riverbed? He continued piecing the puzzle together until his eyes closed. A speed bump nudged him back to reality as he spied the reflective glass of the neoclassical Curtis Green building.

In Haliwell's office, Wilfred Atkins waited. His two-metre height and slight build belied his strength and knowledge of diving. As a retired member of the elite Royal Navy's Clearance Diving Team, he had earned his position as senior diving coordinator. Those who understood diving looked at him with awe.

Wilfred stood when Haliwell entered his office.

"Thank you for waiting. I require your expertise." He motioned for Wilfred to sit. "Please make yourself comfortable. Drink of something?"

"Your secretary has already asked."

Haliwell groaned when he saw the pile of paperwork in his in-tray. Annie, his secretary, had been as efficient as ever.

The office door opened and Annie, holding a wooden tray, entered. "Tea for you, guv, and one strong Americano. I had the kitchen make half a dozen corned beef, pickle and salad sandwiches as I bet you missed breakfast."

"You're a mind-reader, Annie."

She grinned. "In this job, I have to be." She turned and left, closing the door behind her.

Wilfred waited until the door closed. "You said this was a top priority. What's the score?"

"I need you to find a laptop at the bottom of the Thames."

"Where was it dropped?"

"Blackfriars Bridge."

Wilfred rubbed his chin. "Could be worse. A spring tide is due in two days, which means diving will be limited to a few hours each day."

"Not good enough. I need that laptop a week ago."

A worried expression covered Wilfred's face. "If I'm going to risk the lives of my men, I need to know why."

Haliwell told him the barest details.

Wilfred sat there, said nothing and sipped his drink for a few minutes. "To save time the Royal Navy has the specialist equipment to search no matter the tidal flow. The problem is we have to use their divers."

"Why?"

"My men are not familiar with the equipment, and it could take weeks to train them."

"In this instance, I have the budget and authority. Who's the person in charge of these people?"

"Lieutenant Commander Jeff Powell is the man to speak to. I know him from way back. I'll give him a ring if you want."

"Just give me the number."

Wilfred scribbled the telephone number on Haliwell's desk jotter."

Haliwell pressed the buttons on his desk telephone and waited. "Good morning. Police Commander Haliwell. Terrorist unit. I need to speak to Commander Jeff Powell." He drummed his fingers on his desktop while he waited. "No, he can't ring back later."

Wilfred leant across and held his hand out for the handset.

Haliwell passed it across. "Jennie, its Wilfred. Now shift your pretty little arse into gear and tell Jeff I must talk to him like yesterday."

He placed his hand over the mouthpiece. "Jennie and I had our moments a few years back." Two minutes elapsed before Wilfred said another word. His face remained impassive when he said, "Jeff, I need you and your team to undertake a priority job. Designation, Top Secret. The bad news is they keep working until they find the object under discussion. Oh, I almost forgot, bring your Mine Hunting ROV Drones. You will also need searchlights and cameras. Last question, how long will it be before you arrive at the north side of Blackfriars Bridge?" He listened. "If you can't move faster, four hours will do. Right, the site will be ready." He replaced the handset into its cradle. "If these guys can't find this laptop, no one can."

Haliwell tented his fingers and said, "How does it work?"

Wilfred was in his element and leaned forward. "You know what a torpedo is?"

"It hits a ship, explodes and the ship sinks."

"Right and wrong," said Wilfred, with an indulgent smile. "This equipment copies a torpedo, but instead of destroying, they search. Electrical power supplied from shore or surface craft drive them through the water. With fifty-inch monitors, we can see what a police diver might miss."

"Preparations, Wilfred. What do you want?"

"Close the river to all traffic and a large open area close to Blackfriars Bridge to park four HGVs."

"Four?"

Wilfred nodded. "That's what I said. Three carry the drones and their associated equipment, and the fourth is an operations room."

"Okay, I'll update the Commissioner." Haliwell lifted his telephone and reiterated Wilfred's request. As the handset returned to it cradle he turned to Wilfred. "Consider it done. In five minutes, armed officers will close the bridge. For the media only, this is a bomb scare. Let me know when the Navy arrives; I need to be there."

I'll have Wapping River police informed that I want four boats fully fuelled, fitted with portable generators, crewed and ready."

Haliwell nodded as Wilfred left the room closing the door silently behind him. He rubbed his eyes. *This is going to be a long day.*

***

Haliwell arrived at Blackfriars Bridge ten minutes after Wilfred telephoned. His driver stopped when a uniformed police officer signalled. As the window lowered, the police officer bent and said, "Sorry, sir. This road is closed until further notice."

Haliwell opened the passenger door, and as he alighted, removed his warrant card from his jacket pocket and handed it to the officer.

The officer took the card and checked the photo against the man standing in front of him. "My apologies, Sir. The OIC ordered me to stop any traffic."

"Bloody right and make sure you keep any nosey reporters away."

64

Haliwell nodded to his driver who reversed the car and drove away. "Stay where you are, constable. I'll find my own way."

As he approached the four dark-blue painted leviathans, men in standard Royal Navy overalls dragged black cables off their drums towards the river. On noticing a short, well-built man with gold stripes on his epaulettes, he strode towards him. "Lieutenant Commander Jeff Powell?"

The man turned. "Who's asking?"

He extended his right hand. "Commander William Haliwell."

Powell grabbed and shook the proffered hand. "Welcome to my world, Commander. Follow me." He led Haliwell into the waterfront police station and along a hallway to a room marked Conference. "I'm using this as our control room."

In the centre, a fifty-inch screen glowed blue. "There's tea, coffee and biscuits over there. If you have any questions, I'll answer them later. I'll let Wilfred know you're here."

"Before you leave, I have one question," said Haliwell. "Can you find my laptop?"

Powell did not appear offended. "It's a logical question. If it's there, my men and equipment will find it."

"That's good enough for me. Is the coffee any good?"

"That's your second question. I'm told it's hot, black and tastes ok." His face grew serious. "Must go. Oh, I forgot. When we're ready, you can show me where this laptop entered the river."

The last rays of the sun lit the room when Powell returned.

"Any of that coffee left?"

"I made a fresh brew. Take a seat. I'll pour you a cup."

"Cheers, I have a detailed map of the bridge and a red marker pen. Will you mark the initial search area?"

Haliwell handed over a steaming mug of coffee. "It's a guestimate at best." He marked where the patrol found the dead man and drew a small arrow. "I would say in this area, and the tide was flooding."

65

"Pound to a penny it's in the mud under the bridge." He lifted his mug. "You make a good brew of coffee." With a large gulp, he emptied the dregs and returned the mug to the sink. "We'll start in half an hour. You can join us on the river if you want but I warn you, stay out of my men's way. They get uppity with civilians."

"Message received and understood. Lead on and show me where I can park my backside and watch."

Powell, followed close behind by Haliwell, left the rear of the building and strolled along the floating jetty. At the end of the pontoon, Wilfred, dressed in warm clothing, and twelve sailors in their diving wetsuits waited. Tethered to the stern of four police riverboats bobbed the yellow mine-hunting submersibles.

One of the divers turned and faced Powell. "We're ready, Sir."

Powell pointed to the far arch of Blackfriars Bridge. "We start three hundred metres down river and complete a grid search. If we find nothing, we broaden the search area. Any questions?"

The men said nothing.

Powell checked the time. "It's slack water in twenty-five minutes and the tidal condition will be as good as it gets. Let's go. Haliwell, you're with me in the lead boat. Petty Officers James, Dobson and Clyde, you know the drill so don't fuck up."

"Would we dare?" said James.

"Lift and shift. No one has a pint until we find this fucking laptop."

As a group, the diving teams clambered aboard their craft. One by one, the sleek riverboats started their engines. With the submersible secured to the stern the four craft powered across the river.

Once in position, Powell grabbed the radio mike. "Ok, let's get this show on the road. Divers in the water. Standby divers in position. Supervisors, switch on cameras and lights."

At once, the stern of each river craft glowed from the high-intensity beam of a powerful halogen lamp.

66

Haliwell, in the lead boat, sat in the warmth of the covered deck area as each boat's monitor glowed brilliant white. The light dimmed as the equipment descended. At first, the submersibles sank until each operator established neutral buoyancy. He watched fascinated, as swirling brown water ripped across the screen. Before long, the debris-covered river's bottom filled the screen.

Powell gave the order to proceed at one knot upriver.

Each supervisor remained silent as the four floodlights illuminated the riverbed and gave two metres visibility.

"If it's there we'll find it," said Powell.

"Is that wishful thinking?" asked Haliwell.

"No. We just need time. As you can see, progress is slow. Apart from that, it's amazing what Joe public throws off a bridge. So far, I've counted three bicycles, half a dozen buckets. Shit, that's a fucking bomb."

"Silly question but I saw nothing."

Powell's face became a blank mask. "Believe me, it is a bomb. I've seen far too many." He flicked the switch on the underwater communications and pressed button three. "Mike, drop back and take a look at that long cylindrical heap of junk. I think it's a bomb."

"Roger, boss."

Haliwell slid across the seat. "I saw nothing."

Powell's eyes did not leave the screen. "I know a bomb when I see one."

A smile spread across Hallwell's lips. "You did not see a bomb. The priority is to find my laptop."

A silence filled the boat. Powell turned and stared at Haliwell. "What game are we playing?"

"Look, Jeff, I'm sure you've seen that old man wandering around London with the sandwich board that warns the end of the world is nigh. If you do not find my laptop, you might as well go and sit astride your bomb and bang it with the biggest hammer you can find."

"Why didn't you say so?"

The tension drained from Haliwell's face. "Okay, first we look for my laptop and after you may defuse your bomb."

"I agree."

"Thanks, Jeff. Want a coffee?"

A smile flashed across his face. "After what you said, make mine black and strong." He stared at the screen again. "How long have we got until the shit hits the fan?"

Haliwell handed him his cup of black coffee. "No one knows. Could be hours, maybe days, we don't know until your team find the laptop."

"That might be difficult."

Haliwell sipped his coffee. "Jeff, today we don't do difficult. Do what you have to and find it."

"Time is our problem. We're in luck now with the depth of water." With his eyes never leaving the screen he continued. "Do you know, I never worried about the future because I was young and had so much time? So much that what happened tomorrow didn't matter. Tonight, for the first time I realise that the end might be closer than we ever thought. Tomorrow could be Armageddon."

Haliwell crossed his arms and leaned against the bulkhead. "You have a point but until the boffins examine this lunatic's laptop no-one knows anything. If the world decides to end there's fuck all we can do about it."

Conversation no longer existed between the two men. Haliwell dozed while Jeff's eyes remained glued to the screen. Time dragged like a stream of setting cement. Haliwell checked his watch. A minute had passed since he last checked an hour ago, or so it seemed. Sat there with nothing to look at but the back of a man staring at a screen did nothing for his mood. The highlight of the night was when the divers changed over.

Dawn crept across the city as the craft prepared for an even longer sweep of the riverbed.

"Craft two, can you see what I can?"

"Yes, boss."

"Craft two, hold your position."

"Commander Haliwell."

"I'm not asleep."

Jeff smiled as he blinked, closed his eyes, and blinked again. "Okay, you were inspecting the back of your eyelids. This will wake you up. We might have found your laptop."

"Can you see it?"

"My diver is retrieving the object as we speak." He pressed the intercom button. "Diver two, what have you found?"

"One laptop." He held it in front of the camera. "I'm washing the mud off."

"Is that it?"

"The truth is I don't know. And until I do, your men keep searching. The man who owned it is dead and the druggie who dumped it wouldn't know. I have experts to recover the information."

A diver broke the surface, his right hand held a laptop. Powell removed it and handed it to Haliwell. "Happy now?"

Haliwell chuckled. "I think your guys have been in the water long enough. I'll take this to my experts. Meanwhile, the river stays closed, and your men need to sleep." From his briefcase, he removed a bumper roll of paper towels and wrapped the sodden laptop. Satisfied, he deposited the whole in a sealed non-static plastic bag. "If this is what I hope it is, you can go and play with your bomb. For the moment get me ashore."

Powell dragged the diver inboard and disconnected the search equipment, allowing it to descend to the riverbed. "We'll collect or use it again later." He lifted the radio mike. "All boats return to base."

"I'm going to do a runner, Jeff. Please thank your people. I hope this is what we think it is." He reached into his coat pocket, removed his mobile and pressed two keys. "Centre of Blackfriars Bridge."

Powell shrugged and pointed. "So do I, but that bomb is what we're paid for. Can you let me know the score as soon as you can?"

The craft nudged the jetty, and Haliwell stepped ashore. "Of course."

He glanced into the morning sky and watched the police helicopter, its nose down racing towards the bridge. Clutching his prize, he walked fast.

The Lynx helicopter landed, but with rotors turning, the pilot waited for Haliwell. In three minutes, it was airborne and heading towards GCHQ.

Calm, he leant back in the leather seat and shut his eyes.

Fifty minutes later the helicopter pilot shook his passenger. "Wake up. You have a reception committee waiting for you."

Haliwell's eyes snapped open. "Thanks, give me a second to come around."

The pilot laughed. "You must have been tired to sleep in this bag of nuts and bolts."

Haliwell opened the door. "Long night."

The youthful Kathy beamed when she saw him. Haliwell remembered her.

"Kathy James, Commander." She held out her hand. "You have something for me."

"I hope so." He handed her the bag containing the laptop. "This was retrieved from the Thames less than an hour ago. I believe it may solve our problem."

She passed the bag to one of her colleagues. "Take this, remove the hard drive and memory chips. Let me know when the information's available." Neither of the two technicians said a word as they scurried away.

"Breakfast, Commander? We have a first-class restaurant within the facility."

His eyes narrowed. "You're not leaving with the laptop?"

"Those two men are trained in data recovery and won't want me peering over their shoulders."

"You mentioned breakfast."

Kathy smiled. "Follow me."

"How long before we know something?"

She shrugged. "How long's a piece of string?"

# *Ten*

Shattered, Abbey fell into a deep sleep but stirred when daylight peaked through the gap in the curtains. She showered, dressed in her black jeans and oversized blue Shetland jumper. As she slipped a pair of trainers over her small feet, she chatted to her baby. "It's you and me now, babe. We don't need that arsehole, but we can't afford this place. We need to take an inventory of our life. Where would you like to live? No, I don't know either. How about we have a look at what's available?"

She thought she felt the child kick. "So, you are paying attention."

Hungry, she went to the kitchen and made four slices of toast, covered them with raspberry jam and ate them.

Two hours seated in front of her laptop, staring at property adverts online made her eyes ache and head throb. She made a decision on a two-bedroom apartment with riverside views, and private car parking.

She printed the details, closed her laptop and headed out to the coffee shop. With her mind focused on a new start, she strode along the pavement with an air of determination.

The window of Charles and Son, Estate Agents, garnered her interest. On entering, a tall, blonde-haired woman wearing a dark blue trouser suit strolled towards her. In a patronizing manner, she asked, "Can I help?"

"I have a property I want to sell."

"Can you give me the address?"

"Flat number 1, 14 Chelsea Grove Gardens."

"I take it the owner knows you are here?"

The tone of the woman's voice irritated Abbey. "Tell you what, I'll try an agency where human beings work."

A frown filled the woman's face. "One moment, please. I need to speak to my boss."

"Why? Is it above your pay grade? Don't bother, I'm out of here."

"Is there a problem, Debbie?" His tone matched his Savile Row suit, and his face shone with confidence. He smiled at Abbey.

Abbey found him unnerving. He was captivating and spoke the words she wanted to hear but somehow could not trust. Everyone has flaws. He was too perfect.

"Nothing I cannot handle, Barry. This young lady wants to sell her flat."

He turned and offered Abbey his right hand. When they shook hands, she found his grip harsh. "It's my pleasure to meet you." He pointed with his right hand. "Please come to my office, and we can discuss your details in private. Debbie, forget that instant muck. I'll have a fresh peculated black coffee, and for this charming young woman?"

"A glass of water, please."

Abbey watched Debbie stomp away.

Barry guided Abbey to his sanctuary. She walked faster when his hand brushed her thigh.

Seated in an expensive red leather chair, he asked the pertinent questions.

Debbie appeared and slammed a glass of water on the desk. "It's instant or nothing, the machine's broken."

Barry gave her a scornful look, said nothing and with a wave dismissed her. As he completed the forms, Abbey sipped at her glass of water.

"You're in luck. I have a dozen clients in mind for your accommodation. How soon can you vacate?"

She leant back, churched her fingers and stared at him. "Until I find somewhere I haven't a clue."

73

"What profession are you in?"

She frowned. "Why do you ask?"

"It's quite simple. My clients often want a flat close to their office. Saves time on the commute."

"You must be psychic. I have a flat in mind, but it's not with this agency."

"Have you the particulars?"

From her jeans pocket, she removed the details and passed them across.

His eyes scanned the crumpled sheet. "Downsizing, are we? Two bedrooms, Rotherhithe and on the river. Good choice. What I can do, with your permission, is to kill two birds with one stone. That way you will have a smooth transition from your present home to your new one."

She folded her arms. "How much will it cost me?"

He gave a calm, composed smile. "If I sell your place, nothing."

"Can I have that in writing?"

He raised his eyebrows. "Shrewd. If you can wait five minutes, I'll type the agreement."

"I'll read every word."

A smile filled his face. "I've no doubt that you will."

While his fingers rattled the keyboard in front of him, she relaxed.

In a few minutes, he handed her three sheets of paper from the printer by his desk. "If you're happy, please sign at the bottom."

She glanced at him. "And if I'm not?"

He laughed. "Take that to any legal beagle, and they will tell you it's legit. I'd stake my life on it."

She leaned on his desk and gave him a searching stare. "I'll do that." She pointed at her print out. "I need you to arrange a viewing."

"Not a problem." He lifted his mobile and pressed the keys. "Hi, Barry Thompson, Charles and Son, Chelsea. I have a client interested in a property you have for sale. Out of interest, the price appears a tad high. I don't suppose you give discounts for cash?"

"It depends."

"My buyer needs to view this morning. Two bedrooms, Sophia Crescent, Rotherhithe."

"One moment. I can make it. I'll be there in fifteen minutes."

Abbey noticed as Barry spoke his eyes shone. She waited until he finished. "You assume I want you to act on my behalf."

Barry closed his eyes for a moment. "I ask you to put your faith in me. You wish to sell your flat and buy another. I take full account of your needs. No one loses. If you have any problem with me or the way I deal with others we can end this, and part friends."

She raised her eyebrows. "It sounds great until it isn't." She held up the agreement. "I'll talk to my legal beagle. I hope you have a car because I'm not walking to Rotherhithe."

He jumped up. "Your carriage waits. As Nelson Mandela said, 'Your life is in my hands.' Follow me."

Cautious, she looked him in the eyes. "Actually, Nelson Mandela said, 'I, therefore, place the remaining years of my life in your hands.'"

Barry shrugged. "It doesn't matter."

She strode out of the office, waited until he opened the door of his Aston Martin and slid into the passenger seat. "Business must be good."

"It is."

The car took off with the tires screaming but soon travelled at twenty miles an hour through the heavy traffic. "Do you know that you can travel by subway, train, bus, taxi, car, foot or bike, from Chelsea to Rotherhithe?"

"No, I didn't, but I prefer being chauffeured."

Ten minutes later, Barry drove into a visitor's parking space and killed the engine. "Here we are. Depending on the flat, there are great views of the river." They exited the car and strolled towards

75

the property. He pointed to the stairs that led to the first floor of the property. "Glad the agent made it on time."

The man waiting smiled and held out his right hand. "Bill Franklyn, Riverside Properties."

"Barry Thompson." He turned. "My client."

Bill nodded. "Let me show you around, and before you ask, I have spoken to the owners. If you can close the deal in less than three months, they are prepared to drop the price by ten thousand pounds."

"I'm sure they can do better than that," said Barry.

"At this moment that's not necessary," said Abbey. "Bill, please give me the guided tour and if I like it, we'll discuss the price."

Before they entered, she gazed at the blocks of flats side by side. Each was identical to the next, right down to the colour of paint on their Juliette balconies.

"Where's my garage?"

Bill pointed. "You're lucky; it's close to the entrance steps."

"Great view of the river."

"Of course," Bill muttered.

Abbey smiled. "You lead, and I'll follow."

The apartment appeared welcoming with its wide hallway. Parquet flooring complimented the bedrooms and lounge. She made a mental note to have carpets fitted.

Barry waited at the flats entrance and the moment she appeared asked, "Yes or no?"

She was staring straight ahead, but her eyes flickered. "Get me a good deal for cash, and I'll move in the day after you sell my place."

He held out his right hand. "I can do that if I'm the sole agent."

She gave him a sharp look. "I still need to talk with my solicitor."

Barry turned to Bill Franklyn. "Are you in a position to negotiate with your client?"

76

"I haven't told you this, but I know the present owner has a bridging loan."

Barry grabbed Bill's arm. "If you want your bonus this week, shift your backside and get on your phone to the seller."

He shook himself free. "That sharp mind of yours will cut your face one day. I'll do it my way."

"Time's money, my friend."

Bill glared back as he strolled to the building's main door and opened it. "I'm not and will never be your friend." The door slammed.

# *Eleven*

Haliwell and Kathy chatted as they strolled into the dining room at GCHQ. One section indicated a continental breakfast, the other full English.

"I'd rather have my breakfast at home, but you'll know all about unsociable hours." She pointed. "Let's sit over there. One of the staff will come and take our order."

The attractive young woman gave a shy glance as she wandered across. She stood erect with what looked like a mini touch screen in her hand, ready to take their order. As they spoke, she tapped the screen. Then she gave that smile. "Coffee or Tea?"

Ten minutes later, Haliwell sipped a steaming cup of fresh coffee while Kathy drank her orange juice. Bleary-eyed and unshaven, he munched his way through a bowl of Shredded Wheat. The moment he ate the last spoonful, a waiter appeared with his full English, a plate of toast and dish of marmalade.

"You must be hungry," said Kathy, as she nibbled a single slice of toast.

"This is my first sit down meal since breakfast yesterday."

Her mobile's ring tone destroyed the moment. She said little, but a grimace covered her face. "Keep looking."

She lifted her head. "Bad news, I'm afraid. My team can find nothing of interest. They tell me the hard drive has been cleaned professionally."

"So what we found was useless."

"Not exactly. For the moment, access is the problem."

"We're missing something."

"What we cannot find is the file that gave him access to nuclear missiles."

"How do you know it was on this laptop?"

78

"Because he filled a large bloody hole in his C drive."

"I thought you people could recover anything."

"This man has an unusual style, and no stone remains unturned. Look, we'll not stop trying to solve the puzzle. Our difficulty was his method of programming and then saving, and we don't know where to start. I believe he transferred his masterpiece to a private cloud. This uses a dedicated server, and he's made sure no one can find its location. It's a mission-critical system. Press the right button, and it activates."

"Okay," said Haliwell. "You mentioned a dedicated server. Can we check all servers?"

She gave a know-it-all smile. "You really don't have a clue, do you? The basic laptop or a personal computer can host a web server. There are millions of servers connected to the Internet, running continuously throughout the world. What you ask is impossible."

Haliwell yawned. "I'd better go and tell my boss were up shit creek, and the crocodiles have eaten our paddles. Before we go over the waterfall, any recommendations?"

"Wait for whoever has the key to this programme to make their move."

"Could the information have died with him?"

"If I knew the answer, I'd tell you, but I don't. There may be a key somewhere, but we never found it amongst his possessions."

"Time I left. Can you inform my pilot?"

"He's in his flying machine waiting for you. We did give him a flask of coffee and sandwiches."

He shrugged. "Thanks. Keep trying. You never know your luck."

"Don't worry, we will."

"Always worry until you know the answer. Thanks for breakfast."

She stood. "As you're my guest I must escort you out of the building."

"He picked up his mobile. I'm ready."

Together they strolled to the main entrance and stopped. "I'll let you know the moment we find something."

"I'm sure you will." He buttoned his coat against the cool wind and started towards the helicopter pad.

"Did the good guys win?" asked the pilot over the helmet radio.

"No, we didn't."

"Sorry I asked."

The helicopter rotor spun, their rhythmic pulse vibrating the craft. The pilot made his final check. In minutes, they were travelling at high speed back to London.

Haliwell stared through the window as his thoughts wandered. *I hate fucking clouds.* He rubbed his eyes; he was tired of this whole business. Those who worked with complex programmes told him his hacker had left a digital footprint and they would find it. Now the brains told him they could not find anything. Inside his head, the uncertainty grew. His eyes closed, and in moments, his chin slumped to his chest.

"Wake up, Sir. We land in two minutes."

From years of practice, Haliwell jumped awake. He peered through the window and saw the twin towers of the defunct Battersea Power Station. "Have you called for a car?"

"Ordered and waiting, Sir."

"Thanks."

\*\*\*

Haliwell gazed straight ahead, only half-aware of the outside world. The uniformed driver's hands gripped the wheel as she waited for the green light.

Back in his office, he paced the floor, his mind confused as he gathered the few pieces of the jigsaw together. The phone rang. "Yes, Sir. Ten minutes." He frowned as he replaced the handset and stared out of the window. He knew his boss expected results and the cupboard was bare.

Silence filled his office as he contemplated his options. He picked up the phone. "Annie, ask the local plod to pick up those three students I interviewed. I'm missing something, and I'm praying one of them has the answer. The trouble is I haven't a clue what the question is?"

"Tomorrow morning at nine?"

"Nine is perfect but have them in my office at eight. No tea or coffee, they can stew for an hour. I'll have breakfast in the canteen."

"What else have you got on your mind?"

"Why do you ask?"

"I can sense something."

"You know me better than my wife."

"I certainly see more of you than she does. Are you going to tell me?"

"I'm in two minds but just in case, arrange for search warrants to be issued on those students. You never know what we might find."

"I'll have them on your desk before I go home."

He checked the time. "Better go and see the boss."

Annie smiled as he left.

***

Haliwell rubbed his itching arms as he made his way to Arthur Robbins' office. He had no answers and no ideas.

Before he entered, he stiffened his shoulders, knocked and marched inside.

Robbins sat relaxed in his chair. "Give me the news and before you say a word I know there's no good news."

"The geeks are still probing the laptop."

The phone rang. Robbins grimaced as he lifted the receiver. "Julie, whoever it is tell them I'm busy for the rest of the day. Take a message." He turned his head towards Haliwell. "Have you seen

81

the papers? Someone opened their mouth and the rumourmongers are in full flow. One of the comic strips is headlining Armageddon is days away."

Haliwell made a face. "There are some who want this to get worse. I'm sure the defence secretary would love an increase in his budget."

"Thank God no other missiles have launched."

The snowflake generation are the problem," said Haliwell smirking. "Arseholes the lot of them. Always running around with their thumbs up their bums. It the missiles start arriving, they'll wave placards outside parliament and expect them to stop."

"The Prime Minister would like to believe Spinks' murder was fortunate and his knowledge died with him. However, I'm informed half the House of Commons is running around like headless chickens."

Haliwell grinned. "Nothing unusual then."

"Let's pray your assumption is correct. Hold back on the details but have you any recommendations I can suggest to the Prime Minister?"

"Make our missiles hack proof."

Robbins frowned. "You never heard this from me but at this time our nuclear deterrent is out of action until they find your worm and neutralise the damage it may have done. Thank God for the 1987 INF Treaty. As far as we know, the range of Russia's missiles is five hundred kilometres. I'm informed your openness impressed the PM."

"I'm amazed at least someone listened to what I was saying."

The telephone rang. He lifted the receiver and barked. "I told you I did not want to be disturbed." The call ended.

Haliwell gave him a concerned glance. "Problems?"

"No."

"I'm going to interview those three students again in the morning. GCHQ kept talking of a key. It's a gamble but I might have missed something."

Robbins stood, turned his back on Haliwell and strolled to the window. "Keep me informed."

Aware the meeting had ended, Haliwell stood. "Of course, Sir."

# Twelve

Exhausted, Jeff Powell sat in his chair and sipped at another cup of thick, black coffee. *Where was that lifting barge?* His eyes started to close, but a heavy knock on the door forced them open.

A young, fresh-faced police officer entered. "Sorry to disturb you, Sir. Message from Port of London Authority (PLA). Your barge with a crane. ETA Blackfriars fifty minutes."

"Thank you. Could you poke your head into where my team are resting and ask them to get ready?"

"Will do, Sir."

Jeff rubbed the stubble on his chin as he gave thought to the removing of the world war two leftover from the riverbed. Its size and shape determined it was a 500 KG German bomb. While organising the crane his team had cleared the area of mud, debris and readied the rusted relic for lifting. Further investigation proved the removal of the fuse impossible.

An hour later, the officer returned. "I can see the barge, Sir."

"Better get on with it then." He grabbed his foul weather jacket and followed the officer out of the building. His team, ready to dive waited on the stern of a police launch.

He turned to the superintendent. "When can we start?"

"As you requested, full safety restrictions are in place and will remain until you tell us differently."

Jeff jumped onto the deck of the launch and stood next to the boat driver. An aerie silence cloaked the area. No trains rattled across Blackfriars, the river and road traffic non-existent. "Did you volunteer for this?"

"Yes, Sir."

"Doesn't the thought of the bomb bother you?"

"Sir, my arse is twitching like a rabbit's nose."

"That makes you human. What's your name?"

"Sidney, but I answer to most things, but Sid usually works."

"It's high water in an hour. Take me to the barge please, Sid."

As the mooring ropes landed inboard, Sid steered the craft across the river. With Jeff and his team safely on the barge, Sid returned to the station.

While Jeff discussed the operation with the barge captain, the divers readied themselves. Apprehension filled their thoughts but not one man expressed fear.

Located by Sat Nav, the barge glided into position.

Jeff's pulse shifted into overdrive as he checked the time and studied the river. "Divers in the water."

Two men slid into the water, disappeared, surfaced and gave the thumbs up, confirming they were ready. The Chief Diver noted the time in his logbook.

The men on the barge lowered the lifting straps to the divers.

Jeff stood back as his team completed one final check before disappearing below the surface. For those on the barge, the time dragged as they listened to steady breathing from the speakers.

The lead diver's voice came clearly from the speakers. "Ready."

Jeff stood alongside the crane operator. "Depth twelve metres."

"Depth twelve metres, boss."

A flurry of bubbles surrounded the cable.

"Ready to lift."

"Slowly, slowly," said Jeff. "I prefer a nice smooth lift and please do not hit anything."

"I'll try not to," said the operator.

"Clear, clear, clear." Vibrated from the speaker.

Jeff let out a slow controlled breath. It would fool the barge crew, but his team knew the tension he experienced. His eyes moved with the alertness that comes from stress, and his hands remained clenched as the next stage neared.

The hook holding the lifting straps surfaced. "Steady, steady. Keep it at a distance," said Jeff. "Stop. Now, as if you are holding a baby, turn to the left until you're over our floating bomb holder."

"No problem, guv." The crane altered its position so slowly it was difficult for anyone to make out it was moving. Ten minutes elapsed. "Will that do you, guv?"

Jeff smiled. "You're not good, you're fucking brilliant."

"You said a newborn and I love kids."

The two divers surfaced and climbed onto the barge before removing their equipment.

Jeff went and checked the rusted relic before fastening the securing straps. Once back on the deck of the crane, he made contact with the police. As Jeff replaced the handset, a launch cast off from the pontoon. He waited for it to secure alongside.

"You're a glutton for punishment Sid, but my team will take over from here."

"What's the plan, Sir?"

"Using your launch, we tow the bomb on our flotation device downriver to the open sea. In a cleared area, my people will attach explosives, lower it to the bottom and carry out a controlled explosion. As we pass each bridge and tunnel, it will close until we are well clear. Every man and his dog will complain, but there's no other way."

He stopped talking as Sid pointed at the bomb. "What's the odds of it going bang?"

Jeff shrugged. "There's always a chance."

"Jesus," muttered Sid. "How do you remain so calm?"

"It's my job. I couldn't do yours, dealing with the dregs of society."

"It's not all bad, Sir."

86

From behind, the Chief Diver shouted, "Ready, boss."

"Sid, get on your radio unless you fancy a Thames cruise."

Jeff turned to face his small team. "The second Sid is on his way, secure the floatation device. Use the fifty-metre line for towing. How many sandbags did you use?"

"Twenty and secured. Any more and the raft might disappear under the surface."

"Jones, you drive. Let's go before London is completely gridlocked."

Ten minutes later the launch towing its dangerous cargo astern proceeded towards Southend. Jeff and his Chief stood in the stern of the launch. To those who understood, their eyes never left the raft.

Late that night and one mile off Sheerness, a controlled explosion rattled a few windows. Five minutes later, Jeff relaxed on the deck of the craft and using a life jacket as a pillow. fell into a deep sleep.

# *Thirteen*

Abbey trudged along the pavement towards New Scotland Yard, her mind focused. *What does Haliwell want this time?* Her head buzzed, and her heart rate increased. She smiled at her own thoughts. *I'm like a cow walking into a slaughterhouse.* On signing in, an officer escorted her to Haliwell's office. She was surprised to see Michael and Tyler already there.

Haliwell checked the time. "My secretary told you eight o'clock. I'm pleased you found the time." He smiled, hoping his firm tone put the fear of God into them.

She nodded pensively. "Blame the traffic."

"You should have left home earlier. Now shut up and listen."

Abbey took a deep breath. "I'm listening."

Haliwell's tired eyes were interrogative. "This morning I will ask you questions, and you will give me your answers. The difference is it will be as individuals. If I discover your stories are not the same, then the games begin, and you can forget about going home tonight. Do I make myself clear?"

The three of them nodded but remained silent.

Michael, you first. You two will be taken to another room where you cannot overhear." He buzzed his secretary who entered a minute later. "Annie," he pointed, "take those two away."

She held the door open. "Please follow me."

Haliwell cleared his mind and concentrated. "Michael, don't ask to sit. I'd hate to think you were comfortable. The law demands I have to tell you this interview is being recorded." He pointed towards the camera, its red power light blinking. "Now, in your own words, tell me everything about Jacob Spink and his plans to launch missiles. Oh, by the way, the police found him on Blackfriars Bridge."

"You should be asking him these questions?"

"Haliwell rubbed his chin. Bit difficult. He's dead."

Michael's face turned ashen. "What do you mean, he's dead?"

"We received a report that he was stabbed and died from his injuries. The university has been informed. You and your friends crossed the line when you stole money from bank accounts and became members of the criminal fraternity."

Michael smiled. "You'd have a tough job proving it."

"You cracked the system, and I doubt any of the banks would have discovered their loss. So why did Jacob change the game plan?"

He shrugged. "Because he was a nutter."

The questioning continued for over an hour before Haliwell buzzed Annie.

"Yes, boss."

"Take this young man and make sure he leaves the building. As I intend to continue this inquisition, you can bring back Tyler. Michael, go and stay in your halls."

Confused, he followed Annie out of the room.

While he waited for Annie to return, Haliwell strolled around his office, stopped and stared out of the window. He started to ask himself questions. *Why would they lie? Someone has to do this, why me?* A knock on the door spoilt his train of thought.

Haliwell's head throbbed as he experienced the weight of the world on his shoulders. "Come in."

"Where's Michael?" asked Tyler.

With both elbows on his desk, Haliwell churched his fingers. "He answered my questions and left. Now I'm a good listener. Please tell me everything you can remember from meeting Jacob Spink to the present day."

"I've told you all I know but if you insist."

Haliwell snapped. "I do."

When Tyler left, Haliwell sat in silence and allowed his mind to wander. *Both men were mere pawns in a game. Jacob tossed them a few crumbs and they took the bait. Would Abbey be any different?*

Annie entered with Abbey. "Would you like a cup of coffee, sir?"

"Yes, please. Strong and black."

Abbey smiled. "Standing room only."

"My office, my rules."

"What do you want from me?"

"I need to know what your friend Jacob infected with his worm. I need to know how you were involved. I need to know his passwords."

She placed her hands on the front edge of his desk and leant forward. "If I knew I'd tell you, if only to get you off my back."

Annie returned, placed one cup on the desk and poured the coffee from a large stainless-steel pot. "That should keep you awake."

Haliwell glanced at Annie. "Thank you."

Abbey sighed. "What's the point of going over the same ground?"

He peered up at the ceiling and asked himself if the job was worth the hassle. "To see if you tell me the same answers. My old brain tells me I'm missing something, and I believe you know what it is."

She laughed. "Have you forgotten I was the one who informed on Jacob?"

He managed a false smile as he lifted the cup and sipped his coffee. "I'm less complicated than I appear."

A silence filled the room.

Abbey cleared her throat. "Commander, I have enough problems in my life but if I could help you, I would."

He leant back in his chair, hands clasped behind his head and watched her. "Of course, you know Jacob is dead."

90

Surprise filled her face, and the warmth drained from her eyes. "He was a strange man. When did he die?"

He placed his hands on the desk. "You'll be pleased to know his attacker is under arrest. We also discovered his laptop, but the hard drive contained nothing of interest."

Abbey's manner changed. "So why are you still asking stupid questions?"

"It's what I do. When Jacob launched that missile, he sent shivers through the corridors of power. What use is a missile defence system when some university student can operate it at will? Those in power want to know how. The boffins created the internet, and the world's gone mad. You and your associates worked with him and must know something."

"You know what I know."

Haliwell was irritated and checked his watch. "You can go."

He watched Abbey leave and buzzed Annie. She arrived in seconds.

"How did it go?"

He stood up. "What's your opinion of the Lane woman?"

Annie paused before she spoke. "I need to think about my answer."

"Tell me, straight off the top of your head."

"She's a spoilt brat who has had her own way for all of her life. Does what she wants when she wants and with whom she wants. Doesn't suffer fools and from the university reports, she's exceptionally talented. You don't suspect her of more involvement than she admits?"

His gaze met hers. "I think she's hiding something, but I believe in giving someone enough rope."

She smiled. "Go home and have a good night's sleep. As my mum says far too often, tomorrow's another day."

91

# *Fourteen*

When Abbey arrived home, she relaxed on the settee and shut her eyes. Her thoughts wandered to Jacob's murder. Perhaps it was for the best, he was crazy, insane. Inside his head, he believed his bizarre ideas. He had rewritten the ground rules. In many ways, it was exciting until it was not a good idea. Thoughts came and went but one entered her brain. The pros and cons of the argument filled her head.

With a pounding heart, her eyes snapped open. Slowly her breathing steadied. She glanced at her watch. Two hours had passed. She rubbed her eyes, sat up, and stared at the pile of study papers on the coffee table. On lifting the top sheet, she stretched and yawned. *Why do I have to read this crap?* She tossed the page aside, fell back into the comfort of the couch and closed her eyes.

\*\*\*

Barry Thompson removed a buff folder from his desk drawer. He placed it flat before opening and thumbing through his notes. For a few seconds he scanned the pages before lifting his mobile and pressing a memory key. It answered on the fourth ring. "Hi, Terry, I've found another sucker. She's ripe for the con and I'd love to do things with her body."

"What's she good for?"

"A Million. It's a doddle. I'll arrange for you to visit and do the necessary in the next couple of days. Okay?"

"And my cut?"

"Thirty-five."

"I'll wait for your call." The line went dead as Barry removed a pillbox from a locked drawer in his desk. Smiling, he stood, buttoned his jacket and grabbed his car keys. "Right, Miss Lane, the game begins."

*** 

The door-entry buzzer snapped Abbey out of her sleep. She jumped and lifted the handset. "Abbey."

"Miss Lane, it's Barry Thompson, your Estate Agent. I know it's late, but my client wants some photos. She's really keen."

"Why didn't you phone?"

"If it's not convenient I'll come back in the morning." He grinned when the door clicked open.

Abbey opened her flat door and watched him approach. His mouth formed a smile as he held out his hand. She ignored the gesture.

"Thank you. Just a few snaps and I'll leave. I must say the communal area is spotless."

"It should be. The cleaner doesn't come cheap."

She closed the door. "Where first?"

He removed his mobile and set the camera to video. "Right here is great. You lead. I'll follow."

Three distinct knocks on the door distracted her. "Two seconds."

"Hi, I'm Steve Jenkins, basement flat. It's Abbey, isn't it? I'm out of milk. You wouldn't have a spare cupful. Pay you back tomorrow."

She laughed. "I've a full carton you can have, come in. Oh, this is Barry, my estate agent."

Steve chewed his lower lip. "Didn't know you were selling."

"No one does. You're the first. My father died, and I can't afford this place."

She strolled into the kitchen, returned with an unopened carton, and handed it to Steve. As he started to leave, she whispered, "Come back in thirty minutes."

Steve nodded as the door closed.

She found Barry in her bedroom, his hands pressing the mattress on her queen-size bed.

"Great bed."

93

She ignored the comment. "There are three bedrooms. One I use as a study and the other is my junk or guest bedroom."

"I saw the mess. Kitchen, please."

He followed her into a large kitchen. His eyes scanned the expensive bespoke units and granite worktops. Unlike her bedroom, it was tidy.

"You have a great place. Bathroom next. My client will love this."

She opened the door. "My bathroom."

"Well fitted, a modern Jacuzzi, walk-in power shower. I love the fluffy white towels. Last but not least, the lounge."

"I'm going to make myself a coffee. Would you like one?"

"Yes, please. I'm impressed. Most of these buildings have lost their charm, but yours is brilliant." As they entered the lounge, he stopped and looked. "Wonderful high ceilings and the original coving is perfect. Although minimalist, it echoes a world of past grandeur." He continued filming for a few more minutes before sitting on the settee. "This is cosy. What are your plans for tonight?"

She half shut her eyes as if considering her reply. "Why do you ask?"

"I'd love to take you out for a meal."

"No can do. I'm busy." She returned with two mugs of coffee, placed them on the table and dropped onto the settee.

He took a deep breath. "Could I use your toilet?"

A smile played around her lips. "Of course you can. You know where."

A few minutes later, he returned. He liked what he saw, the way she was sitting, relaxed with the lower buttons of her blouse undone.

"Would you like to check my video before I ready it for my sales site?"

As he sidled across she shifted her position on the settee.

Feigning a trip, he stumbled as his hand passed over her coffee cup. "I'd trip over in an empty room." She cringed as he

94

seated himself close. "Take a look. Anything you don't like I'll erase."

She sipped her coffee as he ran the full video. "They make this place appear brilliant. I'm sure when it comes to selling a property, you know your job."

"I'm good at what I do."

The knock on the door startled him.

Abbey frowned. She stretched and rose. "I'd better see who it is." She opened the main door.

Steve stood there, grinning. "You promised you would show me how to install a security programme."

She made a show of yarning. "Sorry, Steve, lots on my mind. I'll get rid of my estate agent. Come in."

Barry was on his feet, looking at his watch. "I just remembered I have another appointment. Thanks for your time. I'll be on my way." He walked to the door, glared at Steve and left.

"Coffee or a beer?"

"A beer, please."

She swayed, bumping into the doorframe as she entered the kitchen. "Steve, I don't feel so good."

"I assume the beer is in the fridge. You go and relax in your favourite chair."

As if drunk, she staggered to her chair and slumped into its soft cushions.

"How you doing?" he asked.

"What the fuck." She lay lifeless on the settee with her eyes wide open. He shook her. "Abbey, speak to me." His mind raced. *Should I phone for an ambulance?* She was breathing and her pulse seemed okay. Steve ran his hands across his face. *Get her into bed.*

With care, he slid her from the chair to the carpet. With no effort, he dragged the carpet across the polished floor and into the bedroom. At the first attempt, he lifted and placed her in the centre of the bed. With the duvet wrapped around her, she was warm and

95

safe. Aware he could do no more, he went, found a book, returned and kept watch.

***

When daylight glowed around the edges of a blackout-blind, Abbey realised she was awake. *Strange. I don't remember going to bed. Why am I still fully dressed? Why is Steve in my bedroom and asleep in a chair?* Using her arms, she forced herself into a sitting position. Her head spun, and hands trembled as she fell back.

"Steve," she croaked, but he did not respond. She stretched out and found her alarm clock. She attempted to toss it at him, but it slipped from her grasp. On the second attempt, it crashed to the floor.

"What time is it?"

She stirred. "Why are you in my bedroom?"

"Last night, you scared the hell out of me collapsing like a sack of rags. I didn't know what to do, so I put you to bed. How are you feeling? Are you an epileptic or something?"

In a whisper, she asked, "What happened?"

Steve shook his head. "Once you got rid of your agent you said you didn't feel too good. I told you to relax while I went to retrieve a beer from your fridge. I spent a minute or two looking for a glass, and when I came back, you were out for the count. I stayed all night in case you were sick. Sorry, I fell asleep."

Abbey breathed deeply. "I remember everything being in free fall and then nothing."

"If I were you I'd stay in bed and rest until you feel better."

"What did you say?"

"I'll make you a coffee. Stay in bed. Black or white?"

"Black, please. My head's beating like a drum."

Steve returned a few minutes later with her coffee, but she was asleep. Making little noise, he tiptoed out of the flat.

***

Abbey ran along an endless tunnel. Her eyes searched the brickwork, checking for a way out. Exhausted, she slowed to a walk.

96

As she progressed, she became aware that her footsteps made no sound. She stopped. *This doesn't make any sense. I'll turn back.* As she turned, darkness cloaked her. She stretched out her arms but found nothing. "Shit," she shouted as the floor gave way, and she drifted in a black void.

A noise in the distance disturbed her. She awoke, blinking away the stupor of sleep. *Who is hammering on my apartment door?* She slipped into her dressing gown. Her head spun as she sat on the edge of the bed. "What the fuck?" and then she remembered. Leaning against the wall, she made the door, secured the chain and cracked it open.

Steve held up a large pepperoni pizza. "You took your time, I was worried. Dinner."

She removed the chain. "I don't feel hungry."

He held her arm as they made their way into the lounge. "I'll blast this in the microwave for thirty seconds. A few mouthfuls of this will do you good."

With the cheese bubbling, he placed the plate on the coffee table nearest Abbey. "Help yourself."

She lifted one slice and nibbled at the edge.

"Oh, I explained your condition with my tutor today, and he reckons someone gave you a date rape drug."

"The only person here was my estate agent, but he left when you arrived. After that, the next thing I saw was you asleep next to my bed this morning."

"It must have been him."

"How do I prove it?"

"You can't, but he was not a happy bunny when I arrived."

"I could go for a blood test."

"After this long, I doubt if they could find anything. It's your word against his. You were lucky; he never got the chance to do anything."

"You're right. This pizza's good." She munched her way through another two slices.

97

"Do you want me to stay, or are you okay?"

"I'm a lot better than I was. It must have been that smug bastard, and you're right, I could never prove it. I'd love to kick his balls so hard they stuck in his throat and choked him to death. One thing's for sure, he'll not be selling my place."

Steve stood and rubbed his greasy hands down his jeans. "I've things to do. Any problems, give me a bell. Make sure your door's locked when I leave."

"You're a pal, Steve. Thanks."

\*\*\*

Abbey was not at her best, but she dumped the remains of the pizza in the bin before sitting at her laptop. Smiling, she planned her revenge. In her bedroom, she slipped into her pink tracksuit and pink Puma trainers. A good run would clear her mind and rid her body of whatever that letch dropped in her coffee.

One hour later, she returned, dumped her clothes in the washing machine and showered. Refreshed and almost human, she sat with her laptop and hacked into Charles and Son, Estate Agents. A read of what was easy to find made her smile, business was not as good as it appeared. With a self-written search algorithm, she entered the system programmer's domain. She laughed at the feeble security as she downloaded illegal pornographic content. With a further series of commands, she concealed her server address. Anyone who had the skill to track her would discover the sender location as a hardware shop in Cape Town. In less than ten minutes, Barry would be looking for another job. There was no way he could talk his way out of this situation.

Next, she emailed Bill Franklyn, Riverside Properties. She gave him her mobile number and asked him to contact her re the sale of her property.

Abbey got up from her desk and filled a pint glass with fresh orange juice and tonic with a ton of ice. In the comfort of her lounge, she snuggled into the cushions of her sofa and relaxed. She was silent but needed to see the results of her handiwork. The

98

evening air was fresh and bracing as she almost ran towards Charles and Son.

As she neared the office, two police cars with sirens blasting the night air raced past. On turning the corner, a police officer stopped her.

"Sorry, madam, wherever you're going, you'll have to find another way."

Filled with nervous excitement, she said, "With the number of police vehicles blocking the road, you must be dealing with a gang of criminals."

"This guy is scum, a paedophile but I never said that. Goodnight."

Her ruse had worked. Someone house hunting had reported the child porn.

One hour later, she went to bed and tried to sleep. At midnight, she was wide-awake. She left the warmth of her bed and made a coffee, switched on her laptop and read the latest news. In seconds, she found what she was looking for. The article in The Mail online read, **A London estate agent named as Barry Thompson was in police custody.** *The police found a cache of child porn on his company server. It appeared that when the public went to the agent's site, child abuse images appeared. He was to appear in court that morning.*

Slumped over her desk, she had no idea when she fell asleep, but when the morning sun woke her, she went for a long hot shower.

*** 

At nine, Bill Franklyn phoned Abbey asking if he might view her flat. As he wandered around, Barry's arrest became the main topic of conversation.

With ample photos and information, Bill promised he would have it on the company's For Sale site that evening. As he was about to leave, he turned to her. "What made you change your mind?"

She looked at him and frowned. "I did not like his mind-set. He was full of his own importance and believed he was God's gift

99

to women. Apart from the obvious, I thought he was a fucking arsehole."

Bill laughed. "We are on the same page. I'll give you a bell tomorrow if you want to change anything."

"I'm sure it's fine." She watched him leave and made the decision to go for a long walk.

Dressed in a dark blue trouser suit cloaked by a beige trench coat, she went out for some fresh air. On passing a cafe, she went inside and ordered a double Americano with a ton of sugar. For over an hour, she sipped coffee and asked herself where was she going with her life? With no answer that made any sense, she downed the dregs, grimaced and left the cafe. Sometime later, she was standing outside Barry Thomson's estate agency. *Strange.* It had not been her intention to go there.

"Not coming in?"

Abbey turned and faced Barry.

He saw the shock register on her face, and an impossible-to-read smile played on his lips.

Her pulse quickened. "Heard you'd been arrested."

The hint of a sneer contorted his lips. "The police released me on bail, but they took my passport. They found some crude pictures on my system. I told them I know nothing about them, but they didn't believe me."

"Did they find your supply of date rape drugs?" The words flew from her mouth before she could stop them. His reaction confirmed she had hit the bull's-eye.

His face tensed in anger, turned red as he buried his rage. "I bet you're a rubbish fuck."

"You'll never know. Will you?"

A smile creased his lips, "Accuse me, and you'll regret it."

"I really don't give a shit. You'll soon be in prison, and someone's pretty boy. If I were you, I'd take an extra-large jar of Vaseline."

100

Barry was tired of word games and raised his hand but then stopped. "Fuck off, bitch."

She laughed and turned away as the first droplets of rain hit her face. She loved the cleansing power of the shower. As she walked, raindrops large and soft plastered her hair to her face. By the time she arrived home, her hair hung in clumps. Once inside, she stripped, tossed her wet clothes into the washing machine and went for a shower.

Later that evening, she stared at her laptop screen. *Why do companies use common passwords? Most software is vulnerable, and they're still using a firewall that originated in the ark.* She jabbed ENTER and waited. In a few moments, her worm crawled into the estate agent's bank account. Satisfied, she had screwed Thompson, she went to bed.

***

Abbey's remark on drugs wound up Barry. If she wanted a fight, he would give her one. He spent the whole night analysing his situation. The future looked bleak. Even if he could prove his innocence, people would say there's no smoke without fire. He studied his mobile's contact data, made a decision and pressed the keys.

"This better be important. What do you want?"

"Hi, Terry. I've a problem and need your expertise. When can you initiate a solution?"

Terry gave a resigned sigh. "Is this some squat you want to buy cheap?"

"It's occupied, and I'd prefer the owner to be out. That detail is up to you. I'll double your usual charge for a quick job."

"Ten thousand, cash upfront and ten more when the place is ash."

"You'll get your money. Have I ever let you down?"

Terry laughed. "What's the address?"

Barry told him. "I'll deliver the down payment on my way to the office in the morning. Do the job when you're ready."

"Listen to the news, and you'll know when to pay me."

The line went dead as Barry said, "Just fucking do it." From the concealed safe in his office he removed ten thousand pounds and dropped it in his briefcase.

# Fifteen

With Barry's money transferred offshore, Terry, a tall, wiry and serious man, was a pro in his business. He parked his Silver BMW a safe distance from Abbey's flat. He always made sure his parking ticket was stuck on the windscreen, while he checked out the locale. A parking fine was the last thing he needed. For him, a rear garden made a quick escape from the property straight forward. His surveillance found an alleyway, which divided the rows of houses. He tried the gate to Abbey's, it was open, but he did not enter.

*** 

Abbey awoke at six and remained in bed for another hour before going for a shower. With a pot of fresh coffee brewing, she checked her emails and answered those requiring a comment. From a drawer, she removed and opened one of her study folders. For the next hour, she read her notes and made the odd spelling correction. On checking her diary, a highlighted appointment with the clinic stood out. Moreover, a couple of lectures required her attendance. In two minds, she grabbed her laptop case, notes and handbag and set off for the doctor's surgery.

*** 

For three days, Terry watched and waited for the whole property to empty. Today and with his clipboard in plain sight, he climbed the steps to Abbey's building. One by one, he pressed the door entry buttons and waited. When no one answered, the door lock clicked open at his first attempt. A gentle push and he was inside. For a few seconds, he stood still and listened. Once inside Abbey's flat, he opened the rear window wide in case he had to make a fast exit. His eyes scanned the kitchen until he found the gas supply to the boiler. Isolating the gas supply at the meter, he removed the metal coupling. "Ready for ignition and lift-off." He chuckled as he stuffed half a dozen sheets of paper under the electric grill.

103

Terry closed the open window. On his return to the kitchen, he switched on the grill, and his right foot booted the gas supply lever to open. Once outside, he waited in his car. A few minutes later the sound of glass shattering reached his ears. Satisfied, he drove away.

***

Within five minutes, the normally quiet street filled with noise and activity when the Fire Brigade arrived. From the damaged windows, shrouds of black smoke billowed towards the sky. Firefighters ran out their hoses, while others prepared to enter the building.

In minutes, the three-man search and rescue team entered the building. In stages, they made their way towards Abbey's flat. At the far end of the street, a gas company employee isolated the gas main. Firefighters played their charged hoses through the damaged windows.

Police cars blocked the street. An officer raised his hand as Abbey went to duck under the blue tape. "You'll have to wait here until the brigade gives us the ok."

"Where? My flat's along this road."

"Number 14."

Abbey's shoulders slumped. "Is it a bad fire?"

The officer stared at her for a moment before speaking. "I suppose someone left the gas on, or it's a tumble drier fault. Don't understand why people leave the damn things running when they go out. Then we all live and learn. As far as I know, the place is empty."

Abbey hesitated. "It's where I live."

The officer gave her a huge grin. "Doesn't matter. You must stay here."

Abbey paced along the adjoining street, her thoughts in turmoil. Had she left something on? She did not think so but then in her condition had she forgotten? Again, she stopped and stared at the street of Georgian houses. Despite the fire, it stood as proof it existed. It remained like a black scar. Scorch marks spoiled the neighbouring homes. Saved by the firefighters, they remained habitable.

Again, she peered at the hard-at-it fire-fighters.

Steve arrived and stood next to her. "Whose house?"

"Ours," she said.

Steve waved his hands in the air. "My mum and dad will be pissed off. It's part of their investment portfolio."

"They'll have insurance," said the officer.

With a sleepy smile, Steve shook his head. "I don't think they'll see it that way. I'm supposed to be looking after the place."

"They reckon it started in my flat," said Abbey.

He hesitated before replying. "Makes no difference. The water damage alone will make my place a disaster zone."

"Look, they're rolling up their hoses. The fire must be out," said the police officer. "Wait. I'll go and ask."

"Thank you," said Abbey.

"We'll need a place to doss down," said Steve. He punched numbers into his mobile and walked away.

The officer returned with a firefighter. He pointed. "These two have flats in the building."

Abbey spoke with impatience. "When can I return to my flat?"

The firefighter gave a short mocking laugh. "Upstairs will have smoke damage to the common areas but with luck no internal damage. The ground and garden flats, one, two months, if you can find a builder."

Steve returned to the group. "Great news. My mate Harold says he's got yards of room and will put us up until we sort ourselves out."

Abbey gave the firefighter a severe smile before asking. "Can I return to my flat and retrieve a change of clothes?"

He did not answer straight away. "Let me talk to my boss. The kitchen floor has gone, but the rest should be ok. We have authorised a carpenter to board the windows. It keeps out those who would strip the place bare." He walked away.

"Seems a straight forward guy," said Steve.

"I don't fancy him. Do you?"

Steve did not laugh and did not smile. "Not my type." They both laughed. A grim-faced firefighter strolled towards them.

When he went to speak, she looked straight into his eyes. "Good news, I hope."

"Not the best but a compromise. One of my team will escort you both into your flats for you to collect clothing and valuables. Both kitchen areas are dangerous. We found the gas pipe in flat 14 disconnected. Have you had any work undertaken in that area?"

Abbey shook her head. "As far as I can remember, the last people to look at the gas supply were there to check the meter. They checked and recorded the meter number."

The man's smile contained no warmth. "Well someone took it apart."

Surprised, Abbey gave his words some thought. "What are you implying?"

"Something isn't right. We were lucky the gas company isolated the supply."

"I never touched the gas pipe. Why would I? Anyway, I have been out all day."

"You might have to prove where you were."

"Not a problem. I had a doctor's appointment first thing. When I left the surgery, I attended two boring lectures. Any chance I can get my things."

"Yes, you can but one at a time. Who's first?"

"You go," said Steve. "I'll wait outside."

The three of them walked fast along the pavement until they were outside the house. Its once pristine white paint now black and scorched around the windows.

"Stay close."

"I'll stay closer than your wife."

"I'm not married, but I know what you mean."

As they entered, she gagged as the acrid stench of smoke filled her lungs. "How do you work in this?"

"Practice and breathing apparatus."

The door to her flat hung on one hinge. She pointed. "That's my bedroom."

"You're lucky you closed all the doors before you went out so the fire never made it this far. We did have to go into each room and check."

She opened the door and saw her carpet covered in black footprints. In an instant, a mental picture of the last six months overwhelmed her. She swore aloud as Gregory Peters words came to mind. *From the end of this month, you will be responsible for the management and repairs to the house and car.* That was months ago. Pregnant and with nowhere to live, she sat on the end of the bed and sobbed.

"I've seen worse than this," said the firefighter. "Once the builders start, they can have this perfect in a couple of months."

She wiped her eyes. "Shit happens, and you're right."

"I'll help you pack."

"Thanks. You'll find two suitcases under the bed."

He dropped to his knees and dragged both cases out and into the open. One he placed near Abbey and the other on the bed. Out of the corner of his eyes, he noticed a lipstick, memory stick and eyebrow pencil on the floor. These he scooped together and tossed them into the case.

Abbey opened drawers and dumped everything in one case until it was full. She smiled when she saw the fire fighter folding and packing her clothes. "Can you help me close this case?"

In ten minutes, they were ready to leave.

"Can I take a peek in the kitchen?"

He shrugged. "Can't see that it will do any harm but don't try to go in."

On their way out, he pulled open the burnt and blackened fire door to the kitchen.

Abbey's eyes stared into a black abyss. Steve's kitchen looked like a tar pit.

"My neighbour will not be happy."

The man coughed and cleared his throat. "No one ever is after a fire and thanks to the gasman we put it out before it took off. Time you let your friend salvage what he can."

Abbey waited for Steve. He did not take long and returned minutes later with a bulging rucksack.

His finger scratched the stubble on his chin. "Most of this stuff needs a good wash, but it's my good gear and should be ok. Come on Abbey. Let's get moving."

When Abbey and Steve turned the corner of their road, he hailed a taxi.

My friend Harold owns a modernised three-bed terraced house. It's not far from Kilburn underground station.

Steve paid the cabby and helped Abbey with her cases.

"His gran died and left it to him in her will. It's a bit of a mess, but it's free. Don't jump when you first see Harold. He's a strange guy, but his heart's in the right place and wouldn't hurt a fly."

She glanced at the terraced house, identical in every way to its neighbours. The once-standard yellow bricks were grubby with London grime. The small front garden contained four wheelie bins of different colours.

Steve jabbed the bell push.

Abbey said nothing when a man opened the door. His long thick beard reminded her of a garden broom. Dark blue jeans and a creased T-shirt covered his thin frame, but his smile put her at ease.

"Come in. Steve told me what happened. Excuse the mess, but housework is not my thing."

Steve followed Harold with the suitcases. Intrigued, Abbey glanced at the many framed black and white photographs.

"My gran's," said Harold. "I haven't the heart to remove them. She was a good woman. Nothing was ever too much trouble."

"You're lucky. I never knew any of my family."

"Look, I don't want to appear unsociable but..."

"Please, tell me where my room is, and I'll leave you in peace."

"Steve, you're in the box at the front. Abbey, you're in the double at the back. Make yourself at home." He nodded to a doorway at the end of the hall. "Kitchen's through there but if you need something to eat, you'll have to order a takeaway."

She smiled. "Thank you for being a Good Samaritan."

"Follow me," said Steve as he grabbed her cases and his rucksack.

Before they climbed the stairs, Abbey glanced into the front room. "Wow," she said, as her eyes caught sight of the many bookshelves, which lined the walls.

At the top, Steve pointed. "That's your room."

"What does Harold do for a living?"

"He's an environmental scientist. You know, global warming and all that stuff. Bit of a boffin from what I'm told."

"No idiot then?"

"Weird, but not an idiot. I need to get my stuff washed. Abbey, when you've sorted yourself out, we'll go to the pub and have something to eat."

"Sounds good." She opened the door, lifted her cases and entered. As her eyes drifted from corner to corner, she smiled. It was as if she had stepped back into an old film set. She dragged a finger across the top of the headboard. To her surprise, no dust. A small chest of drawers stood on one side of the window and a single wardrobe the other side. She glanced out onto an unkempt rear garden. A pink eiderdown covered the entire bed, and the springs squeaked. For a moment or two, the charm of the room distracted her. Then the realisation of what had happened hit her. She removed her shoes, fell on the bed, curled her body into the foetal position

109

and cried. Her world had changed, and she wondered if it would ever be the same again. She raised her head when she heard a tap on the door. "Who is it?"

"Are you alright?"

"Yes."

"Ready for that drink? It might help you relax."

Abbey slid off the bed and opened the door. "Give me a minute or two to wash my face."

He smiled as he saw the wetness surrounding her eyes. "I'll go and grab my coat and meet you downstairs."

She arrived five minutes later. "You're one of the good guys, aren't you?"

Steve rested his hand on her shoulder. "Sometimes."

She kissed him on the cheek.

He seemed surprised. "Why did you kiss me?"

"It's my way of saying thank you. Let's go for that drink?"

He laughed. "My local is four hundred metres away. What's your poison?"

"Gin and fresh orange."

Together they left the house, and as they walked, they chatted about trivial matters. Once inside the lounge of the King's Head, Steve ordered a pint of Seafarers bitter and a gin and fresh orange juice.

The back-street pub was not exactly upmarket. Its ancient floorboards showed through the stained red carpet, and well-used chairs and tables filled the corners.

Abbey sat at an empty table near the window.

Steve returned in a couple of minutes with the drinks and seated himself opposite. "I've ordered two chicken and chips. Is that ok?"

"Perfect."

"Great pub this. A bit rough and ready but never any trouble, and the boss is friendly. Do you know we've been neighbours for two years, and I know nothing about you?"

She gave him a wry smile. "What would you like to know?"

"Anything you want to tell me, and if you don't, that's ok."

"I'm an orphan and never knew my parents. My father lived in America and from what I understand worth millions. He and my mother had a one-night stand, and here I am. Others have controlled my life. As a baby, I had a nanny. When my private schools broke for holidays, someone would collect me and take me on tour. I'd travelled to every major city in Europe before I was eleven. The Far East came and went in my teens. Museums, I've forgotten most of them. The death of my father gave me freedom. No one ever actually cared. To them it was a well-paid job and then I met Brian, another fucking arsehole. What about you?"

He took a large gulp of his beer. "Wow, I can't match that. I can't ever recall anyone visiting your flat since you arrived. What about your friends? Someone must be worried?"

"Have you been stalking me?"

He laughed. "You must be joking. I live in the flat under yours. I hear you walking around, moving a chair and rarely any visitors. You must get fed up with your own company."

She paused before answering. "Never gave it a thought. I felt privileged, liberated. The other girls at school were envious of me. I owned a top of the range laptop, and could buy high-end fashion. Travelling around the world was commonplace. That's my life in a nutshell."

Me, I come from a middle-class background. My mum and dad are both honest accountants and made sure I received a good education. Private schools and all that stuff. As it happens, I also have a head for figures, and when I graduate, I'll be joining the family firm. Almost forgot I play cricket for the university."

She steepled her fingers. "Are you any good at cricket?"

Steve forced a smile. "I bowl well."

"Two chicken and chips."

Steve grabbed the two plates. "Thanks, George."

"Abbey picked up a chip with her fingers and dropped it back on the plate. "Hot."

"Fresh chips and precooked chicken from the microwave. Fills a hole," said Steve. George does a great stew at lunchtime. With homemade soggy dumplings."

"It's hot, tasty and saves cooking," said Abby. "So, you're all lined up to join the family firm."

"I am, but you're not doing so bad. A million-pound flat, a bit singed around the edges. An almost new top of the range Mini. And a rich father. I would say you have a great deal. No worries."

She lowered her head. "Nothing is what it seems. My biological father died a while ago, and I was not included in his will."

"He can't do that. Get a good lawyer, and you could be worth millions."

"I wish it was that easy. My solicitor did mention I could fight but assured me my chances were slim. In fairness, he told me that my father's legal beagles would build the biggest brick walls money could buy. What would I live on?"

"Good point."

"There's something else you should know."

"You're putting weight on in the wrong places, so I guess you're pregnant. Who's the lucky guy?"

"The lucky guy ran back to his wife. More important, I don't think I have any insurance for my flat."

Steve stiffened as his smile vanished. "You must have. Everyone has insurance."

"Everything stopped when my father died. Don't worry, I have money."

Steve ran the fingers of his right hand through his hair. "Not my problem. You'd better hope the report doesn't prove the fire was your fault."

Abbey opened her mouth. "I don't understand. How could it be my fault?"

Steve sipped his beer. "I didn't say it was your fault. Don't worry, my insurance will pay for my repairs. God knows the premiums are high enough. My policy gives new for old, so for me, no problem."

Abbey shifted in her seat. "First thing in the morning I'll go and see my solicitor. He'll know the answer."

"You don't need a solicitor," he said as if speaking to a child.

She stared at him. "You're so wrong, Steve. Since I can remember, Mr Peters always fixed my problems."

"Get real, Abbey. What you need is a good builder, and in London they are like rocking horse shit."

"Mr Peters will sort it out." She lifted her drink and downed the dregs.

"Want another?"

"One more. I need to unpack and have a shower."

"There's one bath, so it's get in, wash and out." He wandered to the bar. *She's a mess.*

Abbey found her thoughts confused.

When Steve returned, she said. "It's my round. How much do I owe you?"

"My treat, but if you don't mind me saying you need to get your life sorted."

She gave a sort of helpless shrug. "At the moment it's a bit of a mess, but I know it will sort itself out."

"Abbey, what planet are you on? You're young, attractive and intelligent. Yet you need to wise up to the real world, fast. The thing about life and not your playing house kind, it pushes you until you break. Out of interest, did you choose to buy or was that your Mr Peters?"

"No. When I left boarding school, Mr Peters had someone from his office escort me there. She told me if I had any problems to contact his office."

"Who paid the service charges and arranged the TV licence?"

113

Reassured, she knew Steve was the sort of person to help. She lifted her drink and sat back in the chair. "I suppose Mr Peters. He or his firm did everything."

Steve's eyes narrowed. "Did Mr Peters tell you the good life is over? From this moment, the poor little rich girl needs to learn the facts of life. The choice is yours, but don't make another decision without running it past me. I may not know the answer, but I bet my father does."

"Thank you," said Abbey. "But why are you doing this?"

He laughed. "You're just the type conmen are looking for. If someone doesn't take care of you, you'll be broke, and on the streets in less than a year."

"You don't believe that, do you?"

"You'd better believe it. Drink up and think about what I said. The choice is yours."

# *Sixteen*

Clutching his briefcase, Barry, his eyes wild, charged along the street. Without looking, he darted across the road. Irate drivers blasted their horns. On entering his office, his staff lifted their heads. Seeing his mood, they turned their faces back to work.

At nine on the dot, he contacted his bank. "Good morning. I need to speak to my account manager."

The woman on the telephone answered, "And who would that be?"

"Ethan Philips."

"Your name, please?"

"Ethan Philips knows me. I'm a friend, he'll speak to me."

"Can I have your name please?"

"Barry Thompson. I arranged the sale of his house."

"One moment, Mr Thompson. I'll check."

Barry drummed the fingers of his left hand while listening to recorded music. "Hurry up, for fuck's sake," he mumbled.

"I beg your pardon."

"Sorry, I was talking to myself."

"Mr Philips is with a client. He says he may be able to call you back this afternoon."

Barry was silent for a few seconds. "Tell Ethan that this is a priority."

"I'm sorry, Mr Thompson. As I told you, he is with a client. I cannot disturb him again."

"Will you fucking tell him I'm on my way to shove a rocket up his arse?" The line went dead. "Stupid fucking women." He stood, grabbed his mobile and dashed out of the office.

Luck was with him as he flagged an empty black cab. It stopped, the driver ignoring the triple red lines. "Where to guv?"

"Canary Wharf, and fast."

"Chance would be a fine thing," said the cabby. "Rarely get above twenty-five these days."

"As fast as you can, please."

"Trying my best, guv."

The cab entered the mass of high-rise buildings and slowed to a crawl.

"You can drop me off here. What's the damage?"

"Fifteen quid."

Barry clambered out of the taxi. From his wallet, he removed his last twenty-pound note. He handed it to the driver. "Keep the change."

"Nice one, guv."

He headed for the Barclays building. As he entered, a security guard stood in front of him.

"Briefcase, Sir," said a thin, uniformed man.

Annoyed at the delay he dumped it on the security desk. "Sorry, I forgot."

A middle-aged, uniformed woman glared at him. "Please open your case, Sir."

He opened it wide.

"Is this your case, Sir?"

"Of course it is," he snapped. "I'm here for a meeting with Ethan Philips. Ring him. He'll clear up this mess."

"Your name, Sir?"

He raised his eyebrows and for a moment stared at the high ceiling. "Barry Thompson. Hurry up."

"One moment, Sir." Her fingers rattled the keyboard. A sadistic smile creased her lips. "You're not on our visitors' list, Sir."

"Okay, do what you have to do, but please let Ethan know I'm here."

From behind Barry, a man's voice said, "Just a precaution, Sir."

His heart raced as unease passed through his brain.

"Body searches are undertaken in private, Sir." The uniformed man stood to his right. "Pick up your briefcase and come with me, Sir."

In a subdued manner, he followed the man into a side room. "What the fuck?"

Seated behind a desk, Ethan Philips smiled. "When you swear at our staff, they have ways of making life difficult."

Barry waited until the security guard left.

"My mistake. This morning, I needed to transfer a sizable sum and found my account frozen."

Ethan opened his file and turned to the keyboard. "I've entered your current account number, and it tells me the account does not exist."

Stunned, Barry remained silent for a while. "Ethan, my clients' property deposits are in that account. If I cannot retrieve them I'm in deep trouble."

"That's not proper," said Ethan.

"That's not your problem. I'll sort it out next week. Now, I need money to operate."

"Let's try another." Minutes passed; the quiet of the room only disturbed by the clicking of keys. He looked at Barry, his expression stern. "Access denied."

"What's happening?"

"I'll get our computer team to check the system. Something is wrong for this to happen. The miracles of technology are great when they work but a pain when they don't."

Barry glanced at his watch. "What do you mean?"

Ethan shrugged. "I don't know, but we need to find out what's corrupting the system."

117

"How long will that take?"

"An hour, a day, a week. The bank needs to find the problem first."

"You're taking the piss."

"I wish. My limited knowledge of computers tells me there's a bug in the system. I wouldn't worry; our experts will enjoy searching and destroying whatever."

"And what am I supposed to do in the meantime?"

"Be patient."

Barry's brain raced. The whole scenario appeared hopeless. "Will the bank cover me if I write cheques?"

Ethan spoke in a low voice. "If I were you I'd close your business for three days, more if you can. Put a sign on the door stating you have a rat infestation. And no, we will not cover unsecured cheques."

"Come on. You know I have the money."

"I know you should have the money, but I cannot confirm that as a fact."

"Thanks for your help. I'll be talking to my lawyer who I'm sure will suggest suing you for loss of business."

Ethan grinned. "You may do whatever you want. Who am I to stop you? Now you're wasting my time when I could be instructing our computer team of the problem."

Barry picked up his briefcase and stormed out. Seconds later he realised he had no money for a taxi. In a foul mood, he flagged a black cab, knowing he could get a member of staff to pay on return to the office.

On entering his office his eyes bulged when he saw Terry in his office. "Debbie, pay the taxi waiting outside."

"I've been waiting for over an hour."

The tension between them filled the room. "Bank business."

"We agreed to my final payment on completion."

Uncontrolled anger filled his eyes before Barry said a word. "You'll get your fucking money."

No pity existed in the man's eyes. "I'm not interested in excuses. You have two days."

"Have I ever let you down?"

"Don't even think about it. Pay me before you have an unfortunate accident."

"In two days this conversation will be a memory,"

Terry smiled, stood and faced Barry, their eyes level. "It had better be." He walked out of the office.

As he watched Terry leave, Barry felt his chest tighten. "Someone get me a coffee."

Debbie arrived with a steaming cup of coffee. "What's going on, you look terrible."

Bloodshot eyes stared at her. Lack of sleep and a splitting headache did little to improve his mood. "Are you that stupid? The way things are, you won't have a job by the end of the week. Go paint your nails or something."

"What's happening?" asked Debbie. "You're not making any sense."

"Every penny I have is in the bank, and with my accounts frozen, I'm technically broke."

Debbie's face paled. "What about us, our plans?"

"I doubt you want to be around a penniless estate agent."

She did not avert her gaze. "Those pictures of children the police found on your computer. I never thought you were into that sort of thing."

"I'm not, never have been but the police think different."

"So, if you're innocent. There's no problem."

"The odds are they'll find me guilty." He shrugged. "How they got in the system I haven't a clue. I would recommend you clear your desk and look for another job."

"There must be someone who can help."

"Fuck off. It's over."

She shrugged. "Shit happens, but a girl must do what a girl has to do. Shame I backed the wrong horse."

119

# Seventeen

The morning sun woke Abbey. For a moment, she was cosy in a warm bed and at peace with the world, and then reality flooded her mind. Tired from a disturbed night's sleep, she grabbed her dressing gown, dashed to the bathroom, and found the door locked. "Steve?"

"Five minutes."

She returned to her room and sat on the edge of the bed. Her thoughts strayed to the fire. *What caused it?* She had left nothing on and as far as doing work on the gas pipe, she would not know where to begin. Her mood changed when Steve shouted, "bathroom's free."

"Thanks." She collected her things and opened the door. Steve was waiting.

"I have some news."

"Is it more important than my bath?"

"I think so. My father's arranged a builder to check on the damage at ten. You should come with me. We can kill two birds at the same time."

"I'll need to talk to Mr Peters."

"He can wait. This builder owes my father a few favours. If he can fit us in, it could save months."

She smiled. "My knight in shining armour."

"Are you coming with me or not?"

"I'll be ready in twenty minutes."

"Good. I'll make toast for breakfast. Tea or coffee."

"Coffee, black, no sugar."

"Don't tell me, you're sweet enough already."

She leant against the door and closed her eyes. "I am what I am."

Steve laughed as she entered the bathroom.

She heard him running down the stairs. Did the necessary, washed all over with tepid water, grabbed a towel and dried. Fifteen minutes later, she entered the kitchen. This morning she wore black jeans, a black jumper and black leather jacket. She pointed. "Is that toast mine?"

Steve nodded. "Smart outfit. Looks expensive."

"Coffee, I need this to get me going. Thanks." She took a slice of cold toast, covered it in jam and devoured it before lifting a second. "Where's Harold?"

"He left early for a meeting in town." Steve glanced at the clock above the door. "Lift and shift. Time we were not here."

"I'll get my coat."

She met Steve by the door. Together they walked to their flats and waited.

At ten on the dot, a black Lexus Coupe stopped alongside them. The driver, a well-built man of average height, emerged from the car. "Steve?"

"That's me, and this is Abbey."

"Albert Cummings. I spoke with your father last night."

He locked the car and walked briskly towards them. He shook hands after wiping them on his trousers. "Been on site."

Well dressed in a dark blue suit, holding a pair of gloves and a clipboard, Albert intrigued Abbey. "Business must be good."

"Couldn't be better but then I do work for the top people in the city, and I charge premium rates. Shall we inspect the damage? Wait, I'll get three hard hats from my boot. Just in case. Better safe than sorry."

Steve punched the door code and then stepped back. "That's odd, the door's open." He pushed and let it swing wide. "Is anybody there?"

"Seen this before," said Albert. "Thieves tend to find out about fires and know the owners will have been absent. They would have visited during the night. Steve, you stay with Abbey."

He returned to his car, opened the boot and removed two pickaxe handles. As the boot slammed shut, he smiled. "This usually scares the shit out of them. Steve, one for you just in case. I'll check around."

They remained next to the door while Albert pulled on his gloves and trudged up the stairs.

Abbey stood close to Steve. "He's a cautious man."

Steve listened as they waited. "Knows the score and doesn't suffer fools."

A few minutes later, Albert returned. "Both flats have been stripped. You had better call the police, although I doubt if anyone will arrive."

Steve contacted the police and told them what had happened. "Someone will be here in an hour or so."

"No point in wasting time. Let's look," said Albert.

"My flat's a wreck," said Steve.

Albert shrugged. "That it may be but I can't assess the damage standing here."

The door to Steve's place hung on its hinges. He laughed. "They found nothing of any value in my place."

Albert removed a torch from his trouser pocket. "I need to check the stairs." The bright beam showed a black waterline a few feet from the floor. "No fire damage and the water has drained away. Hang on to the handrail. I've done this before so let me go first." One-step at a time he descended, testing each one until he reached the bottom. "It's reliable enough. You can come down if you want."

Steve, followed by Abbey, made their way to the bottom with the help of the torchlight.

A confident but relaxed Albert stepped into the hallway. "A ton of water damage but we can supply two or three dehumidifiers and dry it out." He edged into the kitchen entrance. "I'll gut this and then rebuild. No real problem providing the structure is sound. Mind you, they built these places to last."

Abbey grabbed Steve's hand. "Sorry."

"Don't be daft. You didn't do this. Shit happens, you have to deal with it. No casualties and it'll be brand new in a couple of months."

"More like six," said Albert. "There's a ton of work here. Your flat next, Abbey."

The door to Abbey's flat lay on the floor where the fire brigade left it. Albert went straight to the kitchen door and let his eyes survey the scene. "Great, the ceiling's intact. That old plaster might contain asbestos and is at least an inch thick. I'll have to check the joists and make sure they're in good condition. We'll need to gut the kitchen" He wandered throughout the remaining rooms. "A good clean and a paint job should suffice."

Tears ran across Abbey's cheeks when she saw her things scattered across the bedroom. "Bastards."

First things first," said Albert. "I'll get my joiners to supply and fit three new doors and locks. Your door entry needs repairing. Can you let the other residents know?"

"I'll do that before we leave," said Steve.

Albert turned to Abbey. "I understand you let your insurance expire. I cannot skimp on the main repairs, but I'll talk to you later re the kitchen. I have some high-quality second-hand units in my warehouse."

"You're very kind," said Abbey.

He smiled. "I'll make a profit on Steve's place but Abbey, I better warn you, this is not going to be cheap."

"Any idea how much?"

"I don't make a move without checking every angle. You won't get much change out of forty-five-fifty thousand."

"Steve, I've your insurance details. Your father gave me a verbal agreement to complete the repairs. Abbey, I'll need you to sign a contract. What I intend is to complete both flats at the same time. It saves money and labour. Any questions?"

"I'll leave it to you," said Steve.

123

"The contract, when can I expect it to arrive?" asked Abbey.

"We'll talk outside. I need some fresh air," said Albert.

He broke off as a man asked, "Who are you?"

"And who are you," said Albert.

The man held out a plasticised card. "Fire Officer Davis. I'm here to discover the cause of the fire."

Albert explained who he was and that Steve and Abbey were the owners. "We'll leave you to your investigation."

Albert, Steve and Abbey went outside and stood by the front door. "I see the police haven't turned up, said Albert. Don't suppose they will. I'm off to the insurance company for their approval to start. Abbey, my secretary will post the contract sometime in the next couple of days. If you have any questions, ask her. She knows all the answers."

She held out her hand. "Thank you, Albert." His was one of the firmest she had ever experienced.

"I'll let my father know we've spoken," said Steve.

They waited until he drove away.

"Cautious and professional," said Abbey.

"If my father recommends him, he is."

Abbey checked the time. "It's almost lunchtime, and I have to see someone before midday."

"Anyone, I know?"

"My estate agent. I can't afford this place." Her Iphone rang. "I don't need this shit."

"Can I help?" asked Steve.

Her face took on a cruel tenseness. "It's a police officer, he wants to ask me more questions. It's nothing to do with the fire."

"Are you in trouble?"

Her eyebrows appeared to squeeze together. "No, but this police officer can be a pain in the backside."

# *Eighteen*

Abbey's mobile buzzed. "Good morning, Bill. I was about to ring you. I have a problem."

"You've changed your mind."

"No. I've had a fire in my flat. The kitchen's a write off. You'll have to delay the sale until it's repaired."

"That's a shame. I have a client who wanted to view. I have an idea, but I need to speak to an interested party. I'll get back when I have any news."

"Can't you give me a clue?" she asked.

"If my idea bears fruit, I'll call and arrange a meeting. Keep your fingers crossed."

"Okay. Talk later."

Abbey strolled to Parsons Green station. Using her student Oyster Card, she jumped on the District Line to Westminster. Within thirty minutes, she entered New Scotland Yard.

A woman in plain clothes escorted her to Commander Haliwell's office. Neither said a word as the lift ascended.

Annie looked up as Abbey entered. "You'll have to wait, he's on the phone."

"I'd rather not be here."

"You should have been a good girl."

"I did nothing wrong."

"I wouldn't agree. When's your baby due?"

"Four months, give or take."

The speaker on Annie's desk lit up. Haliwell spoke. "Send her in, Annie."

Haliwell nodded to Abbey as he pointed at a chair and wondered if he was over thinking the missile problem. After all, nothing had happened since the murder of the main subject. "I'm told your property suffered from major fire damage."

Surprise filled Abbey's face. "How could you know that?"

"I told you we would be watching you and your friends."

"I thought it was no more than a verbal threat. I didn't think you would actually have me followed."

"It's what I do."

"You still don't believe me, do you?"

Haliwell doodled with a red pen on his notepad. The laptop was a no go. Jacob Spink was dead and no other missile launched. He checked the time.

"I'm closing the investigation. We know Spink fired India's missile. How he did this died with him. Thanks to your friend, our military received the funding to upgrade their systems. The case is closed. I turned up nothing of any use but then perhaps it never existed. You are free to go."

Abbey opened her mouth to say something but bit her tongue instead.

"I said you're free to go."

Her expression did not change. "A phone call would have sufficed."

"You don't seem surprised."

"Told you before, I knew nothing."

"I don't believe you. You're the clever one. From what I'm told you'll get a first without even trying."

"Have you finished?"

"No, and I need a favour."

Abbey glanced at him and smiled. "You threaten to arrest me. Ask a lot of stupid questions, and now you want my help?"

"You can always say no." He opened a drawer, removed her passport and handed it to her.

"So, what's this favour?"

With the look of intensity in his eyes, he said "I need someone I can trust."

She appeared startled. "What, does this mean you trust me?"

"Yes, I do. You informed on Spink. You have ethics, and you're a world-class hacker."

"In that case, who set fire to my flat?"

His gaze remained steady. "I have a sergeant working on that as we speak. He's checking the surveillance tapes. When we know, we'll make an arrest, and then find out why."

Abbey's eyes widened and her mouth opened. "You're a scheming old fart. You know the answer to a question before you ask."

"Yes or no?"

"I'm sure you understand my reluctance. Is it against the law?"

"It's not official. Let's say you'd be working for me."

She paused. *Was this a trap? What did he want?* "Okay, I'll do it just for the hell of it. What's in it for me?"

His eyes fixed on her. "The name of an arsonist."

"I'll not tell a soul."

"Thanks." He smiled and shrugged as his face turned serious. "I want you to hack into our computer system and leave a message for the police commissioner."

"Why?"

"This place needs its computer security updated. I'm aware there are those in the media who use hackers to get information from our files. Most of our tech people live in the past. You youngsters are the future."

"You exaggerate my talents. What sort of message do you want me to leave?"

"I'm sure you'll think of something suitable. Oh, how will I know it's from you?"

"Believe me, you will. When would you want your boss to receive this message?"

"How long does it take to hack into a system?"

She shrugged. "Ten minutes, an hour if the firewalls are robust. I'm at university later."

127

"I don't think you should involve the university."

"Your tech literacy is unreal. I'll use a zombie" server in Moscow or Beirut. Your people will not have a clue until it happens."

He glanced at his watch again. "Regrettably you are right, but, if you ever need the help of a friendly copper, you know where I am. I'll tell you when we find your arsonist."

She smiled for the first time. "If I need to contact you, I'm in deep shit. Bye."

Annie knocked and stuck her head around the door. "You have a meeting with the assistant commissioner, like now."

"Thank you, Annie. Miss Lane is ready to leave."

Abbey stood, turned and walked out without a word.

*** 

Abbey descended into Westminster Underground and boarded the first train to Aldgate East. When she entered the red brick Victorian building, she asked at reception. "Is Mr Peters free?"

"He's been expecting you."

"How come?"

"Didn't you know the local radio mentioned your house fire?"

"Must have been a slow news day."

She lifted the phone and pressed a memory key. "Miss Abbey Lane is in reception."

She paused. "Excellent, Mr Peters. I'll send her straight up."

Abbey climbed the stairs to his office. Peters waited with the door open. He motioned for her to enter. "You look well. What can I do for you?"

He pointed to a chair, returning to his.

"You could tell me my flat is still insured."

Peters nodded as he talked. "Every contract related to your home was void on the last day of the month you became the owner."

"I thought you might say that. Is there any chance my father might help? After all, it's only money, and he had plenty."

128

"There lies the problem. You signed your rights away when you were last here."

Abbey gazed at him. "Can you help me?"

A smile spread across his face. "On your behalf, I will contact and place a claim on your father's estate. I will assert that he has not made reasonable provision for your needs." He wrung his hands. "But, I promise nothing."

"Let me get this right. You're going to contest his will."

Peters grimaced. "I doubt his heirs would appreciate any adverse publicity. I'm a solicitor who learnt to play poker at university with the best. I keep my cards close to my chest and smile. I do not work for them anymore, and I'm looking forward to the fight."

"Thank you. If I don't hear from you, I'll understand."

"Not so fast young lady. Listen to me. These things take time. First, I plant a seed and let it grow. With luck, it might produce a good crop. But as the good book tells us, the seed may fall on barren ground."

Abbey smiled. "I pray your letter works."

Peters sighed, he had a feeling they would ignore his request. "When Pandora's Box closed, all it contained was hope. We have plenty of that."

"It's better than nothing."

"Don't worry; I'm going to devote my full attention to claiming your inheritance."

"I can't pay you."

"If I win, we can discuss my fee. Remember what Nelson Mandela said. It's only impossible until it is done."

She pressed her lips together, nodded. "Whatever happens, thank you?"

The weather had changed. It was now much more refreshing, and the wind gusted. Since talking to Mr Peters, Abbey's mood had lightened and with purpose in her stride, she made way her to the university.

129

# *Nineteen*

Abbey studied the computer screen until her search engine found what she was looking for. She reached into her bag, withdrew a bright pink memory stick and shoved it into the USB drive, and waited for the program to allow her into the dark web.

Two minutes elapsed before two words appeared on the screen. **Required Source**. Abbey keyed in **JUMPING JACK FLASH**.

The screen flashed. **Toko**. She keyed in her user access code. In an instant, **You Have Five Seconds to install your password.** It took four. The screen went white as she keyed in Metropolitan Police official site. She expected to wait, but her bulldozer algorithm breached the firewall in moments. *Must be a crap firewall.* Using a memory stick, she inserted a search programme. Once installed, she gained administrator access. Three minutes later, she opened the main hub index. She scanned the list and opened the police commissioner's logs. Nothing. Smiling, she checked Haliwell's computer. Again nothing.

She laughed. "Clever but pretty basic." She keyed in her hacker codes. The screen changed and in seconds was into the commissioner's files. She chuckled as she copied a rude Wile E Coyote and the Road Runner cartoon into the start-up programme. She closed down, leaving her Trojan in place. *Might be handy.* With her mind on other things, she returned her memory sticks to her bag. On her way home, she popped into Greggs the bakers and purchased two meat filled rolls for supper.

The early evening sun still shone brightly as she approached her temporary home. Her right hand groped in her pocket for the key. Quiet filled the house as she climbed the stairs to her room. She

130

seated herself on the bed, her mind contemplating the future. She needed a place for her and the baby to live, furniture and everything else. Things she had never thought about before. Since her father's death, things had gone wrong, one disaster after another. What was happening? Her life appeared to be spiralling out of control. She focused her thoughts, but the ringing of her mobile irritated her. She glanced at the screen, "Bloody Haliwell."

"What do you want?"

"I'm pleased to say, the commissioner is not amused. Thank you."

"I didn't think she'd see it until the morning."

"She returned from a meeting, switched on her PC and your Wile E Coyote greeted her. From what I heard, her screams woke the whole of New Scotland Yard. '**Find the bastard who did this**.' I must admit I've never seen that rather gross cartoon, but it did make me smile. So much for the innocence of youth."

"It's as old as the hills. You do need to have your systems better protected. Your firewalls are almost non-existent. A first-year computer student could break them."

"I won't say a word. What do I know?"

She laughed. "True. When will you know who torched my place?"

"When I'm certain, I'll give you a call."

"Thank you." She ended the call. Weary, she stared at one of her suitcases still full at the end of the bed. *I must empty that.* With a heave, she lifted and dropped it on the bed, and pressed the locking device. The lid flew back and she smiled. The fire fighter had packed this and his care showed. He had neatly folded everything, making the unpacking and placing her clothes in the draws or wardrobe straight forward. At the bottom, she discovered the lipstick, a memory stick and eyebrow pencil. The lipstick and pencil she shoved in her makeup bag.

131

The USB flash drive she had never seen before. She drew a long breath and smiled as the penny dropped. Her thoughts turned back to the night of her confrontation with Jacob. *Was this his and how dangerous could it be?* She shoved it into a zipped pocket inside her handbag.

***

The moment her alarm buzzed, she crawled out of bed. For a change, Steve was not in the bathroom. She enjoyed an uninterrupted shower. Relaxed and wearing fresh clothes, she prepared to face the day.

Steve looked up when Abbey entered the kitchen but did not stop spooning cereal into his mouth.

She buttered two slices of cold toast. "Steve, do you think Harold would mind if I found another place to live?"

Steve sat back and crossed his arms, his face unreadable.

"Did you hear me?"

"Why? Repairs to your flat are in hand. This place is as good as any, and it's close. You have your own room, and the rent could not be cheaper."

She wrestled with her feelings. Steve was right, but she needed somewhere more permanent for her baby. "You didn't answer my question."

Steve leant forward and stroked his chin before answering. "Harold doesn't care one way or another. He doesn't need the money and lives on his own. I'd give it plenty of thought before you end up in some dingy bedsit."

She hesitated. "I can't have my baby here."

"Why not. What if you go into labour? I can help you."

She smiled. "So you're an expert on delivering babies?"

"No, but I can get you to the hospital or call a doctor."

Abbey flashed a smile. "I'll think about it."

132

# *Twenty*

For the next week, Abbey attended lectures, went for long runs and pondered her next move. Alone in her bedroom, she figured there must be a way out of this mess.

Five days of mundane routine came and went. Abbey had agreed to go to the pub with Steve on Friday night and much to her surprise she looked forward to the evening.

As she opened the door to her room, Steve shouted, "Can I have a word?"

"Problems?"

"Not really. Albert Cummings called. He wants us to clear our flats of personal bits and pieces, like yesterday."

She placed her hands on her hips, "He must be joking."

He held up his hands. "You can leave stuff if you want, but it's going to end up covered in shit."

She seated herself on the bed. "I'll need to hire a storage unit and find someone who can drive a van."

"Wait. You need Space Station. I've used them. They lift, shift and store and are reasonable." From his wallet, he removed a card. "Here's their telephone number. I reckon they'll have your stuff out in half a day."

She rested her head in her hands. "Thanks, Steve. What would I do without you? I've never moved a thing in my life. Someone else always did the thinking."

He chuckled. "Never hurts to ask for help. And as I've told you, if I don't know the answer, I'll find someone who does. Tell you what, I'll give Space Station a bell, and together we'll clear your place. Mine is easy. It's on its way to the tip."

She lifted her eyes. "I've become a bit of a pain in the arse."

"Abbey, shit happens. Believe me, in six months, this will be a bad memory."

She nodded. "I hope you're right. Are we still going for a beer?"

"Definitely."

"I'm off for a bath. What time are we going out?"

"Eightish. When I'm ready, I'll give you a knock."

***

At eight on the dot, Steve knocked and asked if she was ready. Abbey opened the door in seconds.

Steve's eyes glowed. "You look great."

Abbey gazed at Steve dressed in blue jeans and a white T-shirt and smiled. "You don't look so bad yourself."

They both laughed as they descended the stairs.

Abbey and Steve strolled with care along the cobbled street towards the pub. He held her hand. "Don't want you falling. Oh, and by the way, we have an early start in the morning. Space Station will be arriving at nine."

She stopped and faced him. "So long as we finish by midday that's great."

"What have you got on in the afternoon?"

"A lecture. Why?"

They continued walking. "You'll be okay."

Steve held the door open at the pub and let Abbey enter. One table next to the fireplace remained empty. She went and sat on the red leather-covered stool.

"Same as last time?" asked Steve.

She stroked her bump. "A fresh orange and tonic, please. Babe was kicking all night when I had a gin."

"Your wish is my command. What about food?"

She picked up the menu. "Is the Shepherd's pie any good?"

"Tasty."

"Then that's what I'll have."

134

Steve went to the bar and chatted to the blonde barmaid polishing glasses. Next to him stood two men in dark suits drinking pints.

Abbey sat and let her mind wander. She listened to the solitary folk singer in the opposite corner. The crowd were a mixture of women in their thirties having a few drinks before hitting the clubs. A group of men in suits drank beer, told jokes and laughed out loud. Four who did not appear old enough, played darts.

Steve returned and placed a pint of fresh orange and tonic in front of her.

"You were having a good chat with the barmaid."

"Cathy and I have had our moments, and she's a good friend, one of the best."

"Best at what?"

Steve appeared annoyed. "That's not nice."

"You're right. I apologise."

"Two rather hot Shepherd's," said Cathy.

Abbey gazed at the young woman with a friendly smile. Her shapely figure displayed enough bare flesh to tease the male customers.

"Looks good and smells great," said Abbey.

Cathy said nothing and returned behind the bar.

"You'd better tell her I'm not your new girl friend."

"Later," said Steve laughing. "After I've seen you home."

Abbey nodded towards the bar. "Are you on a promise?"

Steve made no comment.

"I'll see myself home."

Steve stopped eating. "I'm many things, but I would never let a pregnant woman walk home alone."

***

The next morning as she strolled along the road, Abbey stared in disbelief at the empty boxes stacked outside her flat. Each with her name in bold black letters.

135

A tall man with grey hair glanced at his watch as she approached.

"Hi, I'm Abbey Lane."

"You're on time."

"I don't believe in keeping people waiting." She climbed the steps and operated the new door entry system. The lock clicked open and she entered. The door to her flat was wide open.

A man in blue overalls appeared from inside her flat. "Who are you?"

Abbey glared at the man. "Who the hell are you?"

He jangled a set of keys at her. "Joe Gittings, Albert Cummings' foreman. I'm making a list of the tools we need to start work. When are you going to clear your stuff?"

She stood erect with her shoulder back. "Today."

"As soon as I can get started," said the grey-haired man.

"The floor in the kitchen's unsafe," said Joe. Everywhere else is sound. I'll be at least another hour."

"No problem," said the removal man. "Miss, can you show me what you want stored?"

"Follow me."

They went from room to room.

"It's a good day's work. We'll pack the small stuff but leave the rest as it is. Our storage facility is the best. I'll give my boss a call."

Abbey gave him a warm smile. "You can't shift the bed and wardrobes on your own and I'd rather not try."

"It's not a problem. I'll ask my boss to send some help."

"I've a lecture this afternoon. Do you need me to stay here?"

"Not really," he said with a smile. "In truth, you'll get in the way. I'll call you when we're finished. You can drop in the office tomorrow and sort out the paperwork."

Abbey glanced at him. "I'm off to buy a cup of coffee. Would you like me to bring you one back?"

He shook his head. "Thanks for the offer but I bring my own in a flask. On my pay, I can't afford three pounds a cup."

Abbey nodded, "No charge, I'll bring you one. How do you like your coffee?"

"Black with nothing in it."

"No problem. See you in half an hour and then I'm out of here."

## Twenty-One

Abbey had finished eating breakfast when Steve entered the kitchen. "You look tired."

He laughed. "You've just shampooed your hair, I can smell the perfume. I'll give my classes a miss today."

"Is that wise?"

He shrugged. "I'm so far behind it won't make much difference. This year's a dead duck. I'll go around again next year."

She stood and poured a cup of coffee. "Want one? It's a fresh brew."

"Why not? Thanks."

She made another cup and sat next to him. "Only a suggestion, but a night in your own bed might help."

"Tell me about it. I can't get enough of her."

"Do you love her?"

"I don't know but there's something about her. When I'm with her she's everything a man needs."

"That tells me you don't."

"I do like her a lot. She's fun to be with."

"So am I but you don't lose any sleep over me."

"You're different."

"What you mean is we're not sleeping together."

Steve opened his mouth but said nothing.

Abby sat back and drummed her fingers on the table. "If you sit your end of year exams, how do you think you'd do?"

"Depends on the questions. Some of it I know backwards, but I've missed far too many lectures. Why do you ask?"

"I can't tell you, but I have an idea."

Abbey glanced at the kitchen clock. "Must go. I've a lecture this morning. See you later."

Steve ran his fingers through his hair. "Okay. If I'm in bed, let me sleep."

She laughed, grabbed her bag and left him pouring another cup of coffee."

***

There was no one in the university computer room when Abbey walked in. She closed the door, glanced around, and waited a few moments before seating herself at the rear of the room.

The screen in front of her flashed, and she typed in an algorithm. The word **password** travelled across the screen, and she entered her favourite. In less than a minute, the names of those who printed exam papers formed a list in alphabetic order. Having memorised the title from the previous year's exam papers, she clicked on the site. Her firewall bulldozer took four seconds to gain full access. She smiled as she opened the printer's exam list for the university. Her eyes skimmed the headings until she found the year and date of the end of term accountancy exam. Using a memory stick, she downloaded Steve's exam papers. Two minutes later, having obliterated anything traceable, she left the room.

Later that afternoon, Abbey sat in front of a screen in the Geeks Internet Cafe. She called up the exam papers and sent them to print. Finished, she strolled to the counter, paid for her time, and printed copies.

"Doing some revising?" asked the fat blond-haired manager as he bit his nails.

"You'd better believe it."

"Good luck. I couldn't understand the questions, let alone answer them."

Abbey laughed. "I'm having the same problem. Have you an envelope?"

"New or used?"

"New please."

From behind the counter, he lifted a white envelope. "On the house for the best-looking girl in here."

139

She folded the sheets, put then in the envelope and laughed. "I'm the only girl in here. In fact, I'm the only person in here. Cheers."

***

Abbey slid the envelope under Steve's bedroom door and went to her room. Pleased with herself, she lay on the bed and closed her eyes. Her mind wandered from the present to her past as she stared at the ceiling. Having few friends never bothered her. Others told her to leave her pain in the past, let it go and move on. She tried to understand why her father acted as he did but quickly realised he had never cared for her. She was a mistake he rectified with money.

Steve interrupted her thoughts. "Abbey are you in there?"

"Yes. Come in." She rolled over and placed her feet on the carpet.

Steve held the envelope in his right hand as he gave her a puzzled look. "Do you know what this is?"

She nodded. "I pulled it from the printer's files. It's up to you whether you use it. I thought it might help."

A grin spread across his face. "Hopeless times, reckless solutions, but it's still cheating."

She gave him a sideways glance. "As I said, the choice is yours. You can toss it in the bin. I don't give a shit. Do you really want to waste a year? Or do you want to be a winner?"

He sat on the edge of the bed. "You make a good point, and another year would be a waste of my time and my dad's money."

"Have you made a decision?"

He stared at her for a moment. "My social life will have to go on hold until after the exams. Thanks, Abbey. Out of interest, how on earth did you break into a secure network?"

"Need to know, and you don't." She glanced at her watch. "I'm going to have a bath and an early night. Baby kept me awake last night."

"You take care," Steve said as he went to leave. "Any problems, give me a shout."

140

# Twenty-Two

The receptionist lifted her head and stared at a tall, well-dressed man. He smiled, but his dark deep-set eyes gave her concern. "Can I help you?"

He saw fear register on her face before she concealed it. As if ignoring her question, his eyes roamed the area while he curled and uncurled his fingers. "I must see Mr Gregory Peters."

"I have no one on his appointment list. Can I have your name, please? I'll see if he's free."

"Please tell him it's important and has to do with a Miss Abbey Lane."

She lifted the telephone and punched in the number. "Mr Peters, I have a gentleman in reception who asks to see you. He says it's with regards to a Miss Abbey Lane."

"Very good. I'll send him straight up."

"He'll see you." She pointed to the lift. "Top floor and he'll be waiting."

He turned and strolled to the lift, waited and as the doors opened, entered. When the buzzer sounded, he stepped out.

Peters held out his hand, but the man ignored the gesture.

He pointed to an open door. "Your office."

Peters nodded as the man walked straight in and stood in front of the desk. With the door closed, he indicated a chair. He settled in his recliner, churched his fingers and asked, "What can I do for you?"

A wicked grin spread across the man's face as his right hand shot out, seized Peter's shirt, and dragged him over the desk. My orders are to give you a choice. Do you want to live what remains of your pathetic life in a wheelchair? Because if you do, I'd be happy to make it happen."

141

Peters gasped for breath. "Who are you? I don't understand. Why?"

"Because you upset my associates."

Dread filled his mind as a wet stain spread across his trousers.

The man roared with laughter. "Fucking typical of a knee-trembling wimp. You sent a letter questioning Miss Abbey Lane and her father's will." With no effort, he tossed Peters into his chair. "You threatened to disclose the existence of a bastard."

Peters went to speak, but a vicious slap across the face silenced him.

"Now that we understand each other, there will be no further letters. If you don't cooperate and I have to return, I won't be so polite." His voice rose. "This is your only warning. If you have doubts, see your receptionist." Without another word, he turned and left, not closing the door.

Stunned, Peters stood and shut the door. On returning to his seat and with shaking hands, he buzzed reception. There was no answer.

Confused, he left his office and headed for reception. As he stepped out of the lift, he could not see Violet. She never left her realm without a relief taking over. He peered through the glass screen and saw her still body on the floor. His face paled as his eyes rested on the hole in the centre of her forehead. A shudder passed through him. His hands trembled as he held the telephone and contacted the police. For the first time in his career, he would have to lie.

He swallowed hard as he attempted to think. For something to do, he locked the main door.

As the last bolt slid home, someone hammered hard and shouted, "Police. Open up."

A tall, well-built man in a dark blue suit entered and stopped. "And you are?"

142

"Gregory Peters, I'm a solicitor. My office is on the top floor. I found the body."

"Graham Ramsay. Chief Inspector." He held up his warrant card. "Where is it?"

Peters could feel his heart pounding against his chest. "What?"

"The body."

"Sorry. In the receptionist's office. Her name is Violet Furguson. She is, sorry was, our receptionist."

Graham turned to two other officers, one male, the other an attractive, dark-skinned female. "You know what to do. Get on with it."

Both officers went about their specific duties.

Graham turned to Peters. "You said your office is on the top floor. Why did you pay a visit to reception?"

"Doctor's orders. I have a circulation problem and he recommended that every so often I go for a walk."

"I assume you never heard the shot. How many other people are in the building?"

"I'm not sure. The top floor only me this afternoon. The first floor, ten or so people work there. They are actuaries, and calculate insurance premiums, risks, dividends, and annuity rates."

"I know I'm a police officer, but I do know what an actuary does. Has anyone told them?"

Peters shrugged. "I haven't, but when you arrived and with the noise of your sirens, I imagine they know you're here."

"How well did you know Mrs Furguson?"

Peters shook his head. "Violet was the receptionist and I'm ashamed to say, I don't even know if she was married, has a family or anything about her."

"How long has she worked here?"

"Over twenty years."

"And you knew nothing about her?"

143

"She worked for the building management company. My firm paid a set amount each year. I assumed that covered her wages."

"Have you the name of the company?"

"Drummond and Co. The office is near Aldgate underground station."

Graham scribbled his notes before looking at Peters. "I need you to introduce me to those on the first floor. After which you may carry on with your work but keep clear of reception"

Peters, followed by the Chief Inspector, climbed the stairs to the first floor. They strolled into the senior actuary's office.

Fiona lifted her head. "Hi, Gregory. Don't often see you in here."

"Bad news, I'm afraid. Violet in reception has been shot."

The officer turned. "Thank you. If I need you, I know where you are. You may go."

Peters returned to his office, his back ached, and his mouth was dry. *Who were these people who could murder an innocent woman?* He tried to steady his nerves, but his hands still shook. Although not a drinker, he opened his small drinks cabinet and removed the five-star bottle of brandy. The liquid splashed over the polished mahogany as he half-filled a tumbler.

Returning to his seat, he held the glass in both hands and sipped the brandy. When the final drop slipped down his throat, he felt more in control. These people were the soldiers of those who never got their hands dirty. Respectable villains never spilt blood or soiled their expensive suits. The man may be dead, but his rules still applied.

He rubbed his hands together nervously and then telephoned Abbey.

She answered on the second ring. "Mr Peters, I didn't expect to hear from you. Have you heard from my father's lawyers?"

"Violet, the receptionist, is dead."

"What has this to do with me?"

144

"My letter stirred up a hornet's nest. It appears that your father did not, as I thought, sit behind a desk making money. The man who roughed me up, shot poor Violet to make sure I obeyed."

Abbey shivered as she listened. "You poor thing. Back off. You've always been good for me, and I don't want to see you hurt."

"Don't worry about me. I got the message loud and clear. I'm warning you to be careful. I doubt having given me notice, they'll come after you, but you never know."

Choosing her words carefully, she said, "I'm not worth the effort. By attacking you they made it clear, I know the score. You don't happen to know the name of the organisation my father operated?"

The line appeared to go dead for several seconds. "American Holdings. I believed they dealt in buying and selling property. Obviously, that's a shell company, but they have branch offices in every major city of the States."

"How did you find this out?"

"I'm a solicitor, not a fool. When your father named me as your legal guardian, I required funds to meet your expenses. They sent cheques to the company bank. In those days, we had branch managers. My financial manager became a friend and for me did some checking. My concern being, was I involved in money laundering? Later transfers became electronic, and I never gave them a thought."

"Thank you. Please don't send any more letters. Over the years, you have always looked after me. You're the closest thing to a parent I ever had."

"Thank you for that. I always thought of you as my surrogate daughter. Don't worry about me. You take care and remember if you need legal advice I'm here. Bye" The line went dead.

Abbey's mind drifted back to what a girl in her school said after a rape. There's many a weirdo wandering around out there. The problem is you don't see them coming until it's too late. She

145

now felt the same. *Don't be silly,* she told herself, and with her mind in overdrive, she made her way from the kitchen to her room.

# Twenty-Three

Not that anyone cared, Commander Haliwell always wrote his reports in longhand. The terrorist threat level was due for reassessment. One thing he wanted to be sure of that those in power understood, it was not about to go away.

His desk telephone rang; he lifted the handset and said, "Haliwell."

"Good morning, Commander. Kathy James."

His mind raced as he recognised her name. "Long time no speak. Have you something on that damned laptop?"

"Yes and no. We found something you should know."

He was silent for a moment. "About time. With the lack of information, I shelved the case."

"We never stopped looking, Commander. From what we have recovered we know you need a trigger which activates the launch programme."

"Okay, what is the trigger?"

"I don't know. It could be anything. What I do know is without the trigger, we cannot stop it operating."

"We must be able to do something."

"You'd need to reconfigure every ICBM launch programme."

"I can't see that happening when governments believe their systems are unhackable."

"I'll send you my report and then it's on your desk."

"Did you find anything else?"

"We recovered bits and pieces, but nothing that makes any sense. I'll keep my people on the case, but I doubt if we'll ever retrieve all the pieces of the jigsaw. The originator did a great job of contaminating the hard drive."

"Thanks for your persistence, Kathy. Someone must have this trigger, but I haven't a clue where to start looking."

"I know the feeling, but if we find anything, you'll be the first to know."

"Thanks. Take care. Bye." As he placed the handset, he wondered if this problem would ever end? Although his office was warm, he felt a chill. Shaking off the thought, he picked up his pen and continued writing.

***

Abbey used what remained of the evening walking back and forth in her room. Her bed beckoned but she spent the whole night tossing and turning, unable to sleep. Tired and irritable, she wobbled into the bathroom. After splashing cold and then hot water on her face, she felt better. Back in her room, she dressed in her black jeans, black jumper, and Doc Martens. On descending the stairs to the kitchen, she was pleased to find it empty. Black coffee and two slices of toast became breakfast.

Physically, she could not attack the problem. She was no longer the girl with a wealthy father, but she was a fighter with a computer.

With the core of an idea, she grabbed her coat and made her way to the university. She prayed the computer block would be empty. When she opened the door a young man, with short black hair and at least two days stubble on his pockmarked face, stopped what he was doing.

He lifted his head and smiled. "Hi, do you know anything about programming?"

"A little."

"Great. Can you help? Whatever I do, it doesn't work."

She glanced at her watch, shrugged and wandered across the room. "Let me have a look. I assume you know the five things required to write a programme?"

The question caught him by surprise. "Variables, operators, conditionals, loops and function calls."

148

A smile spread across her face. "At least you remember the basics. Let me look." Her eyes scanned the screen as she combed the monitor in search of the fault in his programme. She saw the problem and let her fingers rattle the keyboard. "There, try that."

He operated the keys, and the screen flashed and filled with the history of Tudor kings. "That's brilliant. Thanks."

"You mixed up your languages and source code. I do it all the time. By the end of this term, the differences will become more apparent. It's like learning two foreign languages at the same time. Look, I must work on my end of term project. If you're having problems give me a shout."

He held out his hand. "Billy Stone. First-year student, but I guess you figured that out already."

"Abbey Lane, final year. Lots to do, see you around."

She seated herself as far from Billy as she could, leant back in the chair, and connected with the internet. When ready, she typed her access code for entry into the dark web. For a few minutes, she stared at the screen as the white arrow blinked. "Where are they?" she muttered. Her eyes searched the screen until a mess of algorithms raced around the screen. They continued until...

**BLUE TOOTH> JUMPING JACK FLASH**

Abbey keyed in, I HAVE A PROBLEM

**ONLY ONE>IT'S YOUR LUCKY DAY> I SOLVE PROBLEMS**

"DO YOU REMEMBER AL CAPONE

**EVERYONE KNOWS THE STORY**

I NEED TO SCREW A COMPANY WHO THREATENED A FRIEND OF MINE AND MURDERED AN INNOCENT WOMAN

**SOUNDS FUN>HOW MUCH DAMAGE CAN I INFLICT**

IS A TOTAL WIPEOUT TOO MUCH TOO ASK

**I LIKE THE AL CAPONE IDEA> TAX EVASION SCREWS LIKE NO OTHER. NAME THE COMPANY**

AMERICAN HOLDINGS>NEW YORK>I UNDERSTAND THIS IS A SHELL COMPANY

**THIS MAY TAKE TIME> COULD BE PRICEY**

HOW MUCH

**LET ME GET BACK TO YOU> GIVE ME A DAY OR TWO**

OKAY BUT I'LL CONTACT YOU USING BLUE TOOTH

**THANKS**

CHAT LATER JUMPING JACK

The screen went blank. Abbey keyed in an end code. From her bag, she removed a file and continued with her studies.

Two hours later, she finished and turned to Billy. "How's it going?"

"Slowly, but I'm getting there. Thanks again for your help."

"I'm off home. See you around."

She left, her mood buoyant. A guilty smile filled her innocent face.

# Twenty-Four

Abbey filled the next week going over her research and finishing her thesis on the work of Alan Turin. In her world, he was the beginning of computer science and artificial intelligence.

Most evenings she relaxed, but Friday was her night out at the pub with Steve. This evening she called up **BLUETOOTH** on the dark web. He was unavailable.

Moments before she was due to leave, she checked her laptop. The **BLUETOOTH** icon on a new document blinked.

She opened the file. Will contact you at midnight UK time.

One final check in the mirror she grabbed her beige full-length coat and headed for the kitchen. Steve was waiting.

"Nice coat."

Abbey grinned. "It's the only coat that fits me. Babe takes up a lot of room these days. I'll be glad when it arrives."

"I'm told it can be painful."

"I really need to know that. Shall we go?"

As they walked to the pub, he asked. "Is something bothering you?"

"No. Why do you ask?"

"When you came into the kitchen, you had your serious head-on."

"I was thinking about my thesis. It's long enough but is it good enough?"

"I'm sure it is. Are you drinking tonight?"

"I'm on the wagon until babe makes an appearance."

The pub was quiet when they entered, and their usual seats close to the open log fire were free.

Abbey picked up the menu, although she knew what she wanted.

Steve did the same and asked, "What are you having?"

"Steak pie dinner."

"Good choice. I'll have the same. Fresh orange and tonic?"

She handed him a twenty-pound note. "My treat."

He took the money and sauntered to the bar.

When he returned with a drink in each hand, he commented, "Your mind's somewhere else. What's up?"

"I told you, my thesis."

"You know computer science backwards. You teach the teachers. So stop messing about."

Her eyes met his. "It turns out my late father is a bigger bastard than I thought."

Steve shrugged. "He didn't want to know you, so what did you expect?"

"I don't know. Can we change the subject?"

"Two steak dinners," said Cathy. She placed the plates on the table, allowing her ample bust to brush Steve's right cheek. "Need anything else?"

"No, thanks," said Abbey.

"Will I see you later, Steve?"

"You'd better believe it. I'll walk Abbey home and come back."

"Make it before ten-thirty. We have a birthday party, and the boss wants to lock the doors early."

Steve laughed. "Looks like a long night."

"You can lay in tomorrow."

Abbey chuckled and glanced at Cathy. "There was a time not so long ago I partied with the best of them." She rubbed her bump. "Babe and I prefer an early night these days."

"I hope the father's going to pay."

"I want nothing from him. Babe and me are survivors."

152

"If it were me I'd screw him like he's screwed you. Babies change your life, like it and lump it. Well that's what my sisters tell me," said Cathy. "Must go. Customers waiting."

"Her hearts in the right place," said Abbey.

"Salt of the earth."

Neither said another word as they ate.

Steve took their empty plates back to the bar and ordered another pint of Spitfire.

"She alright?" asked Cathy. "Pity she got lumbered with a kid."

"And she's an orphan. No family anywhere."

"You tell her from me that if she needs a friend to talk to, I'm here most days."

Steve paid for his pint. "Thanks, Cathy. I'll tell her."

"Cathy says if you need a friend to talk to she'd love to help," said Steve when he returned to the table.

"She's okay, but I'm not. As much as I enjoyed my dinner, babe's having a game of football. When you're ready, you can escort me home."

Steve walked Abbey to Harold's front door. She smiled as he ran back to the pub.

Back in her room, she hung her coat on the back of the door and sat on the bed. She lifted her laptop, connected to the dark web, and waited. The warmth of the room and comfort of the mattress comforted babe and Abbey's eyes closed.

A distant pinging penetrated her mind. For a few seconds, she wondered why she was still dressed. Reality struck her, and she grabbed her laptop.

She opened the connection.

SORRY BLUETOOTH>DOZED OFF

**GOOD AND BAD NEWS**

WHAT IS THE BAD

AMERICAN HOLDINGS ARE MEGA BAD. DID YOU KNOW THEY HAVE AN INBUILT TRACKING SYSTEM

NO

I WAS WARNED TO BACK OFF, AND THAT MADE ME MAD

WHAT HAVE YOU DONE

I ASKED ALL MY FRIENDS TO INSTALL THEIR MOST DESTRUCTIVE VIRUS BEFORE I CLOSED DOWN. I SENT THEM AN ENCRYPTED E-MAIL WITH A VIRAS ATTACHED. THEIR SECURITY MONITORING SYSTEM WAS CRAP AND WHOLE PILE OF SHIT CRASHED. I WOULD BET THEIR SYSTEM IS FUCKED

WAS THAT WISE

NO CHANCE> I'M IMMUNE TO DETECTION

MOBILE

YOU BET. A TIME AGO GOT MYSELF AN OLD FREIGHTLINER SEMI> FITTED IT OUT AS HOME AND OFFICE

WHAT DO I OWE YOU

**NOTHING>IT WAS MY PLEASURE TO SCREW
THE BASTARDS**

WHAT IS YOUR HANDLE

**FREEMAN**

THANKS FOR YOUR HELP>KEEP SAFE

**I MOVE LIKE THE WIND>DO NOT FORGET WE
ARE HERE FOR EACH OTHER.**

DO NOT BECOME A STRANGER.

Freeman's icon vanished. She shut down and lay back on
the bed. Sometime in the early morning, she awoke, undressed and
crawled under the sheets.

# Twenty-Five

Terry tried three times to reach his contact.

"What do you want?" a man answered.

"Are you busy?"

"Life is quiet at the moment."

"I need a dog put down. If I forward a name and a picture, can you fit this into your schedule?"

"When?"

"I've heard he might be doing a runner. Tomorrow would be good."

"Twenty thousand."

"I'll meet you in your favourite greasy spoon at two tomorrow afternoon."

"Done. Send me the details." The line went dead.

\*\*\*

Barry Thomson, his face tense, glared at the words of the letter from the bank before dumping it into the waste bin. He sighed and for the last time, glanced out of his flat window at the rain. The deluge fell in a steady, unrelenting stream. He was tired of the never-ending investigation by the police. His mind thought of the pending court case along with the possibility of a custodial sentence and the trouble with his bank. Leaving London and starting again was not a difficult decision. He strolled to his office, aware it would be empty. Having wound up and sold the company, his flat and car gave him enough money to survive.

At a brisk pace, he attempted to make some sense of what had happened. Rain ran down his face calming his anger.

On unlocking the office door, he reached for the master light switch. Nothing happened. In the diffused grey light, he could see far enough into the building. The atmosphere was eerie, no air-con hum, no chatter from the staff. He sat in his chair and absorbed the quiet, confident in his future.

Looking at his watch, in one hour his train departed, plenty of time.

Across the road, a short man stood, his frame hidden by a black overcoat. Protected by a bus shelter, he watched. In the dim light, nothing set him apart from any other person. His vision focused on Barry as he locked the door and shoved the keys through the letterbox.

Barry shrugged, lifted his two cases and walked away. The man turned up the full collar on his coat and followed at a tactful distance.

The gap closed as Barry joined the flow of traffic entering Parsons Green station.

The man climbed the steps to the platform, his eyes fixed on Barry's back.

On the platform, he stood a metre behind and waited for the next train to Earl's court to arrive. His eyes glanced at the travel screen, two minutes.

The roar and rattle of the train as it arrived drowned any conversation until it stopped. Those waiting rushed forward, their bodies pressed together.

Jostled by the crowd, he plunged the shiny blade into Barry's back. The razor-sharp point struck the rib cage. With a tug, he pulled it clear and watched his victim stumble, half in and half out of the carriage.

A woman screamed, and chaos ensued as bodies collided in desperate attempts to avoid the fallen man.

Stepping back, the assassin dropped the knife between the train and the platform.

Someone shouted, "It's a terrorist attack." As a round up of stampeding cattle, commuters intent on escaping, charged along the platform. At the top of the stairs, a woman tripped and fell

157

headlong. Like ten pins, one body struck another until a mass of human flesh tumbled onto a concrete slab.

The station manager watched the tragedy explode on CCTV. In a panic, he contacted the emergency services. Struck by the horror, he went and closed the entrance to the station.

The police, fire brigade and ambulances filled the street in minutes. Paramedics checked and treated the dead, dying and injured.

On the platform, half in and out of the carriage, Chief Inspector Davis examined a body. He turned to the station manager. "Tell your bosses that this station is out of action until further notice. And if you don't know already, it's going to be a long day."

***

At two, that afternoon, Terry checked the time as a bacon-filled bap drained butter onto his plate. Three thick cups of coffee later, he muttered. "Fuck him if Simon can't be on time for his money he obviously doesn't need it." Draining the dregs from his cup, he paid the girl behind the counter and walked away.

# *Twenty-Six*

Abbey woke with a start. "Abbey, wake up. I need to talk to you."

She threw the covers off, grabbed her dressing gown and staggered half asleep to the door, turned the key and pulled it open. "Steve, is this important?"

"Do you know a Bill Franklyn?"

She nodded. "Why?"

Steve rubbed his hands together, and his eyes sparkled. "He's been in contact with my father. It appears he's found a buyer for my flat and yours."

"What are you trying to tell me?"

"Your troubles are over. Bill's buyer wants both flats. The fire damage doesn't matter."

"It sounds too good to be true, but I trust Bill. He's a nice person. I wonder why he hasn't contacted me?"

Steve ran the fingers of his right hand through his hair. "Might be good to give him a bell."

"Tell you what. You go and put the kettle on, make some toast; I'll get dressed and give Bill a call. I still think it's too good to be true even if your father believes it's kosher."

Steve frowned. "Okay but put your skates on."

Abbey washed, quickly pulled on some clothes, and descended the stairs and ran into the kitchen.

"Three slices of toast, still warm and a cup of coffee."

"You'll make someone a good wife." Abbey fumbled for her mobile in her bag. "In one minute, we'll know." She opened her list of contacts, pressed Bill's number, and while she waited, nibbled the toast.

159

"Good morning, Miss Lane. You're ten minutes in front of me. I have good news for you."

"I know."

"Pardon."

"I know you have an interested buyer. What are they offering?"

"More than it's worth. As it stands with no repairs, six hundred thousand, but there's a catch."

She slumped in a chair. "What do you mean?"

"It's a take it or leave it offer. You can buy the place you like in Rotherhithe."

"I'm not sure. Can I think about it?"

"The sting in the tail is you have two days, or the buyer moves on."

"Give me time to think. I'll give you a call in a minute." She ended the conversation.

She turned to Steve. "What do you think?"

"It's not up to me. My father thinks it's a great deal, but I'd go for it."

"Look, I know you wouldn't be in this position if it weren't for me."

Steve shrugged. "These things happen, and you weren't even at home. If you get rid of the problem, you can get on with your life. Remember you wanted to find a place for you and the baby. It's your chance to start again where and how you want."

Abbey lifted her head and stared at the ceiling before answering. "Since my father died, and I've been able to be who I want to be, my life has become a mess. You're right, I do want somewhere I can call home for my baby. You've been a help and believe me, I appreciate all that you've done. Before I agree to sell, I must talk to Mr Peters. I trust you, but he's always been there since I can remember. I need him to tell me this is the right thing to do."

"Do what you have to do but time is of the essence."

160

She managed to smile. "This afternoon you'll have your answer. Now let me go and get dressed."

"I'm sure your man will give you the right advice. See you later."

Abbey chose her clothes and went to the bathroom. She showered, and dressed in faded blue jeans, a loose blue jumper, white trainers covered her feet. After combing her hair, she returned to her room, draped a black leather jacket over her shoulders, grabber her handbag and left.

***

"You may go up now," said the receptionist who Abbey had never seen before.

"Thank you."

Peters was waiting as she exited the lift. "You're in luck. I'm free at the moment but would you mind giving me a call in future?"

She looked at his magnified eyes behind his glasses. "Sorry, but I do need to ask you something important."

"Let's go to my office."

He followed Abbey, closing the door behind him.

She noticed his expression appeared troubled. "How are you?"

"I'm coming to terms with what happened, but I'll never understand why he had to kill Violet." He glanced at his watch. "How can I help?"

Abbey explained the situation with her flat. "What would you do?"

He held up his right hand. "You must understand whatever I say is my opinion. I'm not an expert on property."

She nodded.

He cleared his throat. "Can you give me the estate agent's name and telephone number?"

"Of course, but he's not available until this afternoon."

161

He wrote Bill Franklyn's name and number on a pad. "Let me act as your conveyance solicitor. I will speak to Franklyn and ask important questions. What are your instructions?"

"Thank you for helping. If it's a genuine deal, please accept and tell him to proceed. When you have a moment, let me know."

"I have another client soon, but I'll get back to you as soon as I can."

Abbey stood. "The way my life has almost self-destructed lately I'm happy this is in safe hands. I've discovered it's not healthy for me to obsess over the past. I tend to beat myself up for being so stupid. But I know I've got to learn, and try to move forward. I'll be waiting for your call." She walked around the desk and kissed him on the cheek.

He blushed as she strolled out of the office.

The sun was warm and made it the ideal day for a walk. Birdsong drifted on the breeze. For the first time in an age, her life had order. Enjoying the moment, Abbey made her way towards the underground station. Her life had been different to most, too much money always taken for granted. It felt normal to be selling and buying another flat of her choosing. She used her Oyster card, passed through the barrier and headed for the platform. Today she was just another young pregnant woman going home.

Without warning and out of control, she hurtled towards a white tiled wall. Her sight blurred and it went dark. Voices filled her ears, but she could not comprehend the words. Like a cheap horror film, her mind attempted to analyse what was happening. She remembered entering the station and then nothing. Pain ran in circles around her head. *Where was she? How did she get here?* She tried to open her mouth, but something pressed hard on her face. The dark returned, and the hurt faded.

Abbey awoke in a strange bed with white sheets surrounded by blue curtains. The curtain parted, revealing a young woman wearing a nurse's uniform.

"Are, you're awake. The doctor gave you a jab to put you out for a while. How are you feeling?"

"I hurt all over."

The nurse checked Abbey's pulse and noted her breathing.

"Where am I? What happened?"

"You're in hospital. The transport police told the paramedic someone attacked you. You smashed your head hard when you hit a wall. You've been out for a couple of hours. By the way, your waters have broken."

"Is my baby okay?"

"The doctor checked you over, and the wee one is fine."

"Where's my handbag?"

"All your clothes are in the cupboard alongside your bed, but I never noticed a bag. Your money belt and phone are in a safe place. I must say the belt impressed me. A pocket for your phone and sections for cards and notes. Where did you buy it?"

A girl at my uni makes them to order. I've three in different colours. Thank God, it keeps my main stuff safe from muggers. If that bastard stole my bag, all they will find is makeup and odds and sods."

"Before you leave can I get her details from you. At the moment I need your contact number."

Abbey grinned. "That's easy. I haven't got one."

The nurse frowned. "What's that supposed to mean? We all have someone."

"Not me. I'm on my own. Have been all my life."

"I'm sure you must have somebody who wants to know where you are."

"My housemate, Steve, will wonder where I am but please don't contact him unless you must. If you give me my phone, I can give you his number."

Without warning, her first contraction began. The pain was more intense than anything Abbey had experienced before. She screamed as the nurse placed the gas and air mask on her face.

"Breath deep and slow, and it will pass," said the nurse.

Abbey grabbed the nurse's right hand and squeezed as the pain decreased. "That hurt."

The nurse smiled. "You'll be okay. You're young and strong. Use the gas and air when you need to. It does help."

"Do you have children?"

"Two boys."

"Abbey lifted her mobile and the nurse Steve's number. "Would you believe I'm frightened? Can you stay with me?"

"That's normal with your first. I can't stay, but I'll send one of my junior nurses to keep you company. I've other patients to attend to and must tell the doctor you've started."

"I was told contractions could go on for hours."

Every birth is the same, but different. I have a feeling your baby's in a hurry."

Abbey grabbed the gas and air mask as another contraction gripped her.

"More often than not, there's more time between contractions. I'll get the doctor now."

"I'm not due for four weeks."

"Must go," said the nurse.

A shudder ran through Abbey's body, and the fear of the unknown grabbed her.

Ten minutes elapsed before a doctor arrived. He listened to the baby's heart and checked Abbey's progress. "You're well dilated. It'll be best to have you in maternity and see one of my colleagues. You've done well. Arrive in A&E and end up in maternity."

"Doctor, I have a strange urge to push."

He smiled. "I'd appreciate it if you could hold on until we are ready."

"I don't know how."

The impulse to push overcame everything and five contractions later, the baby arrived.

Two nurses cleaned Abbey while another checked the baby,

"That was easy," said Abbey,

"The quickest today and thankfully no problems," said a nurse.

A nurse holding the baby, now wrapped in a sheet, stood beside Abbey. "He's a good weight, and everything's where it should be. What are you going to call him?"

Abbey took and held the child. "I don't know. I haven't thought of a name yet?" She looked into the child's eyes. At that moment, she knew she would protect and love her child with every ounce of her being. "I will call him Noah."

The nurse stared at her unblinking. "Do you have some baby clothes for Noah?"

Abbey stopped admiring Noah and focused on the nurse. "I feel such an idiot. I intended to buy clothes but never did, just in case something happened."

A smile played around the nurse's mouth. "You're not the first to think that way. I understand you have no family in London."

"I have no family anywhere."

The nurse paused. "I shouldn't do this, but if you give me the money, I'm happy to buy what you'll need to care for him."

Abbey nodded and then realised she had little cash in her belt. "Great idea but I have about twenty pounds in cash. I have a housemate who might help. At worst, he'll lend me some money. I'll ring him right now."

Steve strolled in, followed by Cathy. "The sister said it was okay to come in." He held up a bulging plastic bag. "Clothes for your baby. Has it got a name?"

Abbey's eyes widened. "Noah, but how did you know?"

"A nurse phoned and told me you were about to give birth. We went to maternity, and they told us you were here. The clothes are from Cathy's sister."

Abbey took a deep breath. "Thanks a million. I hope they'll fit."

165

Cathy laughed. "He's so small they'll fit. Our plan was to give you these before you came in. My sister had a boy six months ago, and this and much more was waiting in the pub before we got the news. There's also a small buggy, Moses basket and a few toys. What you don't need, give to the charity shop. Oh, and we bought a large pack of disposables. Steve, where are they?"

"Shit, sorry. In your car. I'll go and get them."

"Men," said Cathy.

Abbey laughed.

"Can I hold him?"

"Of course. Abbey let Cathy lift him from her. "Did they tell you I got mugged?"

"I wondered why the side of your face is black and blue. What happened?"

Abbey told her.

"At least you're in one piece, and the little one is fine. Did the bastard get much?"

"Only my handbag, anything of value I keep in my belt."

"Here we are." Steve placed a bumper pack of disposable nappies by the side of the bed. "How long are they keeping you in?"

"Abbey shrugged. "Don't know. I suppose a day or two."

"Suits you," said Steve, as he turned to Cathy. His face turned into a smile. "Nice to meet you, Noah."

"Time you left," said a nurse. "We have a mother and baby to sort out."

"When can I leave?" asked Abbey.

"I understand the doctor wants you to stay for two to three days. Just in case of any problems."

Steve gave her a sideways look. "Give us a bell, Abbey. Cathy, I suggest you give Noah back to his mum."

"I'll take him," said the nurse.

"Good looking baby," said Cathy. "Not that you'll listen but screw the father for support."

"I don't want that bastard anywhere near Noah."

166

"Your decision. See you when you arrive home. Steve can babysit for you while we have a night out."

Abbey laughed. "Maybe in a few months. I need to get used to being a mother."

"Time to go," said the nurse.

"See you," said Steve as they left.

Abbey waved as the nurse left with Noah cradled in her arms. Her mind drifted, she felt different, and it was time she faced the reality of life. Being a mother changed everything.

The ringing of her mobile interrupted her thoughts.

"Abbey Lane," the caller asked in a business-like but friendly manner.

"Yes, who is this?"

"It's Joan Bishop, I work with Bill Franklyn. Can you come into the office tomorrow?"

"I've just given birth. I'll have to get back to you."

"Congratulations, boy or girl?"

"Boy."

"I'll tell Bill you'll be in touch."

"Okay. Thanks." When she put the phone down, she realised life goes on, but something disturbed and nagged her mind. But she forced herself to think about Noah.

A nurse entered the room. "Hi, how are you?"

Abbey nodded. "A bit sore, but happy if you know what I mean."

"I understand. I need to ask you a few questions."

"I don't think I'm going anywhere for a day or two. Carry on."

"Are you breast or straight to the bottle?"

"Can I try the breast?"

The nurse smiled. "Of course."

For the next fifteen minutes, questions and advice on caring for Noah were asked, answered, talked about, and notes made.

167

"You'll be okay," said the nurse. "Let me know if there's anything else I can help you with. Meanwhile, an auxiliary will bring Noah for feeding and changing. Good luck."

Abbey gave her a sleepy smile as she left and relaxed into the pillows.

Left alone, a chill passed through her. Her thoughts focused on Jacobs USB drive in her handbag. What would happen if the thief plugged it into a computer? She fought back the panic that tried to engulf her. The voice in her head told her that finding nothing of value, he would have dumped it in the nearest bin. Should she tell Haliwell about the mugging? Her heart missed a beat when she understood why that was impossible.

The door clattered open, and a plump woman entered. "Time your little one was changed and fed. Do you need help?"

Abbey gave her a smile. "I'll do as you tell me." She slid out of bed onto the cold tiled floor and grabbed the plastic parcel of nappies. "How do I start?"

"Call me Elsie. I try to help the new mums. Let me show you." She lay Noah on the changing table, lifted his legs in the air and in one swift movement removed the soiled nappy. "Next, you clean the mess and with a warm damp cloth wash." She pointed. "There's one by the sink." In less than a couple of minutes, Noah was in Abbey's arms.

"I have to ask every mother. Have you taken or injected drugs?"

"Never," said Abbey

"Good. I assume you have been producing milk so let baby do the work. He will take what he wants. To begin with, it will not be much so I'll leave him with you. Little and often will be the best approach. Now place him in a comfortable position and let him find your nipple."

Noah started to feed as if he had always known.

"You're lucky," said Elsie." When he's full, let him be. Any problems ring the bell."

168

"Thank you."

Elsie left humming a tune.

On the afternoon of the third day Steve and Cathy collected Abbey and Noah from the hospital. Back in her room she turned to Cathy, "You've been busy"

"Steve helped."

Noah stirred in Abbey's arms. "He'll wake in a minute and the fun begins. Clean and feed, cuddle and sleep, that's his life. Steve if you don't mind."

"Do you need something?"

Cathy gave him a gentle shove. "Bugger off, Abbey needs to feed Noah and doesn't want you staring at her tits."

"Oh, right. See you later. For your dinner it's a cottage pie."

"Did you make it, Steve?"

"No, it's a Cathy special she made in the pub."

"It's cooked so just bung it in the microwave for ten minutes." Cathy grabbed Steve's arm. "Time we left."

# *Twenty-Seven*

Abbey sat on her bed while Noah slept in his Moses basket. "In a few weeks, babe, we'll be in our own home. Until then, this will have to do. Don't get me wrong, it's warm, dry and comfortable, and I'm thankful Harold lets us stay." The child stirred but did not wake.

She studied the fading bruises on her arms and face. "It could have been worse. Nothing broken and babe is perfect." She lifted her mobile and rang Bill Franklyn.

"Hi, Abbey. Congratulations."

"She nestled back into the pillows. "Thanks, Bill. I can meet you at your office tomorrow if that's okay?"

"Great. I'll have the papers ready. Just so you know, I managed to push the people buying your flat up to six hundred thousand. That gives you enough to purchase Rotherhithe, pay the bills and have a few pounds leftover."

"That's brilliant. Thank you. What time is good for you?"

"Ten would be good. I'll have the kettle on for coffee. Will you be bringing baby?"

"Of Course."

Turning to Noah, she smiled at her sleeping angel. "We're on our way, babe." She made one more phone call to Mr Peters and explained the situation.

"Good. When the sale's complete, I'll have their solicitor transfer the funds to my client account. Once the purchase of your new property's agreed, I'll repeat the process to the seller's solicitor. Also, I'll sort out the stamp duty payment and have what remains placed in your account. There will be no charges from my company."

"Thanks. You make it sound so easy."

170

He chuckled. "This is not something I usually do. I had to ask for advice. Your estate agent has been most helpful."

"He's one of the good guys."

"You can't be too careful."

"I know. Thanks again." She glanced at her watch, time to feed Noah. Bye." She ended the call.

Noah whimpered but remained asleep. "It's you and me, babe. Don't worry, I'll take care of you, but one day you'll want to do your own thing."

Her mobile rang. She glanced at the screen. "Hi, what have I done this time?"

Haliwell laughed. "Nothing I'm aware of. I need an expert, and I'm offering you the job."

She chuckled. "Has Scotland Yard a crèche?"

"Not that I know of, why?"

"Don't tell me you've forgotten."

"My apologies, but I thought it wasn't due for a while. Boy or girl?"

"A handsome boy."

"Tell me to go away but are you interested?"

"I would have to give it a lot of thought. My finals come first."

"I can live with that. Why don't you come and have a coffee and a chat?"

"I'll need to bring Noah."

"Annie will love taking care of him."

"Are you sure?"

"I'm sure."

"Okay. When?"

"Tomorrow at ten."

"Will have to rearrange my morning but will be there. Oh, and by the way, I don't work for nothing." All she heard before the line went dead was his laughter.

171

Pressing a memory key, she contacted Bill Franklyn. It went to voicemail. "Hi, Bill. Something's come up and I can't make tomorrow. Mr Peters, my solicitor, can sign on my behalf. He has my legal power of attorney. Thanks."

Abbey lifted Noah from his basket, checked his nappy and dressed him in a dark blue one-piece weatherproof outfit. She grabbed her coat, made her way down the stairs and secured him in the buggy. "Time for fresh air, little one."

His eyes opened and closed as she wrapped a blanket around him. For the next couple of hours, she went window-shopping while wondering what Haliwell required from her.

*** 

At ten the next morning, she pushed Noah's buggy into New Scotland Yard reception.

On seeing Abbey, Annie strolled across reception and smiled. "Good Morning. Commander Haliwell asked me to meet you."

"I remember you," said Abbey.

"Wait a moment. I need to see if the boss is ready." Annie went to the counter, lifted a telephone and pressed the buttons. In seconds, she returned. "He's free. And who's this." She pointed at the child.

"Abbey shifted the cover. "Noah."

"I gather I'm babysitting while you and the Commander have a chat."

Abbey smiled. "If he stays asleep, you'll be fine. Awake, he's always hungry. There's a full bottle of milk in the pram bag and a clean nappy."

"No problem. I'm sure we'll get along fine. We'll take the lift. Follow me."

The lift rose at speed, stopping at the floor of Haliwell's office. Abbey followed along a brightly lit corridor pushing the buggy on the thick-carpeted floor. Annie led the way to a small conference room. Inside, Haliwell sat at the head of the table.

He lifted his head when they entered. "You look well. Motherhood must suit you."

"Eight hours of sleep would be great, but that's not going to happen for a few years."

Haliwell laughed. "Been there and done that. Is it okay for Annie to take the little one?"

"I don't think he'll care so long as he's warm and dry."

"He'll be fine. It'll make a change from staring at a screen." Annie pushed the buggy out and closed the door.

Abbey could feel her heart thumping as she sat close to Haliwell. "Why me?"

He leant back in his chair. "Simple. I'm told you are the best at getting systems to give up their secrets."

Abbey shrugged. "Who told you that?"

"Your tutors, and before you ask, you can work from home unless you have something to tell me."

"Okay. What do I have to do to earn my pay?"

Haliwell leant forward on the table. He spoke clearly. "It's impossible to track and monitor extremists who may be plotting attacks. I have tried hard to understand which people in this country constitute a threat. I believe the worst receive instructions and then initiate attacks. There are plenty of them. I want you to discover from where these email directives originate."

Abbey rested her hands on the table. "I would have thought that you already have that expertise in house."

His expression became serious. "We have, but this is an operation where I need someone outside the system. I believe there's a ton of trouble brewing in the Middle East. Call them Isis or whatever but if I do nothing when they strike, many people will die. Invariably, when my people hack into a system they leave a trail a mile long. Subsequently the suspect vanishes. This way you and I know the source and I can act and nail the bastard. I know my superiors would question my methods."

Abbey, her face businesslike, looked into his eyes. "And the pay?"

Haliwell opened a folder and slid it towards her. "It's the best I can do."

"Are you in charge of this operation?" She read the document in front of her before lifting her head. "This contract is for one year and to be fair I haven't a clue what the going rate is for my services."

"Let's put it this way. If it goes wrong, I'll be retired."

"With a fat pension."

He laughed. "Your pay is that of an acting inspector. Will you sign that contract or do I have to look somewhere else?"

Abbey nodded and a smile formed on her lips. "I've never worked a day in my life. I have a baby and need the money. Of course, I accept. Give me a pen and I'll sign my life away."

Haliwell handed her a pen. "You're also required to sign the official secrets act. Annie will send you a mass of emails. You will discover their country of origin. Make a list and deliver the answers to me. No one else. Is that understood?"

Abbey stood. "Yes, boss, but what does that achieve?"

He smiled. "Find the source and I will be able to locate the top agents. You'll find a rather expensive laptop in the baby's buggy. It's the best money can buy. When you finish working for us, you'll return it to me."

She stared at him for a moment. "What do you know about emails?"

"Not a lot. I press send and hope the address is correct. That's why you're on the payroll."

Abbey gaped at Haliwell. "You don't know how an email works, do you?"

He churched his fingers and leant back. "I don't need to."

"Do you want to know?"

"Tell me, but keep it simple."

"Email is the same as a letter. You post it, and it travels from one post office to another before reaching its destination."

"That I understand."

Abbey looked at Haliwell's bright eyes. "That was the simple description, but unlike your paper letter an email leaves a minute fragment of itself at every post office it enters and leaves. There is an excessive number in the system every day. Most of those receiving one read it and dump it in the bin."

"I don't even do that, Annie screens my mail."

"My God, you're the last of the dinosaurs. In a few years, you and those like you will be extinct. Anyway, I digress. Emails are the worst form of transferring information. An average hacker could trace an email in minutes unless the sender configured it in a secure way."

"Can you do the job?"

She nodded. "If I can break through the firewalls and identify the pass-codes, I can write an access programme and walk straight inside. The ones with half a brain will use multi-routes and rogue servers."

"You just hit the button," said Haliwell. "I need to know the location of the sender. For the moment, we will play this as it happens. When you have a few untraceable emails, we can talk about an increase in funding. You'll find fifty emails on your laptop. I expect locations like yesterday."

She shrugged. "That depends on who sent them and what security protocols they wrapped them in. You can be sure I'll do my best. Just hope it's good enough."

He closed the file. "Doing your best will be good enough."

# *Twenty-Eight*

Feeding Noah was never a problem. He loved his food so long as there was enough. Once fed, changed and laid in his basket he remained quiet and content.

"Right, babe. I have to work."

Abbey sat at the small table and opened her new laptop. "Let's see what we have to work with." The screen glowed and one file came up. Starting with the first email, she began reading the contents. Her eyes widened. "Bloody hell. Sorry, babe, you shouldn't have heard that but these people are real nutters."

Her fingers rattled the keyboard as she entered a search and locate algorithm. The screen went blank for a moment before the send IP address and location came up. Jabaliya, Gaza. "Standard security protocols. Amateurs," she muttered. "Instructions on how to make a pipe bomb."

One at a time, she processed each email, eventually compiling a list. When she finished she analysed the results. Most came from Libya, the remainder from locations in the Middle East.

She gazed at Noah. He was asleep. "It's alright for some." On returning to the laptop and listed each email in its appropriate group. One location surpassed all others. Tripoli in Libya.

With a contented smile on her lips, she leant back. This was not the first time she had hacked into rogue systems but somehow she hoped she was doing the right thing. The objective was clear, stop terrorists killing people. She pressed the print button and filed the single sheet of paper. Finished, she contacted Haliwell on his direct line.

He answered on the first ring. "Problems?"

She sighed. "No, why do you ask?"

"I didn't expect to hear from you so soon."

"Well if they don't get any more difficult you're wasting my time. A first-year student could crack these."

"I doubt they teach them to crack source codes. Anyway, may I suggest I meet you in the morning at your home and we take Noah for a walk, weather permitting? If it's raining I'll treat you to a coffee."

"Last of the big time spenders. Why don't we meet in the Silver Spoon? It's on Hammersmith high street. You can't miss it and you can treat me to a large Americano."

"I'll see you at nine."

*** 

Abbey slept for at best three hours. For an unknown reason Noah had gorged on her milk and then promptly vomited the majority over her. Hungry, he demanded more but this time he slept while she cleaned the mess.

Bleary eyed, she showered, dressed in her blue denim outfit and her comfortable Doc Martens. With Noah still asleep in her arms, she descended the stairs to make breakfast.

Steve sat reading the paper but stopped when she walked in. "Here, give me Noah."

She handed the child over who wrinkled his face, filled his nappy but remained sleeping.

"How's the job going?" he asked.

Abbey dropped two pieces of bread into the toaster. "Fine and working from home is ideal."

"What is it you actually do?"

"Oh, I sort out computer problems for the police. Nothing important."

Steve's face showed confusion. "I would have thought they had people to do that."

"They do but I fix the problems they have trouble with."

The toaster pinged and she removed the two slices, buttered and then covered them with jam. "The pay's good and stops me using my savings."

177

She made a cup of instant coffee and seated herself. "I'll need every penny to furnish my new flat. That reminds me, I must give Bill a ring to catch up on progress."

"I'll miss you and Noah."

She finished her breakfast as Noah's eyes opened. "I'll take him." She glanced at the kitchen clock. "From the smell I'll need to change him."

Steve laughed as he handed Noah over. "He's lucky to have you as his mum."

"Food, a clean nappy and a comfortable bed is all he wants. I'm his slave."

Thirty minutes later with Noah safe in his buggy, Abbey made her way to the underground station. The day was fine with a few white clouds in the sky and the sun was warm. She smiled at Noah. It was good to be alive.

The time was almost nine when she entered the Silver Spoon. The staff busied themselves preparing the many tables for the coming day. She sat at a table tucked into a back corner, ordered a large Americano and a Danish pastry.

When Haliwell arrived, he saw her at the table and made his way over to the counter. "A large Mocha, please." He pointed towards Abbey. "I'll be over there."

Abbey watched as he approached and seated himself.

"My first time here, clean and the prices are reasonable," said Haliwell.

Without knowing why, a shiver ran down Abbey's spine. She shook herself to rid the feeling.

"Are you okay?"

"Someone just walked over my grave." She pulled an envelope from the buggy bag. "This gives you all the information you asked for."

Haliwell placed it on the table. "How difficult was it to locate the senders?"

Abbey stared at Haliwell. "Were you testing me?"

178

A thin smile appeared on his face. "Why do you ask?"

"It was too easy. I'd finished the list in less than an hour."

From his other jacket pocket, he removed a buff coloured envelope and handed it to her. "You might find these more difficult. No one in the yard could find the dispatcher yet alone the addressee."

"So, you were testing me."

"Let's be fair. If you had trouble with these," he lifted the envelope and ripped it in two, "you weren't of any use to me."

"When do you need the answers?"

"Like yesterday would be good."

"I follow your reasoning. I'll start on them as soon as I've fed and changed Noah. As a new mum, I can't understand why he's always hungry. Can't wait and lets me know."

"Because he's small he needs to be fed more often. I'm no expert but my wife breast-fed both of ours. They always wanted more than she could give. She always gave them a bottle for their late night feed. By filling them up, we got a good night's sleep. You've nothing to lose by trying. The chemist will guide you on the best food to give him."

"A good night's sleep is every mum's dream. Thanks for the advice." She handed him a slip of paper. "My bill."

He laughed, watched her leave and paid the young woman at the till.

"Is that your granddaughter?" she asked.

"No, just someone who works for the company. By the way, great coffee."

***

Abbey completed Noah's routine and spent the next hour talking to him. Eventually his eyes closed. "Sorry, babe, I've work to do." Without a whimper, he laid in his basket.

She booted her own computer and checked for messages. Abbey realised something was up when she saw – **SPEAK TO ME FREEMAN**

179

She opened the programme to gain access to the dark web and waited. The screen flashed different colours until it went white. Then one word appeared. **HELLO**

She entered her password, waited and then entered FREEMAN.

The screen went blank. Not expecting an instant answer, she placed her laptop to one side and had a look at the emails Haliwell had given her. On first reading, they appeared nothing out of the ordinary but she knew that was not true.

Noah moaned in his sleep causing her to check he was okay. Her laptop pinged. **FREEMAN**

ARE YOU GOOD

**SPINNING> HAVE SOME NEWS.**

GOOD I HOPE

**AMERICAN HOLDINGS ARE CLOSE TO COLLAPSE**

YOUR ATTACK WORKED

**IT DID BUT THEY HAVE EMPLOYED TWO ROGUE HACKERS TO TRACK US DOWN**

THAT WILL BE DIFFICULT

**I AGREE> MY GHOST USERS WENT IN AND DID NOT TRIGGER ANY ALARMS>BE WARNED THEY ARE SEARCHING> UPGRADE/CHANGE YOUR DEFENCE SYSTEMS**

"FREEMAN>THANKS FOR THE UPDATE.> WILL DO

**TAKE CARE**

The screen went blank and Freeman had gone.

Her eyes glowed with satisfaction as she sat back in her chair. *That'll teach the bastards to murder an innocent woman. All I wanted was my inheritance.*

She entered the company into her search engine and read the latest report from the IRS. Investigators had uncovered unpaid taxes dating back years. The report stated that American Holdings were in major financial deficit.

Her fingers rattled the keyboard as she checked her defence algorithms. She went to her electronic prison. It was empty. To be sure, she added another trap for any hacker who tried to dump a worm or virus into her system. For the hell of it, she added the graphic of a raging inferno into which any intruder would metaphorically fall. She grinned. "Anyone hacking into my system will regret they were born."

For the next hour, she worked on the emails Haliwell had given her but she kept hitting a brick wall, which forced her to start again. Whoever sent these had developed a strong encryption, which defied her efforts.

Tired, she stopped, checked Noah and fell back on the bed striking her head on the wall. "Shit." Then she had an eureka moment. She seated herself again and concentrated. There was nothing when she entered a basic search function. As she expected, the screen flashed no access. Into the box, she typed a mathematical algorithm and pressed enter. The screen flashed and she was into the dispatcher's encrypted system. Moments later, she had the location, a village in Afghanistan.

She double-checked the source. It was correct. Noah stirred as she pressed the memory button for Haliwell.

He answered on the third ring. "How's it going?"

"Your emails originate in Afghanistan?"

"Are you sure?"

"One hundred percent."

"Do you know where from?"

"I can give you the coordinates."

"Ready."

She read out the latitude and longitude. "Will you repeat them, please?"

"Not a problem, I've recorded the message."

"Does my info help anyone?"

"You'd better believe it.

"Jesus Christ. That scares the crap out of me."

"In my game, it's a necessary evil. Anyway, thank you."

Abbey ended the call.

# Twenty-Nine

As she was about to close down, a message flashed on her screen. **We will behead you Infidel.** She gasped. "They can't do that. It's impossible." However, she knew these people were not normal.

Abbey speed-dialled Haliwell. "I have a problem. Whoever they are in Afghanistan have tracked and threatened to chop my fucking head off. You need to have your laptop out of here like yesterday." The call ended.

Abbey shuddered as adrenaline flooded her nervous system. However, she continued to stare at a blank screen. "How?" she repeated several times.

The racket of a police siren shook her back to reality. She grabbed the laptop and reached the front door before the bell rang. On opening, a uniformed police officer asked, "Abbey Lane?"

"This is what you want." She thrust the laptop into his chest.

"Thank you. The Commander will collect you and your child. He asks you to be ready." She nodded as she slammed the door.

The officer turned and strode towards his car. The moment he seated himself, the driver accelerated away.

Abbey raced up the stairs. She had Noah to take care of. Frightened, she packed everything that he would need. She glanced out of the window and saw two Asian men wearing dark suits on the opposite side of the road. They stood next to a yellow hatchback pointing at the house. Without thinking, she drew the curtains. Scared, she paced aimlessly back and forth across the room.

When Abbey peeked through the gap between the curtains, the men had gone. Her spirits rose when Haliwell's Black Range

Rover, its lights flashing, swerved into the kerb. She clutched Noah's basket, descended the stairs, and opened the door.

Haliwell grabbed the basket as she hurtled into the kitchen and retrieved two full bottles of Noah's milk. Again, at speed, she climbed the stairs, picked up Noah's belongings and left.

Hurry," said Haliwell.

The driver secured Noah's basket as Abbey, clutching bags, tumbled into the rear seat. In seconds, the car raced away from the kerb.

Haliwell turned in his seat. "Sorry I'm late but had to have the Sat Nav and tracker disconnected just in case someone wanted to discover where I've been."

Abbey checked Noah; she smiled at him sound asleep, oblivious to what was happening. She stared along the road while attempting to read the road signs. "Where are we going?"

Haliwell did not turn around. "A safe house for tonight and I'll move you on to a more comfortable location tomorrow."

"I didn't have time to pack any clothes."

"Make a list. I'll have Annie buy whatever you need. I hope you wear Marks and Spencer because the Force doesn't do Prada."

Abbey hesitated before replying. "What's the rush to move me to your safe house?"

"You and Noah's lives. The location you gave is a mix of the Taliban and Isis. I gather British and American forces give the area a wide berth. It seems they behead uninvited guests."

"How does a bunch of ragheads concern me?"

"You rattled their cage. At that location are the remains of a Russian Communications Centre. Now people are asking what they're doing there. Those ragheads, as you put it, are professional hackers. Last week I was given to understand an email generated from that location found its way onto the President of Israel's desk. It stated, 'Leave the Palestinian lands or enjoy a nuclear holocaust. The first missile will strike Haifa in seven days."

184

Abbey's head spun like a merry-go-round. "I still don't understand."

"God help us," said Haliwell. "Let me ask you a question. When did the Taliban or Isis obtain nuclear weapons?"

Abbey shook her head. "As far as I know, they don't have any."

Haliwell laughed. "Go to the top of the class. Who does?"

Abbey frowned. "Two that I'm aware of, Israel and maybe Iran. They detest each other, but a nuclear war would not be beneficial to either side."

Haliwell talked as his driver drove at speed. "Consider this scenario. Israel fires a nuke into Iran."

"I don't believe they would do that. It would be a suicidal move."

"But what if someone else presses the button?"

Abbey shuddered. "You said Jacob was murdered. Are you sure about that?"

"As sure as I can be. Jacob Spink is dead, and his ashes were scattered in a rose garden, but what if the programme he developed is still out there?"

The afternoon sunlight bounced off the wing mirror into Haliwell's eyes. These narrow roads could be confusing to the unwary but the driver kept his foot on the accelerator. With the skill of a racing driver, the vehicle negotiated every curve without a reduction in speed.

Abbey started to sweat as her mind raced. "We have the Americans and the British Army over there. Why can't we take them out?"

"That's in hand as we speak. These things take time. But until I have you safe none of that matters."

"Do you really believe they would waste their time on me? I'm a nobody."

"Actually, I doubt they are looking for you, but I'd never sleep again if I failed to do my job."

185

The driver turned left off the main road onto a country lane. "Ten minutes, guv."

"Is that where I'm staying?" asked Abbey, as she stared at a large old building.

"You and Noah wouldn't be comfortable in there. It's three hundred years old, cold, damp and empty."

"Nice fountain."

"When did they get that working?" asked Haliwell.

"Haven't a clue, guv. Looks okay though."

They drove past the house and on through a copse.

A thatched cottage came into view. The driver slowed, eventually stopping on the grass outside a white painted picket fence.

The door opened, and an Asian man wearing white scrubs strolled along the path.

In an instant, Haliwell's mood changed. His eyes opened as wide as he screamed. "He's not a member of my team. Drive like hell."

The driver dropped a gear and stamped on the accelerator. Stones and dust filled the air as they departed. Repeated thuds shook the car.

Abbey grabbed Noah. "What the fuck's happening?"

"Shut up," said Haliwell, as he removed two automatic rifles from a concealed compartment.

"Which way, guv?"

"Stop here. I should call for back up, but those bastards will have done a runner before they arrive."

The vehicle slid to a stop. "I could scout the area and check," said the driver.

"Four eyes are better than two. Abbey, can you drive this beast?"

"I can drive a mini in London. Do I qualify?"

Haliwell turned to his driver. "You were a sergeant in the Paras, weren't you?"

186

"Ten years, guv."

"Good. When we hit the ground, you're in charge and I'll follow. The only thing I can guarantee is I usually hit my target."

"No problem. I always hit mine but shouldn't we wait for back up?"

"You have a choice. I can order you to come with me but I won't. I've two men missing, and I'd like to know if they're still alive."

"Can we at least call for back up, guv? It might save our arses if we're caught in a firefight."

Haliwell nodded. "Do it." He opened the passenger door and slid off the seat with one weapon in each hand. From under the seat, he removed extra magazines and ammunition.

"Back up in the air, guv. Twenty minutes."

"Abbey, take the car to the next village and stop. Don't use the radio, just drive. Park out of the way of people"

She nodded, checked Noah, jumped out, clambered into the driver's seat, and slammed the door.

Haliwell and the driver waited until the car vanished amongst the trees.

Those bastards were on target," said the driver. "There are at least thirty dents in the rear door."

"Thank fuck we can still build bulletproof cars."

"Right, guv, head down, and follow me."

Crouched, the two men remained in the cover of the trees and started to walk. With his driver leading, they went forward cautiously until they could see the cottage through the shrubbery.

The driver, a thin, wiry man of thirty years, held up his right-hand, signalling stop.

Haliwell closed the gap between them. "It's too risky to go closer."

"Guv, you stay here. Make yourself comfortable and keep your weapon pointed at the front of the building."

Haliwell gave him the thumbs up as he disappeared. His mind raced. *What the fuck am I doing? I'm past my sell-by date, and I'm playing cowboys and Indians. Every nerve in my body is tight, and to top it off, I need a crap.*

Beads of sweat ran from his forehead, across his eyes and cheeks, but he remained alert. He scanned the area to the left and right of his position but saw nothing.

He knew that meant sod-all. He checked his watch; his driver had been gone for fifteen minutes.

\*\*\*

Abbey drove the beast into Eddington, the first village she came across. In minutes, she drove along Church Lane and turned into the chapel car park. Under the shade of numerous horse chestnut trees, she switched off the engine, turned and checked Noah. He was wide-awake, kicking his blanket off his feet.

\*\*\*

The driver approached the cottage on his stomach. Years of military training taught him to be careful. *If they see me, I'm up shit creek.*

He spotted two men wearing white scrubs standing at the rear of the cottage smoking. They appeared to be arguing about what they should do next. *Fucking amateurs.* The driver checked his safety catch was off and slid closer.

An old tree gave him the cover he needed as he used it to stand. "Stand fucking still," said the driver. The barrel of his automatic pointed at the nearest man.

The second man stooped. A bullet entered his head.

"I told you to stay still." He moved closer and jabbed the barrel into the other man's throat. "You're coming with me, sunshine. One wrong move and you're brown bread. I don't give a shit one way or the other. Understand?"

The man attempted to move. The barrel of the rifle punctured his throat, causing a trickle of blood to run freely.

Shifting his position, the barrel slid into the centre of the captive's back. "Try anything, and you'll be a cripple for life."

188

"My God will protect me."

"I hope he can stop a bullet because if you piss me off, I'll kill you. Look around. No witnesses. I can do whatever I want."

The man pushed back onto the barrel. "Kill me, infidel."

"If that's your last request, no problem. "The man dropped like a stone when the butt of the automatic's stock smashed into the back of his skull.

"Guv, can you hear me?" he yelled.

"Jesus Christ, you scared the shit out of me," said Haliwell.

"Sorry, guv, but I need your help."

"On my way."

Haliwell took five minutes to find his driver. "I heard a shot, are you okay?"

"One went for his AK, so I shot him."

"You did well." Haliwell pointed. "And this one?"

"He wanted to join Mohammed. He'll be an unhappy bunny when he wakes up."

At that moment, the clatter of two helicopters drowned out every word. Haliwell and his driver watched twenty armed men drop to the ground.

Haliwell walked forward but in seconds, armed men surrounded him.

The leader of the squad shouted, "You two, drop the weapons and lay flat on the ground."

A voice rang out. "Steady, that's the Governor."

Men lowered their weapons while their eyes checked the locale.

"Inspector Madden, you made good time. You obviously drew the short straw. One is dead," he pointed, "and this is the other. Get a few of your team to take this creature to the big house and throw a bucket of water over him. I need to have a chat on how they arrived here before I did. Someone on the inside needs their arse kicked."

189

"Right, Inspector, the rest of your men can help me find my people. I know I don't need to tell you but I will anyway, keep your eyes peeled for booby traps."

"I'll lead," said Madden. "Commander, I'd appreciate it if you followed my team."

Haliwell said nothing.

Madden ordered his men to approach the cottage, checking for traps as they went.

Haliwell's driver chuckled. "There are no traps outside."

"Let him do it his way," said Haliwell.

Two men stepped into the cottage and inched their way into the first room. There, strapped to metal beds, were Haliwell's men. They resisted the temptation to relax and took their time checking before cutting the gags from the captives' mouths.

"This room is clear," said the older of the two.

Haliwell strolled in, followed by his driver. "Are you two okay?"

"We fucked up, guv. When they knocked on the front door, we thought it was you. Didn't even glance out of the window."

"Hope you've learnt your lesson but I'm afraid it's back to wearing a uniform. You can stay here until relieved."

"Sorry, guv," said the other.

"Madden, come with me. I intend to interrogate the young man in the big house." He removed his mobile and rang Abbey. "Where are you?"

"In the lounge of Eddington vicarage. I'm having tea with the vicar."

"You're what?"

"Father Vincent was leaving the church when I parked the beast. He came over to see who I was. He took one look at the back of the car and asked why I was driving an armour-plated vehicle."

"Please hand him your mobile."

"Good evening, Commander. Vincent Piper, the vicar of Eddington. Ex-army officer, Blues and Royals."

190

"Thank you for caring for my charges and I've no need to remind you of the rules."

"I understand. My lips are sealed, official secrets act and all that crap."

"Good man. Could you take care of Abbey and Noah until I'm in a position to collect them?"

"How long? If needs must I can have my housekeeper make up a bed."

"Actually, that's not a bad idea. Can I leave them with you until after breakfast tomorrow?"

"Not a problem. I'm enjoying the company and the little one is delightful. See you in the morning."

Haliwell let out a grave laugh as he ended the call. "Come, Inspector, we have work to do."

Madden nodded. "Let's end this once and for all."

"I doubt if our terrorist knows anything of importance. He's dispensable like a chocolate teapot in the Sahara. Now we scare the crap out of him until he cooperates."

"Haven't heard that in a long time, guv."

"Tells you how old I am."

They entered the building and went straight to the interrogation room.

The young man, a stocky person approaching thirty, was sitting on the heavy wooden throne, his wrists and ankles secured to its frame. The first thing he saw when he opened his eyes was the unsmiling face of Haliwell.

"I know you speak English. Full name? Where do you come from? What terrorist faction do you represent?"

Haliwell watched as a thin smile tracked across the man's lips. "Why should I talk to you? I obey orders."

"Because when I smell smoke I search for the fire. You can burn in hell or I can keep you alive."

"You will not harm me. This is England. The police have to follow the rules."

191

Haliwell grabbed a nearby white plastic chair turned it around and seated himself, his arms resting on the back. "No one except those who sent you know you're here."

The man snorted. "You know nothing about me. Kill me and I become a martyr. My name will live forever."

Haliwell's face hardened. "I haven't the time to piss about with part time heroes." He turned to one of his team. "Harry, go get me a hypo full of your special cocktail. Then I can go home. My wife is cooking my favourite tonight, liver and bacon, onion gravy with mashed potatoes."

Right, guv."

He turned back to his captive. "Do you understand the meaning of the word dead?"

"You cannot kill me. It is against the law."

"You really believe that, don't you? We don't ask for permission, we just do it."

Harry returned with a white metal dish holding a few swabs, a bottle of antiseptic and a hypo filled with purple liquid. "All ready, boss. Have you told him it's painless?"

"Thanks for that, Harry. I wasn't going to but then it doesn't matter." He glanced at his watch. "Would you like the privilege? I'm tired and I want to go home."

A pool of urine covered the floor under the prisoner. "I am not a sick dog to be put down."

"That's exactly what you are. Which arm would you prefer, left or right? I would recommend the right, you die quicker that way."

"Harry, if my memory serves, I did the business last time. Your turn."

Harry's face lit up like a mouse in a cheese factory. "To make this easy I will choose for you. I'm a fair man so as my boss suggested, I will inject my cocktail into your right arm."

He handed Madden the tray. "Please, Inspector, hold this while I prepare our friend's arm." He removed two swabs and the

192

bottle of antiseptic. "Of course, you understand we dump your carcass in a pigsty. When they finish with you, it's an unmarked grave, no prayers and ignores your religious customs. We are simple men, dig a hole and add a bag of quick lime. I'm sure you know it kills any smell."

He doused the swabs with the clear liquid and cleaned a small patch of the man's arm. "We have to do this to stop infection. Stupid rule if you ask me, seeing as you'll soon be dead. Inspector, the hypo, please."

Harry took the hypo and with a precise movement pressed the syringe plunger jetting some of the liquid into the air.

The man started shaking. "Why should I tell you anything? You'll kill me anyway."

Haliwell's face tightened. "Because I am an amazing and truthful person. Tell me the truth and you will have nothing to fear."

"Why should I trust you?"

"Just tell me the truth and I'll be your best friend."

"Abu Bakr Abdallah, from the Lebanon. I'm a student at University."

"Which university?"

"Essex."

While Harry held the hypo close to Abu's eyes, Haliwell said, "Inspector, contact the university and check."

"On my way, guv."

Haliwell's face relaxed a little as he whispered, "One lie and you die. Why are you here?"

"I was to assist and learn from my friend. The one your man shot."

Haliwell returned to his chair. "Isn't this civilised? I ask questions and you answer them. What were your orders?"

"To kill a prostitute who cursed our God."

"How did you know where to find her?"

"Our leader gave us the address."

"Who is your leader?"

"He visits our mosque every Friday to issue God's commands."

Haliwell frowned. "I need a name."

Abu looked at him sharply. "We do not question our leader. It is forbidden."

"Your weapons. Did your leader supply them?"

"They were strapped to our motor bikes along with spare ammunition."

"Who gave you this address?"

"It came with a photo of the infidel woman."

"On receiving your orders, you came straight here prepared to kill."

"That is why our God placed us on this earth."

Haliwell shook his head. "So, you are missionaries. You are here to spread the word of God. The last people to do it your way converted the natives of South America to Christianity and then murdered them so they could enter heaven. Hasn't anyone told you it doesn't work that way? Harry, my throat is as dry as a Lebanese whore."

Harry placed the hypo back in the tray. "Tea in five minutes, guv."

"Why do you insult the women of my country?" asked Abu.

Haliwell leant on the back of the chair and stared straight into Abu's eyes. "Because they produce scum like you. There is one unresolved question. Now tell me the name of your leader before I am forced to do something I will regret."

"I told you I do not know his name."

"You are a liar. I believe it is time for you to join your friend."

Sweat soaked Abu's shirt. "It is you who is the liar. You said I had nothing to fear."

Haliwell sat with his arms folded across his chest. "You had nothing to fear if you answered my questions. As it turns out you

194

are bog standard cannon fodder and of no use to me. Inspector, deal with this piece of shit." He stood, turned and walked away.

"If I tell you, I'm a dead man," screamed Abu.

"Whatever you do, you're fucked," said the inspector.

"What if I point him out?"

"Inspector, back off. That's the first thing this cretin has said that's useful. Time for a break." He stood and pointed at Abu. "Give him a drink of water. Inspector, a word please."

"We are going to have a cup of tea." The two men left the room.

"Things have worked out well," said Haliwell.

"Your tea, guv," said Harry as he sipped his own.

"Only if Abu points out his leader," said Madden, making a cup of tea.

"He will now I've scared the shit out of him."

"What if he informs his lawyer that you were going to murder him?"

"I'm sure he will but so far there is no record of this meeting. Haven't you noticed not one of the clocks have moved? For young Abu, time has stood still. When we go back in, Harry will turn the interview sound and camera systems on. We'll be the nicest people you could ever meet."

"Out of interest, what's in the hypo?" asked Madden.

"Mentholated spirit. It has a medical smell."

They drank their tea and made small talk.

"Time to go in," said Haliwell. "Harry, you stay here and do what needs to be done."

"Seeing as we have an understanding, we can remove the straps," said Haliwell. "Make you more comfortable."

While Inspector Madden unbuckled the wrist and ankle straps, Haliwell walked around the room. He stopped at a large mirror, pushed his hair back and then returned to his seat.

"Your name is Abu Bakr Abdallah, from the Lebanon. And a student at the University of Essex. It would appear you are

195

involved with terrorists. Their leader convinced you to accompany another and murder a young woman. Am I correct so far?"

Abu nodded.

"Would you please say yes or no," asked Haliwell?

"That's correct, Sir."

"For the sake of clarity, I'll take that as a yes."

"Is it right for me to say that you wish to assist the police in their duties?"

"Abu nodded again and then said, "Yes, Sir."

"You are aware of Inspector Madden." He pointed. "He will take you to a place where you can rest, have a shower and a meal. On Friday you agree to point out your leader."

"Yes, Sir."

"Thank you for your assistance, Abu. I will see that the courts consider this. Inspector, he's all yours. Don't lose him. I'm going home."

"Sir, I have two armed groups waiting to be dismissed."

Haliwell paused and glanced over his shoulder. "They can go home. Harry, find my driver Peter Grey, so he can take me to the vicarage in Eddington. I need to find my car."

# Thirty

Harry drove Haliwell and Peter, his driver, along the narrow country lane towards Eddington.

As the car rounded a bend, Haliwell saw the towering spire of a church and ancient structure of a building. "Pretty village."

"It's okay if you like that sort of thing," said Harry. "Most villages today have lost their shops, pub and young people. Give me the bright lights anytime."

"Here we are, guv, The Vicarage, in the middle of nowhere."

"Harry, would you believe some people crave for the simple pleasures in life."

"So, do I, guv, but don't tell my wife. I don't see your car."

"You get back to the house and clean the place and check the interrogation DVD has nothing untoward. With luck, I'll keep you on my team."

"I'd like that, guv."

Haliwell, followed by Peter, clambered out of the rear seat. Both waited until Harry was out of sight. As they strolled along the cobbled path, he turned and said, "See if you can find my car."

His eyes roamed over the granite blocks which shaped the vicarage. Old iron frames filled with thick clear glass formed the windows.

A slim man wearing torn jeans, a Black Snake T-shirt and leaning on a cane opened the door. "I guess you're Commander Haliwell."

"Can I see the vicar, please?"

He held out his right hand. "Vincent Piper, at your service."

"I don't know why, but I expected someone older and dressed in a suit with a dog collar."

"Like you, Commander, we do have time off. Come in."

Haliwell followed him into the front room. To his amazement, full bookshelves lined three walls. "The library?"

Vincent grinned. "To be precise, my office. Abbey is upstairs asleep. I'm sure you know this incident has affected her."

"She's a tough woman," said Haliwell.

"She has a baby, responsibility. Something she never had to consider and until today when a stranger tried to kill her. When I first met her, she appeared okay until she sat with Noah in the room. I asked her what had happened, and she started talking. I lost count the number of times she said sorry to her baby. Her sentences became fragmented as her mind jumped from one thing to another. It was when I saw her eyes, they were wild as she asked if everything was going to be okay. I told her not to worry, which was a stupid thing to say. At that moment I understood and kept her talking. The death of her father. Then some idiot who launches missiles, the fire in her flat. And out of the blue the mugging, and you Commander. You came in and out of her subconscious more than anyone else. She trusts you, but in the same breath, you trouble her. Most of her babbling I found hard to make any sense of, but I do know she needs help."

"I would never harm her."

"She knows that but she requires time for the shit inside her head to escape. Can she stay here for a while? The dam has burst, and if we can let the bad water empty, she will be okay."

Haliwell shook his head. "How messed up is she?"

"You'll need to ask her yourself. She wants to see you, but I suggested later."

"What about the child?"

"My housekeeper is great with babies. When Abbey stopped talking, we put her to bed. Tomorrow could be a good day. I hope so."

198

Haliwell closed his eyes and swore. "And I told her to drive my car and wait. Lucky she met you."

Vincent smiled. "I remember from the film The Blues Brothers, Mother Superior said God moves in mysterious ways. I'd like to believe God sent her here."

"You wouldn't happen to know where my car keys are?"

"In my pocket. Whoever fired at you was single-minded. My beat-up Toyota would have died with that amount of damage. I assume you know some bullets can pierce a wagon like yours."

"There are," said Haliwell as he changed the subject. "You don't have to tell me, but why did you leave the army?"

"My squad was on patrol a few miles outside of Helmand, a Taliban IED took my left leg off. Thank God for helicopters."

"And you became a vicar."

"What were my options? Twenty-eight and missing a leg and trained to kill people. Not much of a CV."

"You were an officer. The system would have looked after you."

"What system? The army is the best club in the world when you're a paid-up member. Actually, God and I had a long chat when I died three times during my life-saving operation. Not only did the IED take my leg, but it also planted a few nuts and bolts in other parts of my anatomy. According to the doctors, I shouldn't be here. A chat with the hospital Sin Bosun started me thinking. Two years studying and here I am. So far, so good, and I can help people who are not as fortunate as I am."

"I don't suppose we'll ever have a conversation like this again. Thank you for taking care of Abbey. Right, I need to get home. Can I have my keys?"

Vincent removed them from his jeans' pocket and tossed them towards Haliwell.

Haliwell looked Vincent straight in the eyes. "Pray for Abbey."

199

"I'll pray for you as well, Commander." Vincent went to the main door. He pointed with his cane. "Your car is round the back. Prevents anyone from asking stupid questions."

Haliwell nodded. "I'll give you a call tomorrow."

He strolled through the garden until he saw the car and Peter with his arms crossed, leaning against the bullet battered side.

"Where to, guv?"

"Back to base. I need another car."

# Thirty-One

On returning to his office, Haliwell's problems escalated. An officer leaving the building discovered the duty transport supervisor bound and gagged.

"Search my car," he screamed at the garage mechanics.

"What are we looking for?" asked the supervisor.

"When you find it we'll both know."

Five minutes elapsed before the supervisor presented him with a location device.

"Cheap and cheerful but works rather well."

"That answers one question, but how did those bastards reach my destination before I did? My driver drove like the wind."

"Because they knew where you were going and played the percentage."

To hide what he was thinking, he forced a smile. "For fuck's sake, are you telling me they had people at more than one of our safe houses?"

"No, Sir, but if I need a list of duty officers I go to my ancient computer, search, find and print it out. It's that easy."

Haliwell rubbed his nose. "Show me this machine."

"My office is this way, Sir."

The two men entered a room where the average person could, if they stood in the centre, touch every side.

The supervisor pointed. On the top of a two-drawer filing cabinet stood a grey box and oversized screen. "Old but works."

"Could you produce and print a list of the Mets safe houses?" asked Haliwell.

With one finger, the supervisor pressed the keys. It seemed an age until the document appeared on the screen. With the same

201

finger, he authorised the dot matrix printer. It rattled and groaned but soon finished.

Haliwell lifted the printed sheets and mentally ticked off each location. As he did so, his eyes widened, and his mouth gaped. "I didn't believe you, but this tells me a different story. Thank God the other houses are empty."

His mind whirled. No *one will believe this. The Force spends millions of pounds to maintain and improve cyber-security. I find it hard to comprehend that when we moved to this building, some idiot brought in this relic from the ark. The irony is they connected it to the system, and no one noticed. I'll leave that pleasure of removing it to the IT Officer.*

He lifted the telephone. "Commander Haliwell. I'm in the garage. Put me through to the head of IT at once. Yes, he can call me on my mobile." In seconds, his phone rang. "Haliwell."

"Chief Superintendent Harper, Sir."

"I need your expertise in the garage."

"I'm rather busy. Can it wait until tomorrow?"

"You have five minutes. Any longer and you might need to rewrite your CV." The line went dead.

From the lift strolled a short, fat man of forty years plus. He stopped a metre from Haliwell. "This is no time for games, Commander. I'm a busy man so let's deal with your problem."

"And so am I, Harper." He pointed at the ancient computer. "What is that, and why is it connected to our mainframe?"

Harper lifted the metal box. "Not one of ours and I'm surprised it even works?"

Haliwell fixed his eyes on Harper. "This is an anti-terrorist operation. I will not lose my temper or shout at another officer."

He handed over the list of the safe houses. "The garage supervisor printed these for me. What do you think?"

Harper gazed at the sheets of paper. "I'm not cleared to read this." He handed them back.

"This is a serious breach of your security. I want those responsible found."

202

"I've never seen this equipment before and as I said, it's not ours."

Haliwell grinned. "How come it's connected to your IT system and has direct access to everything?"

Harper crossed his arms over his chest. His small stature made him appear like Grumpy, one of the seven dwarfs. "You can't pin the blame for this on me. I know nothing about it and never approved the installation."

"Stop wetting your pants and become the police officer you once were. Find who it was. Male, female, I don't care but whoever it is almost got my arse shot off. It's in your court, but then you can always retire."

"Commander, things go wrong. I will fix this." He walked into the office and hurled the desktop computer onto the concrete floor. "Sir, I will find out who installed this."

"I doubt that you will," said Haliwell

Harper turned and walked to the lift.

***

In the rear of a white Ford Transit, Haliwell and Inspector Madden sat opposite one another. They, along with their driver and a handcuffed Abu, waited for the sun to go down. According to Abu, his contact always attended Friday prayer.

The mosque stood at the corner of Main Street and the High Road. To its left were a few wine bars and opposite, a tattoo parlour and express supermarket. A few metres along the street stood Greco's, a sizeable Greek restaurant. The large plate-glass windows gave an uninterrupted view of the road.

Parked along the road from the mosque, an unmarked police car waited. Its driver and the woman in the passenger seat appeared to be in deep conversation.

A lone man dressed in rags swore as he picked up used cigarette ends and dropped them into a glass jar.

Abu flinched with pain as his handcuffs bit into his wrists. No one was interested in him as his eyes focused on the rear doors.

203

"Abu, come and sit next to me," said Haliwell. "When your leader arrives, point him out and we will do the rest. He will not know you are here." He shifted to allow Abu a clear view.

"Ten minutes to sunset, Sir," said Madden.

"I did notice more people entering the mosque" said Haliwell.

Abu pointed. "There is my leader."

Out of nowhere, a black van with brakes screeching, stopped outside the mosque. Two figures dressed in black and wearing masks jumped out. Their automatic weapons sprayed bullets everywhere. At speed, and with their guns operating, they ran inside. A minute later, they exited and hurled themselves into the rear of the van. Streams of smoke poured from the vehicle's tyres as at speed, it raced away. In seconds, shouts and screams erupted from the scene.

Haliwell grimaced as he tumbled out of the Transit and the unmarked police car raced after the gunmen. "Inspector, call the local plod."

He dashed across the road but stopped when he saw the broken jar of cigarette ends. The fresh pool of blood told its own story. Using his right hand Haliwell checked for a pulse, nothing. "Bastards."

Shattered lives littered the pavement. Haliwell retrieved a leaflet from the road. It read, **you Isis Bastards, kill one of ours, and we will execute yours.** "Shit, that's all I fucking need."

He turned. Inspector Madden and his driver were right behind him. "We were here and did nothing."

"There was nothing we could do, Sir. It doesn't matter what side they were on, you can't control extremists. There was no way we could have helped these people."

From along the road, police and ambulance sirens grew in their intensity.

"Inspector, take charge of securing a boundary." He pointed. "Get those people well away from here. I'm going inside."

204

Careful not to disturb anything, he mounted the entrance stairs to the Mosque. Here none survived the onslaught. Inside, the wounded groaned and screamed in pain. He turned and left, knowing the paramedics were better equipped to help.

Haliwell found Inspector Madden organising the local police officers. "What can't you see?"

"Can't say I've been looking for anything in particular. What have I missed?"

"Empty cartridge shells. They used automatic weapons. These people were professionals who had this timed to the split second."

"At least everything's on film, Sir."

"We saw it happen, lost one of the team and don't have a sodding clue."

"Excuse me, Sir."

Haliwell turned to face two police officers, a man and a woman. "Where's your car?"

The male officer handed him pieces of misshaped metal. "Triangle nail spikes, Sir. We were on their tail, the rear doors opened and seconds later, we stopped. We have the reg number."

Haliwell rubbed his hands. "Well done. Contact the garage and get a repair truck out here. When it's on its way go back, try and retrieve as many of these spikies as you can. If you miss one, we will have Joe Public going mental."

"Roger, Sir."

"Bright man," said Haliwell to no one in particular. "Shit." He ran back to the Transit. "Thank Christ you're still here."

"I'm safer in here," said Abu. "It looks like a war zone. How many?"

"One is too many."

The roar of sirens drowned their voices.

Haliwell grabbed Abu by the arm. "Come."

"Why?"

205

"This place will be swarming in yellow jackets in a minute. I need you to check the dead and wounded for your man."

"I will be seen by my brothers. You are as good as killing me."

"If I remove the handcuffs, I'll tell those who may ask that you are assisting us with the names of the victims. But try and escape, I'll shoot you."

"You are crazy."

"I know," said Haliwell, "but I get results."

Abu held out his arms and the cuffs were removed.

"Walk next to me."

"Excuse me, Sir," said a young, yellow-jacketed police officer.

Haliwell held up his warrant card. He flashed a toothy smile. "Sorry, I outrank you."

The officer laughed. "You do, Sir."

Together, Haliwell and Abu began checking the corpses which still lay where they fell.

"That is my leader," said Abu.

"Are you sure?"

"I wish I wasn't."

Three bullet holes told Haliwell the worst. He buttoned the man's coat and then shouted to an officer covering dead with blankets. "Officer, come here and give me a hand. I want this man assisted," he pointed, "into that white Transit." He produced his warrant card. "Please, no questions."

The officer, a stocky, bearded man nodded. "I'll cover him with a blanket, it'll look better. Can your young friend help?"

"Of course."

"With reverence, Abu draped the body in a red blanket. The officer bent and lifted the corpse and walked towards the Transit.

Haliwell followed and made sure Abu knew he was still there.

Abu opened the rear doors and helped the officer.

"Thank you," said Haliwell. "One more thing, this never happened."

"What, Sir?"

"Abu inside. Arms out."

"You have no need to put the handcuff on. I won't run."

"I'm driving. It's not a request. Arms out."

\*\*\*

With the Transit parked in its allotted bay, Haliwell jumped out and slammed the door. Smiling, he strolled to the supervisor's office. A police officer stood by the entrance door.

Haliwell produced his warrant card. "Why are you here?" he asked the constable.

The young man took the card. "Your middle name, Sir?"

"You will see I do not have one."

"Just checking, Sir."

"I'd have your balls boiled in oil if you hadn't. Where's the supervisor?"

"Visiting the toilet, Sir."

"I need the use of his phone."

"Carry on, Sir."

Haliwell contacted the Deputy Assistant Commissioner Arthur Robbins. "Working late, Sir."

"Commander, you're back. How did it go?"

"A fucking disaster, Sir. I need you to meet me in the garage like five minutes ago."

"Can you tell me why?"

"Not over the phone, Sir."

"On my way."

Thirty seconds later, Arthur walked across the garage floor. His eyes stern when he saw Haliwell. He stopped in front of him and folded his arms. "I'm listening."

He pointed. "In the back of that Transit, I have a stupid boy who believes Isis is the answer to the world's problems, plus a corpse. I want the boy to believe his leader is alive. I need you to

207

make a remarkable discovery and give me a bollocking in front of him."

"You want me to lie?"

"Yes, Sir."

"What do you hope to gain by this subterfuge?"

"The boy will be allowed one phone call, and with luck, he'll let his terrorist friends know what has happened. But before he does, we search the dead man's house."

"You could do that anyway."

"The moment his associates believe he's dead, the house would be stripped. Let's face it, we don't even know who he is."

"Does the boy know his name?"

"I'm not sure, but MI6 must have a dossier on him."

"When does this terrorist die?"

"Sometime in hospital. I haven't decided."

"I'm not crazy about this idea but what the hell. Let's get on with it."

They walked across to the Transit and Haliwell opened the rear doors.

Arthur, his eyes neutral, flinched when he saw the body. He rested his fingers on the corpse's neck. "Commander, this man is still alive. Call an ambulance."

"He's dead, Sir."

Arthur stood erect with his shoulders back. "Don't argue with me or I'll have you in front of the Commissioner."

Haliwell scurried towards the supervisor's office and made the call. As he returned, he saw Arthur securing Abu to a bicycle rack.

The ambulance arrived in five minutes.

Shielded by the vehicle's rear doors, Arthur briefed them and took several photographs.

When the medics wheeled the stretcher to the ambulance, Abu saw his leader's body covered by a white sheet. An oxygen mask covered the corpse's face.

Both men heard Abu say, "God is great," as the ambulance drove away.

"Commander, take this man for processing and then report to me in my office."

Haliwell appeared to bow as Arthur stomped away. He unlocked the handcuffs and called to the young officer outside the office. "The supervisor has returned so you can assist me in taking this prisoner for processing. He will not fall down the stairs or trip. Do you understand?"

"Yes, Sir."

Abu laughed. "It would be better if my leader had died. Now he has the best reason to kill infidels."

"He has to get better first," said Haliwell with a smile on his lips.

# Thirty-Two

Haliwell listened as his boss Arthur Robbins spoke over the phone to his counterpart in MI6. "Mike, I can't afford a fuck up. Are you positive this man is who you say he is?" As he listened, surprise filled his face. "Okay, I'll ring you back in five."

"Commander, you hit the jackpot. Hanza Khalimov is a recruiter. The US believed he was dead and they are not happy we have him in hospital."

"Do they know he's dead?"

"Weighing up the pros and cons, I guess Mike must have forgotten to tell them. As an associate of the hook-handed Hamza al Masri, MI6 has had him under surveillance for some time. Here's his address."

"I know where the new headquarters of Isis could be. But I'll see what I can find in his house. I can tell you now I intend to rip up every floorboard."

Arthur rubbed his hands. "Be careful. You have enemies where you believe you have friends."

Haliwell laughed. "I'm too bloody old to care. The only thing that frightens me is retirement."

"In the Force, you're as rare as rocking horse shit. I, along with many senior officers, accept your judgements."

"Guv, I started as a copper on the beat and learnt the old fashioned way. My sergeant in those days made sure I understood that without the evidence you're fucked, Sir. I know I'm passed my sell-by date, but I still enjoy locking up the bad guys."

"And you don't give a toss for authority. The Commissioner considers you a dinosaur and wants you out. Your friends control the vote, but like you, we're getting thin on the ground."

"Thank you, Sir. I'm grateful. Another year or two and I'll call it a day."

"Think about it."

Haliwell's mobile rang. He listened and said, "On my way. My team is ready, Sir."

"Good luck."

Haliwell turned and marched out of the office.

***

In a police car with its lights and siren wailing, Haliwell arrived outside Hanzas Khalimov's house.

Inspector Madden greeted him. "The area is as tight as a drum."

"Thanks. It's about time you were promoted."

"I'm happy where I am, Sir."

"We'll discuss your career later. Let's go and rip this place apart and see what we can find."

"What are we looking for?" asked Madden.

In seconds, the big red key destroyed the door. Shouting, "Police, Police," teams of two officers entered every room of the terraced house.

"Neat and tidy," said Haliwell, as his middle finger removed a thin layer of dust from the back of a chair. "Get the ladder. I want to check out the loft."

Officers moved fast and opened the loft access.

Haliwell climbed the ladder, found the light switch and illuminated the whole space. Again, the area appeared spotless. "Who lives like this?" he muttered. "No one. We're in the wrong fucking house."

He descended the ladder. "Inspector, seal the area and get your officers into the houses on the left and right of this one."

"What if the owners object?"

211

"Arrest them."

"Yes, boss."

Excitement and confusion hit one neighbouring house. It's elderly residents invited the officers inside. The woman asked if they preferred tea or coffee.

The house on the right was empty. In seconds, the door erupted from its hinges. Haliwell, followed by six officers, entered. Files covered an old gate leg table. He opened the first, it listed names of those who had converted to Isis. This he tossed aside and began searching drawers. Most were useful to the authorities but not to him. In the backroom, two laptops rested on a chair.

"Inspector. Get everything boxed and across to MI6. Tell them to find me an answer to what these people are planning. I do not want to be somewhere up to my arse in dead bodies like the last time."

Madden glanced around. "What we can see will be on its way in ten minutes. It would help, guv, if you contacted MI6 and let them know. They'll need more than the duty bods to check this lot out."

Haliwell was dialling MI6 before the inspector stopped talking. As he replaced his mobile in his pocket, he roared, "Rip up the floorboards."

"How many, Sir?"

"Every one. I need to know I've not missed anything."

"Yes, sir."

"How goes the fight, Commander?"

Haliwell turned to see the Police Commissioner. "As Steve McQueen once said in a film, so far so good. May I suggest you move as my team will be lifting those boards."

"I'm not staying, but I thought I'd tell you myself. You have my authority to proceed as you consider appropriate."

"That's wonderful. I just wish I knew the right direction."

"Gut feeling, Commander. It usually works."

From somewhere a male voice shouted, "Boss."

"Duty calls, Mam. Who's shouting and where are you?"

"In the kitchen."

Haliwell walked across the bare joists to the kitchen entrance. "Bloody hell. Plastic. How much?"

"Hundred kilo plus. Enough to blow this area off the map," said the officer. "We need this area evacuated like yesterday."

"I'll deal with it, Commander," said the Commissioner. I'll tell the authorities it's a UXB."

"Good idea," said Haliwell.

"Sir, I've found something," called another.

"Where are you?"

"In the front room, guv."

Retracing his steps, he entered the room and saw secured into the fire recess a safe. "Can anyone open this?"

The officer covered in dust laughed. "I can take it to a friend of mine. He's a locksmith."

"On which side of the track does he operate?"

"Is that important, guv?"

"No, so long as you return here with whatever's inside."

"Leave it to me, guv. Now if you don't want your clean uniform covered in crap, close the door on your way out."

"Sir. Sir"

Haliwell let out a deep sigh. "For fuck's sake, where?"

"Kitchen, Sir."

With care, he negotiated a safe path. "Good or bad?"

"Your guess is as good as mine. We were removing the explosives ready for transport when we found this." He handed over an envelope.

"If anyone wants me, I'll be upstairs."

"Okay, guv."

Haliwell removed the contents of the envelope. "That's all I need. pages of a language I can't read." He descended the stairs. "Anyone know where Inspector Madden is working?"

"I'm behind you, Sir."

213

He handed over the sheets of paper. "Could be Arabic but then what do I know?"

The inspector shifted his position, but his right foot slipped, and he tumbled into the void. To compound the problem, his head struck a joist. "Shit."

Haliwell stretched out his right hand.

"My leg's busted, and it hurts like hell."

"I need help," screamed Haliwell. "And I don't care who it is."

Two officers arrived.

"If either of you two as much as smile you'll be on traffic duty until you retire," said Madden.

"Would we dare, Sir?"

"Stop grinning. Hold me under my armpits and lift me out of here."

The men positioned themselves holding the inspector. One nodded to the other as they pulled him clear.

"Jesus Christ. You could have given me some warning."

"It's the best way, Sir. Doesn't give you the chance to think about the pain."

"You're a pair of sadists. Now get me to a chair."

"There's an ambulance on its way."

"Officer, go outside and find the Commissioner," said Haliwell. "She's organising the yellow jackets with the evacuation. Tell her I need another inspector." He waited with Madden until two medics carried him away. He seated himself and browsed the paperwork. He understood none of it.

"Commander."

"Yes, guv."

"The evacuation is well underway. Everyone is blaming the Germans."

"Makes a change from us."

"I'm going home. Call me if you have any problems."

214

"I don't need any more. Is my replacement inspector on his way?"

"She is, Commander."

"Thanks. Must go." Haliwell turned and made his way to the kitchen. "I'm pleased that's old fashioned plastic and not something more volatile."

"We found the detonators. Brand new box along with the drawings for making pipe bombs."

A young man with cropped hair, wearing army fatigues, stuck his head in the kitchen. "I'm looking for a Commander Haliwell. Anyone know where he is?"

Haliwell read the nametag on the soldier's jacket. "Sergeant Simon Porter, Bomb Disposal. A rather pleased Commander Haliwell at your service. The sooner you remove this," he placed his hand on the explosives, "the happier I will be."

The sergeant lifted a block of plastic. "The IRA used this stuff a lot. The Taliban use anything they can scrounge or steal. Anyway, I'll get my team in, and you can get on with whatever you're doing. We'll destroy this on Rainham Marsh's tomorrow morning." He laughed. "Scares the shit out of the seagulls."

Three minutes later, six soldiers arrived carrying steel chests. The joists shivered as each one dropped on some well-placed boards.

"If anyone wants to leave while we pack this stuff away do so now. If you're going to stay, please keep out of our way. This explosive is safe." To prove his point, he dropped a slab on the floor.

"I've seen that before, Sergeant. Great party trick for the inexperienced."

"Sorry, Sir."

His team loaded the Semtex into a chest. When full, two men removed it to their wagon. As the third chest filled, the sergeant turned to Haliwell. "That's it, Sir. We'll be on our way."

215

Haliwell nodded. "Thank you." As the army departed, a woman dressed in a police navy blue coverall, stood in the doorframe. With her ginger hair tied back in a French pleat and no makeup on her face, she smiled. "You look like you're having fun. Inspector Bell, Sir. What would you like me to do?"

"Can you read Arabic?"

"No, Sir."

"Neither can I. My driver's outside. Take this to MI6." He handed her the envelope. "They know it's on its way."

"Her eyes sparkled as she asked, "Do I wait or high tail it back here?"

"You get back here, Inspector." She was more than aware of the effect she had on the alpha males in the force. This was not one of those times.

"Yes, guv."

He shook his head as she left.

With the Semtex out of the way, Haliwell wandered outside for a breath of fresh air. For the best part of the last twenty-four hours, he had been active. Staring at the now quiet and empty street, he mentally reviewed the situation. As his mind wandered, the wail of a police siren could be heard approaching.

The car slid to a stop, and the officer who had taken the safe, jumped out. With a massive smile on his face, he sauntered up the path towards Haliwell and handed him a leather pouch. "Five memory sticks, Sir. I checked the safe for prints. It was clean, so I dumped it in a skip."

Haliwell slipped the pouch into his trouser pocket. "Thank you. You can go and help those upstairs."

"Commander," said Inspector Bell. "A message from some pompous git at MI6. 'Thanks for the paperwork but next time you raid a property could you do it first thing in the morning'."

"Inspector, you got that right, they are pompous gits. Well, they won't like what I have in my pocket. You're now in charge. The

216

order is to strip this house and find anything and everything. One thing more, no one leaves until I get back, and that includes you."

"No problem, Sir"

"If there are any, kick arse."

# Thirty-Three

Haliwell flashed his warrant card when he entered MI6 headquarters. He breezed through the mandatory checkpoints. On entering the lift, he pressed floor eleven and waited. The doors opened onto a well-lit area. With long strides, he approached Eric Carruther's office. Without faltering, he knocked and entered.

Eric and two other men sat at the far end of the room He glanced at his watch. With a smile, he said, "Does the Commissioner know you're working overtime?"

"She has her finger on the pulse. How are you getting on with the pile of paperwork I sent over?"

"Slow down, Bill. Let me complete the introductions. To my left, Adam Watt, he reads and speaks Arabic like a native. To my right, Alf Butler, he's my authority on Isis. Gentlemen, William Haliwell, Commander in the Met. Terrorism is his speciality"

The two men nodded.

Eric placed his fingertips together. "How can I help?"

Haliwell slipped into the chair in front of the desk and tossed the leather pouch towards Eric. "How long until you can figure out what's on those memory sticks?"

Eric rubbed the back of his neck then clapped his hands. "Anyone want a cup of coffee?"

"I'd rather you answered my question, Eric."

"Why are you in such a hurry? Nothing can be that bad," said Eric.

Haliwell shook his head. "How does Armageddon in the middle east sound?"

"Now you are dramatic and anyway, I need a coffee. Tell you what, I'll order a large pot and four cups. Then, my friend, we will look into your computer sticks." He lifted his desk phone and ordered coffee.

"For once, I would like to hit the ground running and not have to explain how we missed world war three."

Eric shuffled in his seat. "Now you are theatrical. As far as we understand the threat of Isis has not gone away, but then we knew that. Where their new base is we haven't a clue."

"I know where it is," said Haliwell.

Eric chuckled. "Bill, I have in this building those who live and work the Isis scenario. We have people on the ground in Syria. Also, a dozen teams are interviewing those captured during the fighting. I respect you for what you do, but there is no way you can point on a map and tell me that is the new Isis base"

"I'll second that," said Alf.

"Get me a map," said Haliwell.

"You're serious," said Eric.

Haliwell managed a smile. "It's approaching midnight. I haven't had much sleep, but if you want to leave this until you can make the time, I'm going home to my bed."

"Okay then," said Eric. He turned to Alf and Adam. "We'll continue this meeting tomorrow at ten. Good night, gentlemen."

They shrugged, gathered their files and left.

"Bill, you know that we record everything said in this room. You could be taking the piss, but then you don't do that. You just have a sense of humour failure, toss the grenade into a room before shutting the door. Do you actually know where Isis is?"

"Ninety percent. I did ask for a map. Afghanistan, a Russian copy would be perfect."

"Why Russian?"

"Because they are better than ours. Alexander the Great sketched ours while on the back of his horse. The Russians produced theirs from satellite images."

"For once I can prove you wrong." A knock on the door stopped him. He pressed a button on his desk, and the door opened.

219

A smart young man pushed a trolley with two coffee pots and a plate of biscuits into the room.

"Would you like me to pour the coffee, Sirs?"

"No thank you," said Eric. "Bill, will you be mum? I'll be back in five."

*Why is it civil servants make me feel like the tea boy?* He always relied on his feelings and instinct, but wondered as he poured two cups of coffee, if he had pushed his luck. He breathed a deep sigh when Eric returned, holding a long cardboard tube.

"Take a look at this." From the tube, he removed a map and placed it on the table. "It's the latest edition." With care, he unfurled a detailed map of Afghanistan.

Haliwell removed from his black leather wallet, a slip of paper. "These are the coordinates I received from an inquisitive young woman."

Eric rubbed his hands together. "Place those empty water bottles on the edge and we can check this out."

With the map secure, they traced the latitude and longitude. Eric marked a faint cross on the map.

"As I thought, in the middle of nowhere," said Eric.

Haliwell laughed. "You didn't expect it to be signposted and on a main road, did you?"

Eric grunted. "Wait, we may have photos of the location." He made a phone call. "It's on its way."

Eric answered the knock on the door. The messenger handed him three large files. "Thank you." On closing the door, he returned to the table. "Two minutes."

He removed a series of detailed photographs. He pointed. "That's the place. A long time ago, it was a Russian Communications Centre. It transmitted its last signal February 1989 after which, it fell into disrepair, and I doubt Isis have the wherewithal to rebuild."

"You're wrong," said Haliwell. "GCHQ has been monitoring emails from that location for ages. I can have copies forwarded if you want to see them. I need a computer unattached to anything but a screen."

"Don't bother." Eric rubbed his chin. "We need to know who financed this and I doubt if it was the Afghans. They haven't two rupees to rub together. Any ideas?"

"If I were searching for a place to regroup, a neglected and abandoned complex would be perfect. But what I think doesn't matter. Where's the computer I can use?"

Eric walked to his desk and removed all the cables apart from the power supply. "Don't worry, I'll have it cleaned before it's used again."

Haliwell seated himself in Eric's chair, sipped his luke-warm coffee, turned on the power and selected one of the memory sticks. In moments, pictures of a military establishment filled the screen.

"I know where that is," said Eric. "That's the Golan Heights army base." The video lasted ten minutes.

Haliwell picked up another memory stick. This time, he did not have a clue. Line after line of formulae rolled down the screen. The final few seconds made them jump. In silence they watched, their eyes unblinking, a nuclear explosion.

Both men shook their heads.

The third stick showed the naval port of Haifa. The forth, contained Isis propaganda. The fifth, the Islamic revolutionary guard training Isis troops.

"No-one will believe us," said Eric. "Iran has historically been the enemy of the Taliban and their like. Even if we challenge the Iran government, they'll deny any association. It's a perfect storm. Isis receives a ton of Russian weapons free of charge and training. Whenever it happens, Iran can sit back with their arms folded and a huge grin on their face. They can tell the world they may have detested Israel but they had nothing to do with its destruction."

"You have two choices. Do nothing or destroy Isis."

The links blended in Eric's mind. "What we need is proof. In fact, we'll request an Anglo-American surveillance of the area."

Despite the worry lines and crow's feet, Haliwell laughed. "Don't you people ever make a decision?"

"More than my job's worth," said Eric. "Look what happened to Tony Blair when it went wrong. The country remembers him as the man who declared war on Iraq. Those who earn the money will agree with my suggestion to investigate the Russian Comcen."

Haliwell glanced at a grandfather clock stood in a corner. It read twenty minutes to five. "I'm getting old," he muttered. "I've done my bit. You know all there is to know. Now it's up to the Whitehall Mandarins. Please, don't fuck up."

# Part Two

## One

For a while, the skies threatened and then the rolling wall of sand hit them. Sheltered by a mountain, they waited. The night temperature continued to drop, and five men cloaked as if in the arctic, said nothing. The wind howled, and sand pummelled the canvas canopy.

In the light of a pencil torch, Sergeant Major Harry Martin and United States Marine Sergeant Todd Miller studied a map.

Harry broke the silence. "We might be fucked if we stay put but driving in this is suicide."

"You can bet your ass on it," said Todd.

"Right, Todd, tell your men to hunker down. Some of these storms can last for days."

Todd flashed a smile, peered at the sand-covered windscreen and shrugged. "Good job when we stopped you ordered guidelines fixed."

"Been here before. When nature calls and you go for a crap, without safety lines you're as good as dead. I'll tell my men, you tell yours. Okay?"

"On my way, Harry."

Todd wrapped his scarf over his face, parted the rear awning and slid through the gap.

JG, a corporal gunner, zipped the canopy shut. "The yank seems alright, sergeant."

"Todd's okay. He's the same as us, doing his job. Get some rest. It'll be a long day tomorrow."

\*\*\*

The dawn sun sent shafts of light through the sand-streaked windscreen.

223

Harry woke and stretched, his boots disturbing his crew. "Lift and shift. JG make a brew. I want to be out of here in one hour."

"Right, Sergeant," said JG, as he brushed the sand-covered canopy clear.

Harry followed JG out and appraised the scene. Mountains surrounded them, and sand covered everything. For centuries, invading armies had marched across this hellhole. *Why?* he asked himself.

"Morning, Harry," said Todd.

"We were lucky parking up when we did. At least we can still see our wagons. We're having a brew. You're welcome to join us."

Todd laughed. "My guys prefer coffee. Thanks anyway."

"Whatever. Weapons check one hour and don't forget radio silence."

"Dead right." He turned back to his trucks. Already his men were clearing the sand away from the wheels.

One hour later, Harry stood and received a nod from six drivers. "Move out."

His driver, wearing goggles, gazed at the Satnav. "Which way, Sergeant?"

"Go left, Don."

JG stood behind his cocked and loaded heavy machine gun. Harry scanned the way ahead. They were deep into Taliban country, and everyone knew they shot visitors.

Private Steve Winters, his SA 80 Mark 2 assault weapon ready, protected their rear. His eyes searched the ground for Taliban soldiers who had a habit of popping out of holes in the ground after you passed.

Hours later six Long Range Vehicles parked inside a derelict stone structure. The crumbling walls gave respite from the burning sun. Harry watched as his and the Americans camouflaged their trucks.

He beckoned to Todd as he spread out a map on the bonnet of the nearest vehicle. His finger pressed on a position. "We're here and you can see the Russian Comcen tucked into the mountain. In front of it is a village and that might be a problem. I propose we post two men, one from each unit, in two shifts to watch the target."

"I agree, "said Todd. "Can I ask you a favour?"

Harry smiled. "You can ask, but you might not like the answer."

"This is a recon job. To the stupid, this is a walk in Central Park. I never think that way, and you're not stupid. How about we split the two teams and make it a true Anglo-American exercise?"

"I like it. How do you want the split?"

"I always knew you were an okay guy. We can swop drivers and one team member."

"Yes and no. My driver stays with me. You can have JG, my machine gunner, instead."

"No problem. Let's go and give them the good news."

That night, after their long drive, Harry found the silence unnatural. He stared at the Milky Way as it carved a broad swathe through the cloudless night sky. The light from the half-moon cast a strange glow over the landscape. He shivered. This was his final mission. "Those who must, one cigarette."

Two men crouched against a wall and lit their cigarettes. Each man shielded the glow with their hands as they inhaled the pungent smoke.

He strolled to the gaping hole that once held a window and peered into the valley. On three sides, the high peaks of the mountains sheltered the ancient settlement. The derelict communications base stood at the bottom of an escarpment.

Harry held his night vision glasses to his eyes and gazed into the dark. Pushing forty-one, his uniform failed to conceal his muscular frame. "Jimmy, Hank, count the satellite dishes." Tension resonated in his voice.

"What satellite dishes?" said Hank.

225

"Exactly."

"What the hell is that place?" asked Jimmy,

"Would you believe the Russians fought hard to hold this country?" said Harry.

"And look what happened to them," said Hank. "The mother-fuckers got their asses kicked and cleared out."

"I can understand why they buggered off," said Jimmy. "Who in their right mind wants to exist out here? This is not living, it's purgatory and about as far from civilisation you can get."

"Look, the Brigadier received orders for us to check this place out and we will. Those who know believe this is the new home of Isis. It seems they have resurrected the communications equipment and threaten cyber attacks. It's a new style of warfare. In the future, soldiers like us will be redundant. From what the boss said, these rats bury bugs into our automated programmes. The idea is to stop our equipment working."

"Well, so far I've seen sod-all, Sergeant. I reckon it's deserted."

"You two keep your eyes open. I'm off for a kip."

"You can count on Hank and me, Sergeant."

"You wouldn't be here if I couldn't."

Harry checked the time. With sunrise at 0500, they might see some movement tomorrow. He crawled into his tent and lay on his sleeping bag. In minutes and from years of practice, he slept.

\*\*\*

The sun was over the horizon when Harry awoke. Still half asleep, he crawled on his hands and knees to the observation position. He rubbed his eyes and stared at the bleak landscape. "You're up early, Todd."

"Take a look, there's some movement in the village."

"Can I have a pee first?"

"You sure can," said Todd with laughter in his voice. "And don't forget to wash your hands."

"I'll piss over them and use your shirt for a towel."

226

"I bet you would."

Thirty seconds later, Harry, his binoculars in his hands, scanned the village. He watched an old man fill a trough with water from a well. This completed, he opened a rickety gate allowing goats to sate their thirst. A young kid ran off. The old man started waving his arms moments before the explosion occurred.

"One old but live minefield," said Harry. "Now why would anyone plant mines in front of a village in the middle of nowhere?"

Todd rubbed his chin. "To stop people like us from walking in the front door or the villagers leaving."

"I'll go along with option one," said Harry. "The old man is the village and his job, to keep the goats fed and watered. But where are the rest?"

"What's the next move?" asked Todd.

"We continue watching. Tonight a few of us go for a stroll, and if we find nothing, tomorrow we go home. Until then, two of you will stand watch. The rest of you relax and don't drink too much water."

For the rest of the day, everyone avoided the sun, but sweat still soaked their uniforms.

Later towards evening, the sun dipped, and cool breezes blew from the mountains.

"I need five volunteers. Todd, you're in charge while I'm away. If the shit hits the fan, you and the rest get the hell out of here. I want no heroics rescuing dead men."

"Harry, you won't see my ass for dust," said Todd.

"Typical yank," said JG. "Isn't, let's get the hell out of here, your favourite saying?"

"Right in one, Limey."

"Shut the fuck up, both of you," said Harry. "We're a team and rely on each other."

"Where are my volunteers?"

All apart from Todd raised their hands.

"You're fucking mad. Okay, JG, Hank, Lionel, Steve and Joe, check your weapons, load with double ammo and the moment the sun dips below the horizon we leave."

"Where are we going?" asked Joe.

"I want a closer look at the village."

"What about the mines?" asked Hank.

"That's easy, don't tread on any."

***

At nine in the evening, Harry checked his team. "Don't forget, ten metres between each man and remember, I do the talking."

Harry followed an old animal track he had seen earlier. The dark deepened but using his night-vision goggles his eyes scanned the area. In this barren landscape, all he could see were rocks.

His team trod in his footprints as best they could until they reached the solid rock of the mountains. "JG, make an arrow."

Using five small stones, he marked the way up the hill.

Hank turned to Harry. "Sergeant, I've got to know how you knew where to tread."

Harry smiled. "Today we checked out the locale. That dead goat told us the location of the minefield. The Russians are no different to us. They mark the minefield with signs to stop their own men fucking up. I noticed where the stumps of the posts were and gave them a wide berth. The old trail made it easier."

"Now you know why he's the sergeant," said JG.

"There endeth the lesson," said Harry. "Keep your distance and keep close to the base of the cliff. Let's go."

Harry led his men, following a track that skirted the edge of the village. From his brief, he understood this place dated back hundreds of years. Mud brick structures were the houses of those who once lived there. The scars of bullet holes and grenade attacks were everywhere. He wondered who fought whom.

Dry stonewalls provided good cover, as each man moved like a ghost, drifting on the night wind. Goats stirred as they passed. Somewhere a dog howled.

They halted at a high wall topped with rusted razor wire. It appeared indestructible. From aerial photos, Harry knew this formed a large square around the main building. He considered his options. The locale was as quiet as a country graveyard. His fingers gripped the stock of his weapon, as oxygen flooded in and out of his lungs. Concern for his men churned his stomach. In seconds he calmed, and that scared him more.

Silently, they walked forward and turned a corner. Fifty metres further they came across two enormous steel gates. Harry ran his hand across the rust-covered metal. "Can't risk blowing this open. That's it. Time to go back."

"Shit," muttered Joe as his foot slipped on a stone. His head struck the gates. Six men stood open-mouthed as one swung on their hinges.

Harry wanted to laugh but signalled silence. Without touching the metal, he edged inside the compound. Taking a defensive stance, he covered his team as they entered.

In silence, they hugged the wall, stopping when Harry pushed open a door with his foot. Cautiously he looked inside.

"Okay," said Harry, with a note of confidence in his voice. "This place appears abandoned. JG, come with me. The rest of you keep your eyes peeled. Steve, you're in charge."

***

Harry, with JG covering his back, scouted the whole of the outside area in less than thirty minutes. The barracks were easy to identify being of a fundamental nature. The actual communications centre they guessed was inside the main building. "JG, stay here. I'm going inside." The door opened again without a sound, and that bothered him. In Helmand, dry hinges soon produced the classic sound effects of a horror movie. He wiped the hinge with his finger and found it covered in grease. Inside the first room he entered, layers of dust and sand covered everything. He took a gamble and used his pencil torch. The light confirmed the footprints on the floor belonged to him. On entering the main hallway, disturbed sand led

229

further into the building. His heart pounded. Someone had been here.

JG jumped when Harry tapped him on the shoulder. "Night vision goggles, follow me and cover my back."

With their night vision operating, the two men went deep into the building. They stopped when the trail vanished into a tunnel cut into solid rock. The roof was approximately five metres high, and the passage three metres wide.

"Stay close," said Harry.

JG said nothing as his eyes scanned the tunnel.

They had covered fifty to sixty metres when the roof dipped.

Harry continued to edge forward but then stopped. Ahead, the dull glow of light became visible.

As the two men moved stealthily along, the light grew in its intensity.

Harry held up his right hand and listened. Faint voices bounced off the passage walls making it difficult to assess numbers. Neither could understand a word.

With their backs to the wall they inched forward. Harry held up five fingers and pushed JG back. As they exited the tunnel, sighs erupted from their mouths.

"Five guards, JG, but what are they guarding?"

JG rubbed his chin. "For once the brass might be right."

Five minutes later, they arrived at the gates.

"Find anything?" asked Steve.

"You'd better believe it," said JG. "The place is crawling. The sergeant made a wise decision, and we high tailed it out of there."

"Shut up," said Harry. "No more chit-chat until we're safe back at base."

On entering their camp, Todd had a meal of corned dog hash waiting. As the wanderers tucked in, he sat next to Harry. "What's the next move?"

In between mouthfuls, Harry said, "We need to find out what's going on before we leave."

"So. you're going back?"

"We're going back but not tonight."

## Two

During his watch, Harry wandered through the camp. Gentle snores came from his team. As the day crept over the horizon, he shook JG. "Nothing's happening. Keep your ears and eyes open. Wake me in an hour."

JG grabbed his assault rifle and stood, giving his eyes time to take in the surroundings. "Okay, Sergeant."

Harry went to his tent, switched the safety catch of his weapon to **off** and lay on the sleeping bag. His eyes closed, and with practised ease, he allowed his body to recharge.

*** 

JG roused everyone as the sun peaked over the dark horizon.

Harry checked the time, five o'clock. "Get some food and water in your stomachs and go for a dump. During the next few hours, we'll not be stopping."

"You have a plan," said Todd. "Care to let me inside your head?"

Harry grinned. "I have a thought. If that place is an operational ComCen, how did they get the equipment here? It's too far for a helicopter. My guess is with a convoy. Have you seen any roads? My aim is to answer that question and return to base."

"So, we do a recon in daylight. What if they see us?"

"I bet they'll keep their heads down. You forget, we aren't supposed to know this place exists."

Todd shrugged. "Should be fun or a fucking disaster. I'll cover the rear with JG, your machine gunner."

"Deal done and dusted. Now can I eat my luxurious breakfast of dry biscuits and warm water?"

Todd chuckled as he strolled away.

For the first hour, Harry led his team to a distant plateau well clear of the minefield. There was no protection from the sun or the dust. They circled the base of the mountain that, according to

232

their map, backed onto the village. The group stopped in a line and studied the terrain. A road of any description was not visible.

As the morning progressed, the heat became intense. The slight morning breeze was long gone. "One mouthful of water," said Harry.

Todd strolled across. "Harry, I agree with your premise, but I don't see a road or anything like one."

"We need to get closer."

"How about we split up and I cover that end?" He pointed, "you this end and we meet in the middle."

"Agreed, and if we find nothing, we go home."

"This heat's a pain in the ass blurring my vision. Go home, no one would argue that."

Harry watched Todd's team move out before ordering, "Let's go."

They drove towards the base of the mountain searching for anything resembling a road, a path, a track. Harry glanced back; one of his team had stopped. At speed, his driver turned.

"Problems, Leroy?"

"I've found your road or at least why we can't find one."

"Harry glanced around at the stone-covered ground. "Give me a clue."

"Donkeys."

"I was lucky and spotted these stones. There's been a large team of donkeys and motorbikes here." He picked up a pebble. "Dried donkey shit. Been here a long time, desert dust and the sun have made it almost unrecognisable. Most would find it hard to tell between this and actual stones. Dried oil on the larger rocks shows where they stood their bikes."

"How long do you reckon?" asked Harry.

Leroy crunched a lump with his heel. "Six months to a year."

Harry glanced towards the mountains, but as far as he could see, there was nothing. "That makes sense. They transported

233

everything the way they have since time began. Gruelling, and if undertaken at night, unseen."

"Well spotted, Leroy."

"I'm still a country boy at heart."

Todd returned with his team. "Problems?"

"No," said Harry. "Leroy spotted what we all missed, dried donkey shit. And you don't need a road for donkeys."

"What's the next move?"

Harry studied his team. Sweat soaked their clothes and dust clung to them. The glare of the sun created images that did not exist. "It will be cooler nearer the base of the mountains. We still need to verify that Isis has established a comcen. I say we rest a while, complete a final scout of the area and then head for home. Anyone a better idea?"

"I'll second that," said Todd.

"Whatever we do has to be better than being cooked by the sun," said JG.

A general mutter of agreement came from the men.

"Let's find some shade," said Harry.

Ten miles later, they parked between two huge rocks that formed an arch and precious shade.

"Harry," said Todd. "This is an ideal spot to rest up for a couple of hours. Can you tell me why we couldn't see these oversized pebbles from ten miles out?"

"Heat haze. I've never known it this bad. On your own, you'd go mad in hours walking around in circles. Thank fuck for compasses and Satnav. Get some rest."

The men camouflaged their vehicles and relaxed in the shade. For as long as they lay still it was not that bad. Hot swirls of air spiralled and collapsed around them.

At five that evening, Harry decided it was time to lift and shift.

"Sergeant, I know your eyes can play tricks on you out here, but I'm sure I saw a flashing light. It lasted a few minutes, but then I fell asleep."

"Joe, was it a flash or pinpoint?" asked Harry.

"Flashes."

"Someone moving around was wearing a watch. Show me where," said Harry.

Joe laid on the ground, with his head on a pack. He lifted his right arm and pointed. "If you take a gander at the side of the mountain you can see two pointy bits. Just in front of them."

Harry and Todd grabbed their binoculars and focussed on the direction given.

"I can see the two pointed rocks but nothing else of importance," said Todd.

"I agree, which means we must get closer. According to our map, we're fifteen miles away. Okay, stow the gear and check your weapons. We're going to take a gander. Mike, take your toy out of its box."

Harry split the team into two groups. He led while the other remained a mile behind. As they moved forward, he continued to scan the base of the mountains. After two miles, he signalled with his right hand, "Stop."

Harry turned to his team as the other long-range patrol vehicles drew up on either side of him. "Can you see the cave?"

"I did wonder if it was a trick of the light," said Corporal Mike Jones.

"Where?" asked Corporal Sid Green.

"See that dark streak rising from the base? That's shadow and the entrance."

"Got it," said Mike. "But on its own, it proves sod-all."

"Got it," said Todd.

"I wish you were wrong, Mike. It's time you had a play with your toy. I suggest we advance to a mile from the base of the slope. That way if they have basic AKs and RPGs they can't hit us."

235

"Are you sure about that, Sergeant?" said Mike.

"I'd better be as I intend to be the closest vehicle. Mike, I want you one hundred metres further out, and you Steve, the same again. Todd, if they open fire hit them hard. This will be a slow pass. If we're lucky someone on their side will fuck up."

"What happens if they don't?" asked Sid.

"Then life gets difficult, and we activate plan B."

"We have a plan B?" said Todd.

Harry grinned. "By then I will have thought of one. Now shut up and let's get going."

At one mile, six patrol vehicles stopped. Each maintained one hundred metres from each other.

"Mike, this is your moment."

"Give me ten minutes, Sergeant, and I'll be ready"

JG rotated his machine gun while they waited.

"Ready, Sergeant," said Mike.

"How long will it stay in the air?" asked Harry.

"Fifteen minutes at fifty miles an hour. The company laptop is set to record what the camera sees, so please don't touch."

"Launch when you're ready, Mike."

No bigger than a briefcase, the white drone sat on the ground, its six rotors spinning. Mike operated the controls, and it lifted into the air.

Harry stood and watched the screen. In two minutes, it was filming the area next to the cave entrances. "Do you want me to enter the caves, Sergeant?"

"Scan the entrances only."

Mike reduced the speed of the drone. Hovering, it crept to the first entrance, entered, and withdrew. With accuracy, Mike dropped to a few feet above ground level. The drone approached the second entrance and entered.

"Mike, I see something," said Harry. "Can you go further inside? Shit, the picture's gone."

"The drone's down," said Mike.

"Are you sure?"

"No signal. It's dead."

"Why, when it was working perfectly."

"Maybe someone shot it out of the air."

"Take another look at the last couple of minutes."

"Did you see that flash? Pound to a penny it was a shotgun."

"Okay, pack up. Let's return to the shade."

*** 

Dusk came, followed by the dark of night. The men sipped their water as Harry briefed them.

"I don't know what this place is or might be. At best, it's what the Brigadier thinks it is. At worst, it's a group of Afgan villagers sheltering from the heat. The easy option is to call up the RAF and ask them to target the caves with Pathway bombs. In this instance, I don't think reaper drones could do the job. What I don't want is to kill innocents."

"Last I heard you can't tell the difference," said Todd. "Friend or foe, they blasted our drone."

"I agree, but I need to confirm whoever's in that cave is Isis."

"How?" asked Todd.

"My team will return to the Comcen and enter the tunnels. We'll deal with any resistance. Todd, you and yours drive within three hundred metres of the cave," he pointed. "Once in position you can blast the crap out of the entrance this end with your heavy machine guns."

"With radio silence, how will I know when you're ready?" asked Todd.

"I'll press twice on my transmit button. At that moment, you let loose the barrage from hell. You leave when we leave, but as sound travels at night, I recommend we muffle our exhausts."

"Any questions from anyone?"

"How about a week's R and R when we return to base?" asked JG.

237

"Wait and see," said Harry. "Now get ready to move out."

*** 

Two hours of driving in the dark elapsed before Harry's team reached the village. Knowing the place was abandoned they drove as close as they could.

The drivers remained behind to guard their vehicles. Ghost-like, Harry led his team through the village and into the derelict building. At the entrance, he stopped and pressed transmit on his radio. One of the waiting drivers sent two blips on the main broadcast.

*** 

On receiving the signal, Todd gave the order. At once three heavy machine guns commenced their barrage.

*** 

Harry and his team donned their night vision goggles before they entered the tunnel. As before, they stopped when it turned left. Harry peered around the corner. Three armed men sat on chairs around a table using the light from a gas lamp to play cards. He drew back and raised three fingers.

JG tapped two men on the shoulder as he withdrew his hunting knife from its sheath. He held up three fingers. The other two nodded, handed their rifles to another and slithered forward.

As one, they sprinted towards the unsuspecting guards. Against the wall, rested AK 47s and backpacks.

JG closed on the nearest man, dragged his head back and sliced the soft skin of his throat. A second man dropped to the floor with a knife in his head. One, the biggest, started to run but did not get far. A classic rugby tackle forced him to the ground. Before he could fight back, JG raced across and severed the man's throat.

Harry and the rest of his team walked forward. He lifted the AKs. "Well worn but still effective," he whispered. "We're wasting time."

JG lifted an Isis flag. "Here's your proof."

238

Harry nodded and with the glow of the gas lamp, they went further into the mountain.

The tunnel widened and electric lighting lit the area. Harry signalled a halt. "Listen. Diesel engines to power lighting and transmitters." To his left and right rough wooden doors prevented access. Sounds within the confines of the tunnel appeared loud. He lifted a latch and nudged the door. No sooner than it was ajar, he pulled it shut.

He signalled for his team to retreat.

Back where the three guards lay, he stopped.

"That was a dormitory. From my split-second look-see, it was full of men sleeping. Time we were out of here."

"Couldn't we toss a couple of grenades and wake them up?" said JG.

"I'm not smiling, JG. Shift your arse."

"Sergeant, you're dead boring."

"Better that than dead."

Twenty minutes later, Harry transmitted two blips. As they drove towards the leaning rocks, the men started to relax. After two hours of hard-driving, they seated themselves in the relative safety of the rock structure.

"We made a lot of noise but not one bullet in retaliation," said Todd.

"We found them. It's a barrack block covered in thirty metres of stone. It's going to be difficult. Time to contact the nut crackers."

# *Three*

Harry took his time writing the situation report for Helmand. When finished, he gave Todd a copy for comment.

Todd shrugged. "No different to what I'd say."

With the daily user code correct, he handed it to his radio operator. "Flash signal for the base headquarters. Leave the receiver on. I expect an answer tonight."

"What's next?" asked Todd.

"Wait for those in command to make a decision."

"Most of them couldn't organise sex in a brothel."

"I tend to agree with you, but we wait. Have you any coffee? I actually fancy a cup."

"I'll get one of my guys to make a pot. How do you like it?"

Harry's eyes twinkled. "Hot, strong and sweet, like my women."

"None of them out here but your coffee's on its way."

The two men on guard duty wandered around the camp while the rest relaxed and slept. Harry, along with Todd, gave up waiting for a reply and grabbed some rest.

***

The glow of a new day peaked over the horizon when Harry's driver woke him. "Message from Helmand."

Harry rubbed his eyes. "Does it tell us to come home?"

"No, Sergeant."

"Somehow I didn't think it would. Thanks."

He stood and strolled to where Todd slept and gently nudged his side.

"You woke me in the best part of my dream."

"Don't tell me you were about to get your leg over."

"How did you know?"

Harry laughed. "Out here we all have the same dream. Bad news I'm afraid." He handed over the signal.

"Typical Air Force assholes," said Todd. "They get a good night's sleep in an air-conditioned bedroom. I bet they have a curvy bed-mate to make love to and have the audacity to tell us to be ready at eleven."

Steve checked the time. It was approaching five in the morning. "Rise and shine, my merry men, Robin Hood needs you. It's time to earn the money the sheriff pays you."

"Ten more minutes, Sergeant."

"Rustle up breakfast. It's going to be a long day."

While they ate, Harry briefed his team. "Those who know better than us have decided we split into two groups. Group one will assist the Flyboys direct their laser-guided bombs at the main entrance. Group two will return to the village and capture any escaping Isis members. Please understand, if they raise their hands in the air, we accept their surrender."

Todd stood. "I'll take the easy job and position the lasers for the attack and join you back in Helmand for a couple of beers."

"Thanks, Todd," said Harry. "Okay, eating, drinking and your other requirements have at most thirty minutes. Then we leave."

"I'm not happy about this surrender business," said JG. "How do we know they aren't wearing an explosive vest?"

"Believe me, I'd much rather you all lived to fight another day. If you have any doubt, shoot the bastard," said Harry.

"Why didn't you say that in the first place?" said JG.

"I briefed you on our orders as I must. Out here, I am the OIC and deal with the situation as it evolves. So, give them what they deserve and good luck. Understand?"

"Yes, Sergeant."

"Well, shift your arse and start clearing away. If I'm needed," he pointed, "I'll be behind that rock doing my own thing."

"Too much information, Sergeant."

As one, six Long Range Patrol Vehicles left the safety of the rocks. Todd headed towards the mountains by a diverse route. Harry's driver drove as fast as it was possible over the rough terrain.

***

Todd led his team until they were out of sight of the cave entrance. At this point, he changed direction towards the mountains. They stopped in a concealed hollow to remain hidden. In minutes, Todd's men cloaked each vehicle with camouflage netting. He studied his map and estimated their goal was five kilometres distant.

He glanced at the sun as he wiped the sweat from his face. "Let's make a move. I want this done and dusted before those flyboys arrive." In single file, Todd led the way with his men spaced five metres apart as they advanced along the dust-covered track.

Rocks of every size covered the ground, and the men's winding path rose and dipped. In one area, the climb was so steep they had to crawl. Each man, except the radio operator, carried many weapons; RPGs, grenades, and a supply of ammunition.

It took them two hours to reach a position which gave them good cover, along with a view of the target.

Todd laughed when he saw a semi-circular area stretching a few hundred metres from the entrance. "I propose we stay clear of that. It's a killing zone."

"How do you intend to set the lasers?" asked Hank.

"Can you see any guards?"

"No."

"So, where are they?"

Hank rubbed his chin. "If it were me, I'd be as far back into that cave as I could get. You'd have the drop on anyone approaching."

Todd chuckled. "That's why we'll approach from this side. And then fire three RPGs straight into the cave, create mayhem and enter. Drop our laser beacons and then do a runner."

"Just like that," said Joe.

"I'm open to suggestions," said Todd.

"You're the boss. I'm a grunt and always will be"

"Right," he pointed. "You three, RPGs locked and loaded. You two, carry the laser beacons and stick close to me. The rest of you act as a rearguard and cover our backs when we run out of there. Any questions?"

"When do we start?" asked Hank.

Todd glanced at his watch. "Ten thirty." He scanned his preferred approach to the cave using his binoculars.

The men cleared the smaller rocks away and set up their positions. When completed, they had a clear view of the cave but remained undetected.

Todd calibrated four laser beacons. Those with the RPGs checked, loaded and locked them ready for use. They all sweated buckets as they prepared everything for the assault. The magazines for their M16s had double magazines loaded and spares at hand.

The men drank tepid water from their canteens as Todd checked each weapon again. He glanced at his watch. "Ready for a stroll? Let's go."

Todd nodded to his team as they left the safety of the rocks. Silently they walked along the base of the cliff. In five minutes, they were standing to the left of the entrance. He tapped his RPG carriers on their shoulders. As one, they unlocked, ran to the centre of the cave entrance, dropped on one knee and fired. They did not wait for the detonation but charged to the left for cover.

Dust and debris erupted from the cave. Todd, in company with his men, charged with their M16s on rapid fire. To their surprise, return fire remained light. Five grenades silenced the Isis survivors. At speed, two men positioned the four laser beacons.

"Move out," shouted Todd. In good order they withdrew, each man covering another. In less than five minutes, they dropped behind the boulders shielding the rest of the team.

Todd glanced at his watch, ten-fifty. "You two keep an eye on the entrance. The rest of you find a hole. It's going to get noisy and messy." He scanned the sky and spotted four specks approaching. "Sam, contact the pilots and tell them lasers in place and then hide."

Behind huge boulders, Todd and his men hugged the ground. The roar of the first Typhoon from Cyprus, followed by an explosion, made the land shiver. Three more followed. In less than ten minutes, the entrance to the cave vanished.

Todd stood, brushing the dust from his hair and clothes. "Grab your weapons. Let's check on the damage."

"Sergeant, you can see everything from here," said Hank.

"What ..." shouted Todd as a crack as loud as thunder filled the air and the ground shuddered.

Everyone turned as the mountain face split apart. Rock slabs the size of buildings accelerated towards the ground. Clouds of debris filled the air as it spewed outwards. Todd and his men crawled under rocks and prayed.

When the noise abated, men covered in stones and dust stood and stared.

Todd counted his men. None were missing. He grabbed his water bottle and rinsed his face before attempting to speak. His voice was caring as he gazed at the once empty space in front of the entrance. "Anybody hurt?"

"The term feeling lucky comes to mind," said Leroy.

"Someone up there loves us," said Hank.

"Dust off. Let's go home," said Todd.

"It's good to still be alive. You lead, and we'll follow," said Joe.

They retrieved their weapons, and began the journey back to their LRPVs.

Harry's team drove into the village and parked their vehicles in the shade. Each man checked his own weapons, fitted grenade pouches and filled ammunition belts. Into their pockets, they shoved a basic first aid kit. Don grabbed the water bottles, went and filled them from the well.

Harry and Don completed a cursory check on the area, finding the goat herder sleeping in a chair. They woke him and using sign language told him to shelter inside his hut.

On their return to the rest of the unit, everyone was ready.

Harry drew a sketch of the old communication building and compound. He pointed out the officers' quarters, barracks and main building. "There's one way out, but we stop any survivors from outside the compound. This we use to our advantage." He had one hour until the RAF arrived. "Right, grab your gear."

Led by Harry, his team trotted through the village. At the massive metal gates, they stopped. "JG, Steve, you can have some fun blasting holes through this wall. It's not thick so be sparing with the explosives." He turned. "You two, open those gates in case someone is awake in there."

After the first detonation, Harry went and checked the opening. "That's great. It gives a clear field of fire. Three more and we'll be ready." A second blast told him to start positioning his men. "Remember, I'll fire the first shot. If that doesn't stop them, it's your turn."

Glancing at his watch, he waited as the second hand moved towards eleven and readied himself. For a while, nothing happened. A black-clad fighter emerged from the building and at once returned inside. *Had he noticed the holes in the walls?* Harry wondered.

A few minutes later, at least twenty individuals wearing black Burkas and holding white flags in their right hands, appeared. As a group, they shouted, "Peace, we come in peace," as they inched across the compound.

"They're sending their women out first," said JG.

Harry scanned the group with his binoculars. "Those women have bombs strapped to their bodies." With deliberation, he aimed at the leader and fired one shot.

The explosion produced a domino effect. In a flash, body parts plastered the compound. A few metres in front of Harry the bottom half of a leg landed.

"How did you know?" asked Steve.

"I saw a wire leading to a clenched left hand."

"Who the fuck sends their wives out into the open with explosive vests strapped to their tits?"

Harry shrugged. "They do. Their next attack might be more determined. Keep your eyes peeled."

Minutes later, heavy fire came from the upper floor of the centre. It focused around Harry's position but firing at a hole in a wall had its own problems.

"JG, get your RPG."

"Ready, Sergeant."

"Choose your target and fire."

JG fired his RPG, absorbing the recoil as it kicked into life.

The missile flew, entering a top floor window. The explosion sent clouds of dust out of every window. "They now have full air conditioning."

"Shut up. Two more."

JG obeyed the order but chose different windows.

"Steve," said Harry. "Go tell the men to ceasefire. We can't afford to waste ammo." He scurried away and returned in minutes.

Without warning, a group of men, their AKs on automatic, charged from the centre. Although they did not stand a chance, it was effective in forcing Harry's team to duck back. Then one man tumbled, and then another until all were dead or dying from their wounds. The smell of blood was everywhere.

"How many more?" asked Harry. "What the hell?"

The ground vibrated, and a gush of debris shot out of every opening of the centre. As if in slow motion, the walls of the building collapsed outwards, while the reinforced concrete roof fell on those sheltering inside.

"Wait," ordered Harry. "Survivors can still pull a trigger and kill you. Steve, go and check our boys for casualties."

The minutes ticked by.

Steve returned. "One flesh wound from a rock splinter. Nothing else."

"We wait until I'm ready," said Harry. After thirty minutes, he smiled. "Time for a walk. JG, Steve, follow me."

They opened the two steel doors and peered inside. The slaughter made them empty their stomachs. Every part of the human anatomy lay scattered on the ground like the waste from an operating theatre.

The three men walked towards the rubble that was once the centre. "If anyone is alive in there they won't last long. We've carried out our orders. Let's go."

***

Back at the trucks, they relaxed, drank copious amounts of water and ate their rations.

"I've informed base mission completed, and no casualties," said Harry. "Let's rock and roll."

In a few minutes with the heavy machine guns manned, the three vehicles began their long journey.

# *Four*

Haliwell was giving advice to Inspector Madden when his phone rang. He lifted the handset. "Who is it, Annie?"

"It's the Commissioner, and by the tone of her voice, she's not in a good mood."

"She never is. You'd better put her through." Haliwell leant back in his chair. "Good morning, Commissioner."

"Haliwell, my office, and in case you misheard me, that means now, not at your convenience."

"Yes, Mam."

"I'm waiting."

He strolled into Annie's office. "What have I done wrong this time, Annie?"

She peered up at him and smiled. "If I knew I'd tell you."

"I know."

Taking his time, he took the long route. On entering the Commissioner's outer office, her secretary smiled. "What have you done wrong, Commander?"

"You must mean working more hours than God almighty."

"You'd better go in, she's waiting."

"Wish me luck."

He knocked and entered, closing the door with a gentle click behind him. "You wanted to see me, Mam."

She made an impatient gesture. "You may stand or sit."

He smiled as he seated himself. In front of him was a plump woman aged forty-five, with brown hair, cut short like a man's, and her bright red lipstick shimmered in the light. Her uniform was immaculate. The collar of her blouse so stiff with starch the wearer could decapitate herself.

"Haliwell, there are those in M16 and elsewhere who believe in your methods. In my opinion, you're a dinosaur who should have retired a long time ago. I met with the Home Secretary this morning. She advised it would be to my advantage if I promoted you to Deputy Assistant Commissioner. She also gave me this envelope, for your eyes only, and asked that you reply within the hour. Pound to a penny it's an invite to the Queen's garden party. I received an invite but advised it was inconvenient to my planned schedule. Your promotion is effective immediately. However, I expect you to remain in the same office until you leave the Force."

Haliwell stood and nodded. "Excuse me, Mam. I need some fresh air."

"Make sure you're wearing your rank badges the next time we meet."

"Yes, Mam." Haliwell never ever appeared smug. But he did wonder what was happening as he wandered back to his office.

"Couldn't have been all bad," said Annie as he entered.

"She promoted me. It's not a dream because the words came straight from those lacquered lips."

Annie rested her elbows on her desk. "Congratulations. It's about time."

He smiled. "And you'll get a pay rise."

"Every penny helps."

He grinned. "This might be out of order, but can I take you for a drink at lunchtime?"

Annie pursed her lips as she tapped her long pink fingernails on the desk. "I'll have to think about it. You might want to drag me off to some dark corner and have your way with me."

Haliwell's face flushed.

Annie laughed. "I've worked for you since you made Chief Inspector. You never forget my birthday, and I receive a Christmas present every year. Yes, I'd love to have a drink with you."

"Oh, I thought..."

"Sometimes it's better not to."

"One o'clock."

"I'll be ready."

He walked into his office, tossed the manila envelope on his desk and stared out of the window. Bewildered, his thoughts turned to Abbey. The last time he had seen her, she was at the vicarage. The vicar was correct, she was a mess. Relaxing in a peaceful village was the best thing she could do.

He strolled around his desk, settled into his chair, and saw the envelope. Using a letter opener, he sliced the top and removed the single sheet of paper. His chin dropped as he read its contents.

Dear William Haliwell

I will be honoured if you could attend 10 Downing Street today at one o'clock for a chat.
I'll say no more.
Looking forward to our meeting.
The Prime Minister.

The signature was unreadable. Some moron was extracting the urine. Then he remembered what the Commissioner said.

He contacted the exchange operator. "Don't hear from you very often, Commander. How can I help?"

"Can you connect me to the appointments' secretary at 10 Downing Street?"

"No problem."

"Downing Street, exchange."

"Sorry to bother you but I have a meeting with the PM at one. Could you please confirm?"

"Your name please?"

"Commander William Haliwell."

A few seconds elapsed. "That is correct. Do you need a car to collect you or will you drive your own?"

"I'll walk. Thank you."

250

"Please be on time." The line went dead.

He stood and went into Annie's office. "It appears I have to meet the PM at one o'clock."

"Well, you can buy me a drink after work," said Annie.

"I will, and that's a promise." He glanced at the wall clock. "Better make a move."

***

Cleared by the police at the entrance, he walked along Downing Street. At this point, he remembered that the door of Number 10 only opened from the inside. The constable on duty gazed towards the gate, nodded, and the door opened.

"Good afternoon, Deputy Assistant Commissioner Haliwell. Warrant Card, please." She gave it a quick glance and handed it back. "Please follow me."

He noted a man position himself by the entrance door as he followed his guide.

"The Prime Minister's study." She opened the door, moved for him to pass and then pulled it shut.

"Good, you're on time. I remember you from that SIS meeting ages ago. In fact, you were the one person who made sense." The Prime Minister motioned. "I'm sure you know the Chief of Defence Staff Sir John Martine."

He shook Haliwell's hand. "A pleasure to meet you."

The Prime Minister seated herself in an old armchair and crossed her legs. "Be seated, gentlemen."

Haliwell sat in the other chair alongside John.

The Prime Minister smiled. "William, I'm pleased to see that you accepted your promotion. My sources informed me you might not. Anyway, down to business." She glanced at her watch. "I have a busy afternoon and an appointment at Mansion House this evening. John, the floor is yours."

"A couple of days ago I read a report kicked off by you when you stuck a rocket up Eric Curruthers' backside. Out of character, he sent your information to the Troop Commander in Helmond...

"The combined UK and American Special Forces group found Isis. With the RAF dropping a few bombs, they destroyed an Isis communications centre. Since then, we have waged a quiet war in the mountains. Isis has nowhere to hide. Not one of us thought they might split into smaller factions. Their use of caves and tunnels, which litter the rugged terrain, was a good move. You have saved hundreds of lives. Isis is running around like a headless chicken. It's an absolute triumph from our point of view."

"Thank you, but that's my job."

"You've been doing your job, as you put it, for forty years. This is the time your hard work and dedication has earnt a reward."

"Haliwell rubbed his chin. "Prime Minister, I didn't do it on my own. It has always been a team effort."

"Who led the team? You did, and next week you'll become a Knight Companion of the Most Noble Order of the Garter."

He tried to think of the right words, but his mind went blank.

The Prime Minister smiled. "If everyone did their job, as you put it, the world would be a safer place."

"Prime Minister, when I awoke this morning I thought the sun's shining, can't be bad. I never imagined that today my life would change."

The Prime Minister read her notes before lifting her head. She wondered how he remained so calm. "You will receive your knighthood from Prince Charles next Thursday. The ceremony will take place in the drawing room of Clarence House at ten in the morning. Your wife and other guests are welcome, maximum four." She glanced at the antique clock on the mantelpiece. "Sorry, have to dash. Thank you."

Both men stood as the Prime Minister left the room.

"William," said John. "I have a proposition for you, but I stress it is your decision."

"I'm listening."

"MI6 have a vacancy for someone with your doggedness of character and honesty."

Haliwell smiled. "Thanks, but no thanks. I'm too old and set in my ways."

John raised his hand to interrupt him. "That's exactly the point, William. Today we have young whiz kids who are full of their own self-importance but they can never see the wood for the trees. You observe, reason, calculate and examine the evidence and then make a decision. Many of those who work for us can crack codes but will never decide if they want one or two slices of toast for breakfast."

"I'm honoured that you've considered me for the position. I could recommend others if you wish. For the moment, my boss will not be a happy bunny when she discovers my imminent knighthood. She expected to be in this year's birthday honours list. So, I'll make sure, where appropriate, members of my team get promoted and continue chasing the bad guys."

"You could work part-time," said John.

"I'll think about it."

"Good man."

The door opened. "Any idea when you will be leaving, Gentlemen."

"At once," said John. "My car's outside. Want a lift?"

"No thanks. I promised to buy my secretary a drink, and I need one."

On his return to the street, he gathered his thoughts, breathed deeply and strolled forward. His eyes wandered, his focus scattered like his nerves. With a friendly wave to his uniformed associates, he left the security of Downing Street. The blast of a horn made him turn. The driver was screaming at him. The Shogun swerved out of control but in that moment, the front of the vehicle knocked him to the ground and crashed into the side of a passing car.

Out of control, Haliwell hit the ground, breaking his nose. Blood covered his white shirt. The pain made him realise he was still alive. An armed police officer cleared the crowd.

"Don't move, Sir," said the officer, "an ambulance is on its way."

"My fault, didn't look. Let the driver go on her way."

"I have her details, Sir. But she hit another car. The breakdown wagon's on its way."

"Please give them to me. I'll deal with it later. Now help me to stand."

"You're bleeding, Sir."

"Officer, you have been given a direct order by a senior officer. Help me stand, please."

The officer waved to one of his associates while supporting Haliwell under one arm.

Another officer arrived and took the other arm, and between them, they assisted Haliwell to a chair inside the gates. When they seated him, he said, "That hurt."

With its siren screaming the ambulance arrived. The gates opened to allow access, closing as it passed through.

The paramedic strode with his bag towards Haliwell. Almost in automatic mode, he checked eyes, vision, limbs, and head, pushed and pressed Haliwell's body where he did not want it touched.

"You're a lucky man. Your nose is broken so we'll take you to A and E."

"All this fuss. Anyone would think I'd been run over. Please hurry, I need to return to my office."

"Sir, they can fix your nose in a few minutes. I recommend you do as you're asked."

Haliwell stared into the man's eyes. "You don't give up do you?"

"Like you, Sir, I have a job to do."

"I give in. I'll walk to the ambulance and wait until you've helped those in the other vehicles."

"It a deal."

# Five

Annie kept her eyes fixed to the screen when Haliwell entered the office.

"Good morning, Annie. You may look, and you have my permission to laugh."

"I bet that hurt. You were lucky from what I heard from Traffic."

"My mind was on other things, and I stepped in front of the car. How stupid is that? It appears I've a broken nose, two cracked ribs and a mass of bruises."

"We've all been there. How did your chat with the PM go?"

"Next week I have the honour of Prince Charles conferring a knighthood on yours truly."

"Are you for real?"

"You'd better believe it, and I would like you to be there with my wife. Let's face it. I see more of you than I do her, and anyway, she thinks you deserve to be there. Moreover, for your ears only, there's a position waiting for me at MI6. What do you think?"

Annie gazed at him, her eyes wide. "It's not for me to say."

"If I accept, I would like you to come with me."

"And if I'd rather stay here?"

Haliwell flashed a grim look. "Sorry, I shouldn't have put it that way."

Silence filled the office for a few seconds until Annie spoke. "What happens to my pension? What are the hours? Will I be working for you, or will I be stuck in a pool? I need to know before I jump ship."

He paused as the phone rang. "It's the boss for you, Sir."

He took the handset. "Good morning, Mam."

"I hear you were in an accident."

"A few cuts and bruises and six hours in A and E but otherwise I'm fine. I still bounce when I fall over."

"You should take a few days off, rest, watch television and recuperate."

"Mam, I can't think of anything worse than spending my time watching television."

"Your decision." The line went dead.

"Coffee?" asked Annie.

"My morning lifesaver. Thank you."

"I've three messages. Inspector Madden says he is in the building today if you still want to see him. Oh, and Abbey Lane asked if you can give her a call when you have a moment. You're in the high court tomorrow morning re the case against Abu Bakr Abdallah, from Lebanon."

"In order of preference. Coffee. I'll see Madden in my office at eleven but my driver midday. And, not for discussion, I turned the job down."

Annie stared at him with a determined gaze. "I'm pleased; believe it or not. I enjoy working with you."

He laughed. "Ditto, Annie."

*** 

Haliwell rang Abbey.

"Thanks for calling. I need to talk to you."

"Is it important?"

"It's private."

He flicked the pages of his diary. "How about Friday morning. I can't be more precise than that. I assume you're still at the vicarage."

"You should never assume, but I am. See you Friday. Bye." The call ended.

*** 

Haliwell was in another place, staring over the London vista from his office window.

257

"Sir, I have Inspector Madden waiting."

"Thank you, Annie." Grimacing with pain from his cracked ribs, he returned and seated himself. "Send him in."

"Good morning, guv. And congratulations on the promotion."

"Thanks. Park your backside. We need to discuss your promotion. The last time I asked, you said you were happy as an Inspector. Well, I'm not. In the next minute you will decide your future. As you know, I have the authority to hire and fire. Say yes, and you walk out of here a Chief Inspector. What's your answer?"

Stunned, Madden asked, "Can I have time to think it over, Sir?"

"No."

Madden scratched his cheek and furrowed his brows. "Will this mean a change of department?"

"Certainly not. You're stuck here with me."

"You strike a hard bargain. I accept, Sir. Thank you."

"Congratulations, Chief Inspector. Now I have a favour to ask."

"You're asking me for a favour?"

"Please listen. My driver, Peter Grey, is an ex-Para and is wasting his time. Could you find a place in the team? I've checked him out, good military record and I like him."

Madden spread his hands. "I will be forwarding my recommendations for an inspector and a sergeant to you. He joins at the bottom, and the rest is up to him."

Haliwell rubbed his hands together. "Good, he should be waiting outside for an interview he doesn't know about."

One-hour later, Police Officer Peter Grey became a member of the elite task force.

.

***

Haliwell, dressed in a crease-free blue suit, white shirt and black tie, nodded to the clerk of the court as he entered. His eyes scanned the courtroom before he seated himself.

Abu Bakr Abdallah in the Dock did not acknowledge his presence.

The judge entered, and everyone stood until motioned to sit. The process began with the opening remarks from the defence and prosecution lawyers.

Two hours elapsed before they called Haliwell. He reiterated the facts from the moment his car received damage from shots fired by the prisoner.

The recently qualified defence lawyer stood. "Commissioner Haliwell, are you telling this court the truth?"

Unflustered by the question, he glanced at the judge and then the young lawyer. "You saw me swear the oath on the bible."

"But are you telling the truth?" he asked again.

"You already have my answer to the question."

The judge intervened. "Is there a purpose to your questioning? Commissioner Haliwell has been clear with his answer."

"Your honour, the prisoner informed me that the police threatened to kill him. I am attempting to discover if this is correct. Commissioner, is there any truth in this accusation?"

Haliwell spoke loud and clear. "I was in attendance when a member of my team disarmed the accused. Abu Bakr Abdallah used the AK47 in his possession to fire at my vehicle. I conducted the interview by following the current guidelines. I'm sure you have seen and listened to the DVD recorded at the time. Did the prisoner have any bruises or marks to indicate violence towards him? What I will say is," he pointed toward Abu, "the prisoner cooperated by answering my questions. From what he told us led to further arrests by police forces across the country."

"Commissioner, I only require an answer to my question."

"My apologies," said Haliwell.

Laughter rippled around the courtroom until the judge silenced it with his gavel.

"No further questions."

Sir," said Haliwell. "I have other police business to attend to. May I stand down?"

The prosecution and defence lawyers nodded to the judge.

"You may."

Haliwell left but noticed a man staring at him. Outside the courtroom, he stopped one of the court's security team and produced his warrant card.

The smartly dressed officer asked, "Can I help you, Sir?"

Haliwell drew her to one side and pointed. "In court number one, there's a man who for whatever reason, did not take his eyes off me. I need to know his name and anything else you can find out about him."

"Can you point this person out, Sir?"

They walked towards and opened one of the many doors. "He's the one wearing a dark suit with a horrid red tie. He appears to be of Asian descent."

They closed the door. "Where will you be, Sir?"

"In the local greasy spoon along the road enjoying a bacon roll and a cup of stewed tea."

She smiled. "I'll meet you there when I have your information."

"Thank you." He turned and exited the building and strolled along the street to Tiffany's.

This insignificant but well-known establishment fitted between new city properties. On the menu, mugs of tea, chips with sausages, beef burgers, eggs, bacon, black pudding, white pudding, and fried bread. The dozen or so customers lifted their heads as the door opened.

Haliwell seated himself at a table farthest from the door. He did not look out of place. Barristers, judges and courtroom staff often used Tiffany's for lunch. Some, before returning to their solitary city pads, purchased an evening meal.

The one waiter sidled across. "What's it to be, luv?"

"One large mug of tea and two bacon rolls, please."

"Been in court 'ave we?"

"I'm a police officer."

She gave him a charming smile. "Get a lot of them in 'ere. The wanderers I call them, 'ands everywhere but where they should be. "Give us a tenner, the tea's on the 'ouse."

He handed over a ten-pound note.

"Back in five."

The security officer spotted Haliwell devouring a roll as she entered. She apologised for not arriving sooner.

"Do we know who he is? Sorry, would you like a cup of tea?"

"Yes we do and, no thank you, but one of those bacon butties would go down a treat. I missed my lunch break."

Haliwell waved to the waiter and pointed at the roll in his hand. She gave the thumbs up.

"Your man is Abdullah the elder brother of Abu Bakr Abdallah, the man in the dock. I must say from appearances he doesn't look like his brother."

Haliwell stroked his chin. "Interesting. Thank you. I'll have the system check him out. Pound to a penny he groomed his brother."

"One bacon roll. Five-pound, guv."

He handed over three two-pound coins. "Keep the change."

"You're a star, boss."

"Enjoy your lunch, and thanks again."

"Makes a change, Sir. Why do these rolls dripping in bacon fat always taste so good?"

"Because they're bad for you. Must dash." He strolled into the street, looked left and right and crossed the road. He pressed the speed dial on his mobile. "Madden speaking, Sir."

261

"Can you check the elder brother of Abu Bakr Abdallah. I understand his first name is Abdullah."

"What am I looking for, Sir?"

"Chief Inspector, when you find it let me know."

"Of course, Sir."

***

Haliwell checked the time and contacted Abbey.

She answered on the second ring. "Hi, I need to talk to you, and what's happening with my temporary job?"

"I've put you on sick leave until you feel like returning."

"Can I resign?"

"Return to work and then give your notice."

"Can I have time to think?"

"That's why you're on sick leave. Being shot at is never a good experience. Believe it or not, it still scares the hell out of me, and over the years, it's happened a few times. Bearing that in mind, how's baby Noah?"

"He's having the time of his life with Vincent. Everyone in the village says he's adorable. Mind you, no other baby exists for miles, so he's spoilt rotten."

"Abbey, I'll need to end this conversation in a few minutes. What else is on your mind?"

"I rather we talked in private. It's sort of personal."

"I can't make it before Friday. Must go. Bye." He killed the call and shoved his mobile into his trouser pocket. The pain from his ribs made him grit his teeth as his mobile rang.

"Hi guv, it's Inspector Madden."

"Chief Inspector."

"I'll get used to it, guv. Anyway, your man Abdullah doesn't exist. I didn't believe it, so I dug deeper and still found zilch."

"A man who has no police record and I've seen him. Good chance he's illegal, and I doubt if he's Abu's brother. I'll return to court and have him taken in for questioning. Meanwhile, you might find him on some database."

"Okay, guv." Madden ended the call.

Haliwell walked into the court entrance and produced his warrant card to a member of the security staff. "I need you to seal," he pointed, "that courtroom. No noise and no shouting, I intend to detain a young man who is inside."

In five minutes, two security staff barred each door.

"Ready when you are, Sir," said the senior staff member.

"Let's get on with it."

The man nodded to his team members who opened the door. Abdullah had gone.

"Thank you," said Haliwell to security. "It now becomes that much harder to find him, but I will."

On leaving the courts, he swore. The roar of a powerful motorcycle bounced off the buildings around him. He recognised the helmetless rider and stepped back behind the black painted bollards as it roared past, its rider laughing.

Haliwell shrugged although he had the strong suspicion he would see this man again. He glanced at the time and decided to go home.

***

Sometime Friday morning the weather changed from fair to rain. It bounced off the roads as Haliwell drove into Eddington village. When he saw the grey stone church car park, his mind wandered. *I bet this place hasn't changed in centuries. I'm going to have a look inside.* As he approached the iron-studded door, the sound of singing lightened his mood. *Choir practice in the morning, most unusual.* He opened the door and entered, it was empty apart from Vincent Piper, the vicar.

"Good morning, Vicar."

Vincent turned and beamed with pride as the harmonies soared around the building. "Great to see you again, Commander. Abbey's waiting for you in the house."

"Any idea why she wants to see me?"

263

Vincent smiled. "That's up to her, and I respect her privacy."

"The acoustics in here are fabulous. Play something else, and when it finishes, I'll go and talk to Abbey."

"I have a recording of Morning Has Broken, as sung at Aretha Franklin's funeral."

The two men sat opposite each other as the music filled every nook and cranny of the church.

When it ended, Haliwell stood. "As much as I enjoyed every moment of that, I must go and talk to Abbey."

"Will you tell her I'll be at least another hour?"

"Of course," said Haliwell as he strode along the aisle to the door.

The rain continued to bucket down as he knocked on the vicarage door.

Abbey smiled when she saw him. "Thank you for coming."

"As you're on sick leave, why wouldn't I?"

"Come into the kitchen. The coffee percolator has finished doing its thing."

"Perfect timing."

"I saw you parking your new beast."

Haliwell sat in a well-used kitchen chair while Abbey poured two coffees.

"There you are, black as you like it."

"How are you doing?"

"Back to normal, whatever that is. Vincent is a marvellous man. He knows how to drag problems into the open without asking questions."

"I can't hear Noah."

"Having his morning nap so with luck we won't be disturbed."

"I'm all ears, Abbey."

She seated herself and took a sip of coffee. "I've known Vincent for five weeks, and he's asked me to marry him, and I said yes. What do you think?"

Haliwell grinned. "What I'm going to tell you might surprise you. The day I met my wife, I knew she was the one for me. Don't ask me how but it took me a week to ask her out and do you know what she said?"

Abbey shook her head.

"What took you so long? We got married six months later. I won't tell you it's been easy, but we overcame our problems before they became something else. If you know it's right, go for it. Have you named the day?"

"Not yet. I'm happy to live here with him, but the villagers might disapprove. So, it will be as soon as we can arrange the details. If I ask, will you and your wife come?"

"I'll ask her, but I'm sure she will be happy to buy a new dress for the occasion."

"That's great."

"I must ask the question. Are you sure?"

She smiled. "Yes. We need each other and deserve that chance. One thing's certain, you don't know where love will take you. With Vincent, I've learnt to accept the realities of life and death."

"Oh, by the way, I have some news. It's not as important as your's, but I'm now a Deputy Assistant Commissioner. And their Lordships have given me a knighthood for my services to the Force."

"Sir William Haliwell, Deputy Assistant Commissioner, sounds great. I'd ask you to give me away, but Gregory Peters, who was my legal guardian, has already accepted."

"How is Gregory? I haven't seen him in years."

"He doesn't change. Do you know, he's the nearest thing to a father I ever had?"

"Is there any coffee left?" asked Vincent.

265

"I've told Sir William our news, and he's pleased for us."

"What's with Sir William?" said Vincent.

"Thanks to a lot of help from Abbey, it appears I've discovered the location of a few Isis soldiers. Those who decide these things have offered me a knighthood. Keep that under wraps until it happens."

"All I did was track the source of a few emails," said Abbey.

Haliwell smiled. "That started the snowball rolling down the hill. And could have got you killed."

"But it didn't. Anyway, all's well that ends well."

"That's a cliché I never use, but then I have my reasons. He stood, "Right, Abbey, come see me and tell me you're resigning and I'll have it processed. Let me know the date of the wedding. Must go. Keep in touch."

Abbey and Vincent watched as he drove away.

"He's one of the good guys," said Vincent.

A squeal from upstairs caused a big smile from Vincent. "Your son calls."

# The Destiny of the other Characters in order of appearance

**Mr Gregory Peters.** He never recovered from the attack in his office and retired. These days he devotes his time to helping the less fortunate.

**Tyler** managed a 2-1 at university but works in a newsagents and cares for his invalid mother.

**Michael** left university and became a surfer. He travels around the world usually with an attractive woman hanging from his arm.

**Chief Inspector Madden** promoted to Chief Superintendant and retired a few years after. Relocated with his wife to Spain and established a hire car company on the Costa del Sol.

**Annie** retired when William Haliwell resigned from the Force. Loves being with her grandchildren and has completed the London Marathon as a senior citizen.

**John Newton** died of a drug overdose while serving his sentence for the manslaughter of Jacob Spink.

**Estate Agent Bill Franklyn** purchased twelve buy-to-let properties and owns a letting agency.

**Lt Commander Jeff Powell** retired from the Royal Navy at fifty-five. Operates a diving school where he and his wife live in Gibraltar.

**Steve Jenkins** gained a first class honours degree. He married Cathy and while she cares for their three children, Steve runs his father's business.

**Abu Bakr Abdallah** served half a ten-year sentence for terrorism. On his release travelled to Libya. His whereabouts are unknown.

**Father Vincent** married Abbey in his church. The Bishop of Ipswich officiated at the ceremony. Abbey assisted in the writing of a programme for the MOD to nullify Jacob Spink's programme.

**Abdullah -** He's still out there.